DANGEROUS ABDUCTION

Book 2 of O'Connor Brother Series

By: Rhonda Brewer

This book is dedicated to my two beautiful children, Laura and Colin. You are my greatest creation and have cheered me on everyday, giving me the courage to follow my dreams. I love both of you with all my heart.

Acknowledgements

There are so many people who made publishing this book possible and saying thank you just doesn't seem enough. First, I want to thank my critique partner Amabel Daniels. As a new author she supported me and shared her experiences and ideas with me. Next, thank you to fellow author Zoe York for creating the beautiful cover for this book.

I also want to thank the many authors who helped me along the way with advice, experiences and the pep talks to make this possible. Abbie Zanders, Em Petrova, Susan Stoker, Kathleen Brooks, Rhonda Carver, Cynthia D'Alba, Victoria Barbour, Kate Robbins, Eve Jagger, and Lynn Raye Harris. They are amazing authors and amazing ladies.

To my beta readers, thank you for their time and input. Especially, Michelle Eriksen and Mayas Sanders. They gave me great advice.

Last but certainly not least, thank my husband whose encouraged me every day. To my parents, nobody could have a better mom and dad. Also thank you to my Aunt Gertrude Holwell, who throughout my life has been there for me any time I needed her and has always been like a big sister to me.

Chapter 1

The house was so dark Marina could not see the lamp that sat on her bed side table. Estimating exactly where it was, she managed to find it and turn the switch. Nothing. *Damn it.* She slapped her hand around the top of the stand until she finally found her smart-phone and accidently knocked it on the floor. Luckily, the screen lit up so she was able to hop out of bed and find it quickly. She tapped the flashlight app and it illuminated her room. It seemed to be the only light to be seen as she moved to the bedroom window and pulled back the curtain. The entire road was completely blacked out.

"Great! A freaking power outage." She sighed because one thing Marina Kelly despised was being alone in a blackout.

With her phone lighting the path, she made her way to the kitchen. She only tripped once and stifled a curse when she stubbed her toe on a chair that she was sure she'd pushed in earlier. She praised herself for her obsessive habit of making sure everything had a place when she put her hand on the battery-operated lanterns she kept in the cupboard. She needed to save the battery on her phone since the cordless phones didn't work without power. Of course she hadn't listened to her mother and gotten a corded phone like her mother suggested. *Mom was right again.*

She hated the dark, and if Danny woke up, he'd panic. Her son was terrified of the dark and always had a bright nightlight in his room. She grabbed two of the lanterns and turned to make her way towards his room but a loud crack echoed through the house, making her stop in her tracks.

"Marina!" A male voice rumbled and it sent fear to the depths of her soul. She knew that voice as if she'd only heard it yesterday.

"Oh God. No!" Her voice was a whisper and her breathing came in pants as she gasped for air. It couldn't be him.

"Marina, don't hide. It'll only make things worse on you." Chills rushed down her spine and she tried to move, but it was as if she were walking through water. She needed to get to Danny before he did. Her son had never met his father before and he wasn't going to meet him if she had anything to do with it.

"Marina, you better fucking answer me. I'm taking my kid." The words sounded more like it was coming from a growling animal than from a man. Marc wasn't getting Danny. She'd die before she let him near her son.

She tried to tip-toe out of the kitchen to get to Danny's room before Marc found them both, but another loud crack from the foyer made her freeze in her tracks. Then something pulled her towards the sound and away from Danny's room. She couldn't stop moving towards the ominous crash. A flash of light lit up the foyer, and a dark shadow filled the open doorway. At least she could be a distraction and keep Marc's attention away from Danny. It didn't matter if he hurt her again. She could take whatever he dished out because all that mattered was Danny stayed safe.

The room was suddenly filled with a bright light allowing her to see more than she wanted. He was in front of her and her heart pounded in her chest like a jackhammer. He was bigger than she remembered, and his lips were turned up into a sadistic, evil, smirk. She turned to run but she couldn't move. Then her entire body began to tremble and she couldn't control it.

"Did you think you'd be able to hide from me? That I wouldn't find you out here in the boonies? I found you here once before, bitch." Marc spit at her and his face twisted in anger, turning blood red. He didn't look human.

"Marc, please, please leave us alone." Marina forced out the words but they came out in a whisper.

"Begging, Marina?" He sneered.

He slammed her against the wall, and his fist connected with her stomach, making her buckle over. Then he pulled her up by her hair and wrapped his other hand around her throat. Adrenalin must've been coursing through her because there was no pain from his assault. Even when he released her hair, pulled his hand back and slapped her across the face. She wasn't even shivering anymore.

Then both of his hands closed around her throat, making it harder to breathe, but he was squeezing so slowly it was as if it was all in slow motion. Marina raised her gaze to meet his and gasped at the red glow emanating from his eyes. She clawed at his hands but he was too strong.

"Mommy!" Danny squealed. *Oh God, no.* She shot a desperate glance at Danny's bedroom door. He was struggling to get away from Marc. *What?* Marc was still choking her. How could he be holding Danny? "Mommy, wake up!"

Marina bolted upright in her son's bed gasping for air. Sweat covered her face and her heart thundered in her chest. Danny was next to her staring at her with wide frightened eyes. *It was a dream.* It was another freaking nightmare, and Marc wasn't in the house trying to take her son. When were they going to stop?

"Mommy's okay, baby." Marina pulled him into her arms and kissed the top of his head. "Mommy just had a bad dream."

This was the third night in a row she'd fallen asleep in Danny's bed, and it seemed to be the only time she did fall asleep. Between getting hardly any sleep because of the nightmares and work, exhaustion was setting in. She had to do something about this before she made herself sick. For a while the nightmares had only come one or two nights a month, but for the last few weeks they'd been coming almost every night. It was pissing her off because she thought she'd finally gotten the fear under control.

A loud knock on her front door made her whole body go rigid. She glanced at her watch. It was after ten o'clock, which was late for someone to be just dropping by. Who would be at her door this late? *Marc?* Before she knew what happened, Danny jumped off the bed and ran out of the room.

"Danny! Stop!" Marina ran after him, but he'd already opened the door. The sight that filled her doorframe made her heart thud for another reason altogether.

"Marina, are you okay?" James looked sexier than any man had a right to. He had become part of her dreams as well. The ones that starred him, though, were anything but nightmares.

"She's fine, Unca James. Jus' a bad dream." Her son jumped into his arms and then he had to go and kiss the top of Danny's head. Marina felt as if she'd melt into the floor.

"It's fine, pal." Marina focused on those beautiful, intense, blue eyes. "You did exactly what Uncle John and I told you to do." James lowered Danny back to the floor but his gaze never left hers.

"Danny, go get back into bed. I'll be there in a minute." She tousled Danny's hair as he darted past her.

"Night, Unca James." Danny waved as he disappeared into his room. That left her alone with the only man in four years to ignite a need that burned to her core. James O'Connor. *Fuck.*

"Are you okay? Really?" His deep, velvety voice made her shiver.

"I'm fine." Why did Danny call him? She glanced down realizing all she was wearing was a short pair of pajama shorts and a tank top that her body would be considered too curvy to wear in front of anyone. It wasn't meant for others to see, and it was comfy to wear to bed. Wait a minute. Danny called James? How the hell did he call James?

"Danny was frightened when he called." James scanned up and down her body, making her want to strip naked and run for cover all at the same time.

"Okay, I've got two questions." Marina needed to change gears because the deep stirrings he caused were getting hard to fight, especially when he was so blatantly taking in every inch of her.

"Shoot." James leaned against the doorjamb, shoved his hands into his front pockets and met her eyes. Even that was hot. She was so pathetic.

"What did you mean when you said, Danny called like you and John told him?" When his face flushed, Marina couldn't help but smile.

"So… Well… okay here it is. Stephanie was worried about you being in the house alone with Danny. Nobody really knows for sure if Marc is still on the mainland," James pulled his hands out his pockets and walked farther into the house. Closer to her. So her sister was responsible for this.

"That still doesn't explain how Danny called you." Marina tried hard to keep her voice steady but when James was around she was mush.

"John and I taught him my phone number because I live the closest to you." James stared down at the floor like a little boy caught with his hand in the cookie jar. It was adorable.

"Why is Stephanie so worried?" Was there something going on she didn't know about? Had Marc been in touch with one of her family?

"She's just worried he'll come back. She doesn't trust him." James glanced up and met her eyes again. His gaze scared her and turned her on at the same time.

"Marc was pretty clear he wasn't going to bother us again." Her ex-husband had written a letter to tell her he wouldn't be in touch with her again and dissolved his parental rights.

"She's just worried, but at least we know Danny remembered what we taught him." It seemed her son was keeping secrets from her and he wasn't the only one. Stephanie would be getting a phone call in the morning.

"Wait! Who's with Mason?"

James was a widower and his son was a few months older than Danny. James would've had to get a babysitter to come check on her because she knew he wouldn't leave his son at home all alone.

"Ian is staying with me for a few days." Ian, another of the seven O'Connor brothers. "Besides, if he wasn't there, I would've taken Mason with me."

"Thank you, James. I'm sorry Danny made you come out for no reason." Marina was grateful but the attraction to him scared her senseless.

"It wasn't for no reason. Danny was scared, so a thank-you isn't necessary. Its what family does." It seemed the whole O'Connor clan had taken her in as part of the family.

"I didn't mean to scare him." It wasn't as if she could control the nightmares but if it wasn't the nightmares about Marc, it was dreams about James and although they were scary they would disturb her in a whole different way.

"You want to talk about the dream?" His concern was sweet, but he really needed to get out before she jumped the man.

"Not really, but thanks."

His gaze locked with hers and for the thousandth time she wished she'd met James under different circumstances.

"Okay, I'm going to go, but if you need anything, call."

Marina nodded as he disappeared though the front door. She closed it quickly and leaned against it as she took a couple of deep breaths to will her pounding heart back to a normal beat. He always did this to her and he didn't even know it. What was she going to do?

Chapter 2

James jogged back to his house and tried to tame down the erection straining his zipper. All he could picture was her in those damn shorts that showed her firm thighs and hips that were built to grip while he pounded into her. Then there was that top clinging to her full breasts and giving him a perfect view at the outline of her nipples. *Jesus*. It was getting worse. If that was even possible. He couldn't even be in her company for more than five minutes and his dick had a mind of its own.

"God damn it." James slammed the front door when he entered his house.

"Whoa there, bro. Are you trying to wake Mason?" Ian sauntered out of the kitchen.

"No," James snapped and headed straight to the fridge. Ian chuckled but when James glanced at him, Ian was texting. "What's so funny?"

"Sandy." Ian's face flushed as he shoved his phone into his back pocket.

"Why the hell don't you just ask her out?" James asked.

Ian and Sandy had been dancing around each other since they met, but Ian was gun-shy. Who could blame him? Ian's long-time girlfriend left him six years ago without a reason. Ian had been devastated and didn't date much since.

"I could ask you the same question." Ian raised an eyebrow.

"Sandy isn't my type." James pushed Ian's shoulder as he ambled past him on the way to the living room. He needed to find something to take his mind off Marina and her sexy nighttime attire.

"Very funny." Ian followed him. "I'm talking about Sandy's cute neighbor, or we could call her John's sister-in-law, or Stephanie's sister, or the woman you've been drooling over for the last four years."

James pointed his index finger at his brother. "One, I don't drool over anyone, and two… well, there's no two, but I don't drool." James flopped down on the sofa and propped his feet up on the coffee table. He leaned his head back against the back of the couch and scanned the room. Anything to distract him from thinking about her. His dark blue plush couch and loveseat complimented the beige walls. Across from the couch was a stone fireplace that he'd refurbished when he and Sarah had first moved in the house and above it hung a series of photos of his son. From the day Mason was born up to his recent fifth birthday.

"Bro, you may not drool, but you do look and who could blame you? Marina Kelly's hot." Ian plopped down next to him. "I'm not the only one to notice. A.J. and Nick couldn't keep their eyes off of her at John and Stephanie's wedding."

"They better keep their fucking eyes and hands to themselves. Marina doesn't need their kind of shit," James grumbled.

"Maybe she does." Ian nudged him and without a second thought James grabbed his brother by the front of his shirt.

"I swear to God, Ian, if you don't shut it now, I'm gonna pound the piss out of you." James clenched his fist as if he was ready to do that very thing.

"I'd love to see you try, bro." Ian narrowed his eyes and James let go of Ian's shirt with a shove. James could hold his own, but Ian could definitely kick his ass. With a third degree black belt in Karate and a wall of solid muscle, Ian was probably the most ripped doctor anyone had ever seen.

"Go text Sandy." James snatched the remote from the coffee table and flicked through the channels. When Ian started to laugh on his way out of the room, James clenched his teeth.

He was wound so tight it wasn't even funny. Between drooling over Marina, and yes, he did drool over her whether he was going to admit it or not, and dreaming about her, he was so sexually aroused all the time it was as if he was an over-sexed teenager. Marina had him in a spin and she didn't even know it.

Marina was the first woman to turn his head since Sarah died and if the sexual frustration wasn't enough he was weighed down with feelings of guilt. Sarah had been gone almost four years, and Sarah made him promise that he would not close himself off to finding love again. Of course he made that promise when they found out she was going to lose her battle with breast cancer and he would have said anything to make her happy. He just didn't know if he could keep that promise. At least not until he met Marina Kelly, but she had her own demons. Her ex-husband was a drug-addicted asshole who hurt her both physically and mentally. James wasn't sure if anyone could ever get over that kind of thing.

As a police officer he'd arrested men like Marc O'Reilly on a daily basis. Some of the conditions the victims would be left in would make James sick to his stomach. It took every ounce of strength to keep himself from pounding the assholes into the ground. He and his six brothers couldn't stand men like Marc because their father had always told them women should be treated with nothing but love and reverence.

Marina's sister, Stephanie, was married to his twin brother John. Stephanie was always setting up dinners to give James and Marina a chance to get to know each other. Stephanie would say it was because she wanted the families to be close but John had given him the real reason after the first meal she'd invited him to. The only problem was, Marina always seemed to keep her distance. Proof she was nowhere near ready to get close to anyone and if he was being honest, he didn't know if he was ready. If only his dick felt the same way.

"I'm hitting the hay for the night," Ian pulled James out of his head.

"Yeah…Okay…Night." James mumbled.

"Ask the woman out, for Christ sake." Ian was not one to be making suggestions.

"I could say the same to you, bro." James shot back and Ian held up his hands in defense. It made James chuckle because he and Ian were quite a pair. Neither of them had the guts to ask out the two women they wanted. The only place James could ask Marina out was in his dreams. Except in his dreams he and Marina were doing a lot more than just dating. *Fuck!*

James woke hunched over on the couch. He didn't remember what time he closed his eyes, but it was way after midnight. Falling asleep on the couch had become the norm for him. He couldn't even remember the last time he slept in his bed. He avoided sleeping in the bed because for some reason he tended to dream more when he slept in it and that meant dreaming of Marina.

He glanced at his watch. "Fuck it," he groaned. It was a just before six in the morning and knowing his son, he would be up any minute. Mason rarely slept in.

At least he had the day off and he could drop Mason at school and spend some extra time with him. Hopefully he'd get the errands done that he'd been putting off all week. There never seemed to be enough time for anything these days. His work schedule was typical for a police officer. Three twelve-hour shifts and then three days off. If it wasn't for his family, he didn't know what he'd do. Thank God he had no more overnight shifts. James had a feeling his Uncle Kurt had something to do with his permanent schedule change.

After Sarah died, working overnight shifts were difficult since he couldn't spend much time with Mason. Then Sarah's parents moved to Alberta with Sarah's brother, which meant James had to depend on his own family even more. He'd put in a request for a leave of absence until Mason was old enough to enter daycare but when he got called into the office, Uncle Kurt, who was also his boss, told him his schedule had changed to day shifts. It was a huge blessing and made life easier. Now that Mason was five years old, he was in kindergarten and part-time daycare. Things were certainly easier than when he was a baby

Maybe it's why he felt such a connection with Marina——she was also a single parent. At least she had Stephanie and her parents to help, and now that Stephanie was married to his twin brother, Marina had the O'Connors for support. If only she would accept it.

"Daddy, can I have a cookie?" Mason stood at the bottom of the stairs in his underwear and his hair totally out of control. His son may have Sarah's beautiful dark brown hair but the poor kid had inherited the wavy locks of the O'Connor clan.

"Do you think cookies are a good thing to have for breakfast?" James always tried to give Mason the choice to make right decisions. It was something he and his brothers were taught as children. His mother always said most of the time kids made the right choice and when they didn't you guided them towards the right one.

"No." Mason sighed, plopped down on the bottom step and rested his chin in his hands.

"So what do you think we should have for breakfast?" James stood up and went to the kitchen.

"Waffles?" Mason followed him.

"Okay, big guy, waffles it is." James pulled out the waffle-maker and the ingredients. Sure there were easier ways to make them, but Mason enjoyed the homemade ones and nobody could beat his waffles.

"Can I help, Daddy?" Mason was already pulling a chair over to the counter.

"I think you should probably go put on the clothes I laid out on your chair last night and then you can help. I'll wait for you." Mason was out of the kitchen and up over the stairs in seconds.

Chances were when he came back down something would be inside out or backwards.

"Coffee, lots and lots of hot coffee." Ian walked into the kitchen rubbing his hands together as he blew on them. No doubt he'd been out on his daily run by the redness of his cheeks and nose. The man was up at five every morning and ran for an hour. James was all for keeping in shape, but jogging in October was not on his list of workouts. He'd stick with his treadmill and weights until the warmer weather started.

"Good run?" James filled two cups and held one out for Ian.

"It's fucking freezing outside." Ian pulled off his hooded sweatshirt and hung it over the chair.

"Nanny's gonna put pepper on your tongue for saying bad words, Unca Ian." Mason ran into the kitchen and James chuckled as Ian rolled his eyes. Kathleen O'Connor obviously kept the same rules with her grandson as she did with her sons. Growing up, if they used what she called bad words, Kathleen would put pepper on their tongues and they'd have to keep it there for as many minutes as their age. It burned like hell.

"Yeah, Uncle Ian." James helped Mason stand on the chair while they mixed up the waffle batter.

"I'm sorry." Ian gave an exaggerated sigh.

"I won't tell, but don't say it no more." Mason stirred the batter and James turned his head to hide his grin.

"I won't, buddy." Ian held the cup in front of his mouth probably to hide a smile as well.

"Daddy, when are you going on a date with Danny's mommy?" Mason turned to James after he jumped down off the chair. The bowl of batter James held tipped and some spilled onto the counter. James heard Ian choke back a laugh and he wanted to whip the bowl at his head.

"Why would I go on a date with Danny's mommy?" James wiped up the spill without turning to look at Mason or Ian. He really didn't want to turn around since he knew Ian was waiting for him to answer Mason's question probably with a huge grin.

"Auntie Cora said you and Auntie Marina were gonna go on a date." James should've known where that came from. His aunt, also known as 'Cora the Cupid' by his family, had been on his back since she met Marina. The story was she knew when people were meant to be together and as far as he knew, she was never wrong. According to Cora, he and Marina were meant to be together.

"You know if Aunt Cora said it, then it's true." Ian chuckled. James spun around to glare at his younger brother.

"Maybe we should ask Aunt Cora about Sandy." James raised his eyebrow and Ian clamped his mouth shut.

"So where are you goin' on the date?" Mason wasn't going to drop the subject until he got an answer.

"I don't know if we are, buddy. We'll see." James hoped that was the end of the topic. It really wasn't comfortable having this conversation with his five-year-old son or anyone for that matter.

"Nanny Betty says you're jus' gun-shy." Mason climbed up on his chair as James put the plate of waffles in front of him. "But you're not 'fraid a guns."

Ian had completely lost it and wasn't even trying to hide his laughing. James had to admit the whole conversation was amusing and was struggling not to laugh as well.

"No, Mason, I'm not afraid of guns." James chuckled.

"Nanny's so silly." When Mason started to dig in to his food James silently thanked God the kid found something else to do with his mouth. James needed to have a chat with his mother, grandmother and aunt about those conversations in front of Mason. Not that it would change anything but all he needed was Mason to say something in front of Danny or worse, Marina.

Chapter 3

Elizabeth Avenue on a Friday evening could be considered the equivalent of hell. Marina estimated she was driving about a meter every ten minutes, although, it was more like crawling. It was ten minutes past five and construction crews were on just about every road, trying to finish the last of the road work before winter hit.

Her knuckles turned white as she gripped the steering wheel in frustration because at the rate she was going, the daycare would be complaining about her not being there on time. Of course she couldn't call, because as usual she'd forgotten to charge her cell phone at the office. One of these days that slip was going to get her into trouble. It wasn't as if she was late picking Danny up every day, but the staff meeting ran late, and she had to send in her final edits to her boss. That took longer than normal because the article she'd edited was about the police force in the province, and of course her uncontrollable thoughts kept bringing up images of a certain sexy police officer she couldn't get out of her mind for more than ten minutes.

"Come on, move." She yelled at nobody really. She just needed to yell out to alleviate her frustration.

The traffic was one of the reasons she moved out of the city to Hopedale. It was a nice town and up until her sister moved there, she'd never visited the small ocean-side community. Stephanie had gotten a job as a physical therapist and personal care attendant but ended up falling in love with her patient and was now married to him. John O'Connor was a great guy and treated her sister like a princess.

He was nothing like Marc.

Marina shook that thought out of her head. He was the last person she wanted to think about right now. A shiver ran up her spine as her nightmare from the previous night flashed in her thoughts. She really needed to talk to someone about them, since they were becoming more frequent instead of less. It didn't make sense for the dreams to return because Marc hadn't contacted her in years.

Marina pulled into the lot of the Little Tots Daycare, and parked her car opposite the door. She stepped out of her car. The hairs on the back of her neck prickled.

She scanned the parking lot but nothing seemed out of the ordinary.

"Great. Now I'm getting paranoid," she mumbled as she pulled open the door leading to the daycare center.

The caretaker waved to her as she walked inside. She glanced around to catch sight of Danny, quickly found him at a desk fully entranced on whatever he was colouring. He was almost five years old and since his birthday was in January, he couldn't start kindergarten until next September. He was so upset when he found out Mason would be going and he wouldn't.

He was growing so quickly and constantly surprising her with things he said and did. Like the surprise phone call he'd made to James the night before. She still wasn't over that embarrassment, but it was nice to know help was close by if she needed it. She didn't know why everyone was so concerned about Marc but it was starting to make her think they knew something she didn't.

Danny was the only good thing to come out of her marriage and the last thing he needed was to know just how mean his father had become. Being around the O'Connor family was good for him because he got to see how a man should treat a woman. He also had some amazing male role models in the seven brothers.

"Mommy!" Danny squealed and launched himself into her arms almost knocking her off her three-inch heels. She hugged him tightly as she barely caught herself from falling flat on her ass.

"Did you have fun today?" Marina kissed his cheek as she put him back on the floor. He nodded and turned around to grab his things out of the small wooden box on the wall that Danny called his cubby. Each of the kids were assigned their own to put their belongings in.

Danny was babbling about something when Marina pushed open the door and held it for a woman entering the building. With one hand holding his backpack as well as Danny's hand and the other holding the door, Danny managed to pull from away from her and darted into the parking lot.

"Danny! Stop!" Marina screamed and dropped everything to run after him just as a car turned into the parking lot. Another car was backing out next to the two cars he ran between. She lost sight of him for a moment as a large truck almost clipped her when it tried to turn into a parking spot. Marina frantically scanned the lot. The screeching tires of a car had her spinning around just in time to see someone scoop Danny up and head towards her. Marina covered her mouth with her hands, and her attention locked on Danny as they got closer.

"You know better than to run away from your mom, buddy." She knew that deep sexy voice. Marina looked up and all the air gushed out of her.

James.

"I'm sorry, Mommy." Danny's arms wrapped around James' neck as he dropped his head.

"Thank you so much, James," Marina tried to say but it seemed all the air was gone from her lungs. She pulled Danny from his arms and hugged her son to her.

"As you know, I've got one just like him." James tousled Danny's hair.

"He's such a handful sometimes." Why did her voice always sound so breathy around him?

"They certainly are." James smiled showing his dimples and perfectly straight white teeth and she wanted to melt. That man could be a freaking model.

"I forgot Mason attends this daycare too." Marina tried to avoid staring at him and glanced towards where her car was parked but a gust of wind brought his clean scent around her face and without even thinking, she inhaled deeply.

"Yeah, it's the closest one to his school and the only one that will pick him up after school." *Why the hell does he have to smell so amazing and why does he wear my favorite men's cologne? Stetson.*

"Mason's my buddy." Danny boasted.

"I think you're his too, big guy." James chuckled.

"I get my share of Mason stories everyday, especially when they stay with John and Stephanie." Marina let Danny down on the ground but kept a firm grip on his hand.

"I don't know what those two do but when Mason comes home, I can't settle him down for hours." James rolled his eyes.

"They spoil Danny rotten." Why were her hands shaking?

"I guess since they're having trouble getting pregnant, they're trying to overcompensate with the boys." She could hear the obvious compassion in his voice and it only made her want him more.

"I know Stephanie's trying hard not to lose hope." Marina's heart went out to her sister and John. There weren't two people in the world who loved kids as much as they did.

"Nan always says you'll have what's for you when it's for you." James smiled down at Danny. "I better go get my little terror."

"It was nice seeing you again, and thanks for grabbing Danny for me." Marina turned towards her car but stopped before James was out of sight. "James?"

"Yeah?" His gaze met hers and that flutter in her stomach started again.

"Thanks for last night too." As much as it annoyed her that Stephanie set it all up, it was nice to know that someone was there if she needed them.

"Anytime. It was really great to see you again, Marina." James turned and disappeared into the building but not before she checked out his firm ass. Damn, the man looked good in everything and knew how to wear a pair of jeans.

She enjoyed the drive from St. John's to the small town of Hopedale. It was a close-knit town where everyone knew each other, and it was the same place where James and his brothers grew up.

Stephanie and John had bought a house a few roads away so John suggested Marina buy his old one, and she jumped at the offer. She loved the relaxed atmosphere of living in a small town because it was quiet and Danny had a huge back garden where he could run around and play.

James wasn't the reason she moved to Hopedale, but it was a bonus having him less than one hundred paces away. Ninety-eight steps to be exact or at least that was what she was told by Danny and Mason. It was as if the two little boys were joined at the hip. It wasn't surprising to see Mason sitting in her living room with Danny watching television or having a snack in the kitchen.

It must be hard for James, raising Mason on his own. Sure, he had an amazing family, but she knew from experience how hectic it was as a single parent, especially, when that parent had to work long hours. Even when you had family, it was still overwhelming.

The first night she'd met him, he'd driven her back to her parent's house after Marc showed up at John's. The same house where she and Danny now lived. James had been quiet at first, but when they'd pulled into the driveway, he said something she'd never forgotten.

"Marina, you don't know me or my family, but you need to know something. Stephanie is part of our family now. She gave my brother back to us and he loves her very much. That makes you part of our family too. So if you need anything, and I mean anything, just pick up the phone and call one of us. We'll move heaven and earth to help you."

His whole speech moved her to tears and every time she thought about what he said, she'd feel that lump in her throat. The O'Connor family always had her back, through the crap with Marc, involving Danny and her in their family gatherings, and of course on those nights she screamed herself awake.

The only thing that made her uncomfortable was Stephanie, not so subtly, dropping hints about how great James was. Like she didn't already know how absolutely amazing and sexy he was, but Danny was her only priority. However, her sister seemed to think Danny needed a father in his life and James was the perfect man for the job. Marina didn't deny James was a great father and sweet to Danny, but she didn't know if she was ready to open her heart again. Marc had shattered it and she still wasn't sure if she'd put all the pieces together or if she ever would.

Stephanie had eased off on her lectures lately, but sometimes James would be thrown into the conversation. It wasn't that she wasn't attracted to him, because she'd have to be dead not to be. All the O'Connor brothers were hotter than men had a right to be, but the only one to appear in her dreams was James, and none of them were G-rated.

It scared her the way James looked at her sometimes because his gaze had an intensity that made her tremble with desire. Marc had that same intense gaze, and it terrified her. She knew James was nothing like her ex-husband but Marc hadn't always been the monster he'd turned into at the end of their marriage. It was as if she married one man but divorced another. When she married Marc she had said until death do they part, but she had no idea that the death was almost hers.

She opened the front door and walked into the foyer of her small bungalow. Danny darted around her and went to the living room, plopping himself in front of the television to watch his favorite show. Something about dogs that was on Animal Planet. He was obsessed with dogs and had asked for a puppy numerous times, but Marina didn't feel he was ready to have a pet. However, she did promise to think about it once he turned five.

Marina turned into her huge bedroom. John had renovated it since he and Stephanie lived there. It had been transformed into an enormous bedroom with an ensuite. She loved to ease into the huge soaking tub once Danny was in bed for the night and relax. Then she'd curl up in her bed to read, work or even walk out onto the back deck that was off her bedroom.

The spacious kitchen was her favorite part of the house mainly because through the large bay window she had a full view of the ocean. Of course Hopedale was surrounded on three sides by the ocean, but she thought the best view was from her garden. When her anxiety started to overwhelm her, she'd stand on the deck and let herself get lost in the sound of the waves splashing against the rocks.

The feelings had lessened over the last four years, but lately they'd returned with the nightmares.

Marina changed into her clothing of choice, jeans and T-shirt because it was how she felt the most comfortable. She was never a fan of business attire, but in her line of work she had to be professional. So, the fitted business suits and the torturous high heel shoes were what she wore at the office. Both she and Stephanie were never girlie girls mostly because they'd spent so much time growing up on construction sites with their father or digging around the garden with their mother.

Marina glanced into the living room as she made her way to the kitchen, Danny sat crossed-legged in front of the television amongst the toys he hadn't picked up before they'd left that morning. She reminded him to pick them up and to move back from the television, but she knew he didn't hear her. The bunch of puppies running around a garden appeared on the screen, and Danny was enthralled. She shook her head and proceeded to the kitchen.

Getting home after six in the evening was always a pain. Throwing something together to make a quick supper, then homework, then bed. During the week her time with Danny was short but Friday bedtime wasn't as strictly enforced. It killed her to miss so much time with him. She wished she could work more from home, or possibly even write herself.

"Yes Marina, you stay home and be a famous writer. What are you going to write about? How to cook supper in less then thirty minutes?" She muttered as she pulled open the freezer door.

She pulled out Danny's favorite—chicken nuggets in the shape of animals. He'd make the noise of each one as he ate them, but not before he'd ask over and over if the nuggets were made out of that specific animal. She'd have to assure him they weren't and was glad the company had seen fit not to make a nugget in the shape of a chicken. Danny would never eat anything again. She'd just spread them out on the pan when her phone rang.

Marina pulled her phone out of her pocket as she turned on her oven. "Hello."

"Hey, Rina." Her sister always sounded so cheery. It was nauseating.

"Hey, Steph, Whadda ya at?" A typical greeting for Newfoundlanders, which meant 'what are you doing,' and Marina said it without even thinking. Before she moved back to Newfoundland, she lived in Ottawa. It was amusing when she greeted people in the same way, they had no idea what she was saying.

"I'm cooking supper and wanted to invite you and Danny," Stephanie said.

"I was just starting supper." She was really too tired to walk the two roads to her sister's house.

"Put it away and come have supper with us. We're leaving for the airport at nine, and I want to spend some time with you and Danny before we go on vacation."

"I almost forgot you guys were leaving today." Stephanie and John were heading to Hawaii for three weeks, since the doctors told Stephanie sometimes stress could make it hard to get pregnant. So thanks to John's Aunt Cora, and her vacation home in the tropical paradise, they booked a relaxing trip to lessen their stress level and just enjoy each other.

"So can you come over, please?" Stephanie was in full begging mode, and Marina knew it was pointless to argue.

She was going to miss her sister, and Danny would definitely miss both of them. John was just a big kid with Danny. Marina hoped the couple were able to have a baby of their own, because anyone could tell John desperately wanted to be a dad. He'd come from a large family, and it was obvious they were extremely close.

She turned off the stove and calmed Danny enough to get his coat back on and then headed outside to her car. It seemed so lazy to drive the two-minute walk to her sister's house, but chances were Danny would be almost ready for bed by the time they returned home. That meant he'd only have one mood, and that mood would be cranky.

Danny was strapped in his seat and she was about to get in the car herself. She thought she saw something move out of the corner of her eye, but when she turned her head the only thing she saw was the line of trees across the street from her house. She turned in the other direction but nothing.

Not Nothing.

Something was making the hair on the back of her neck stand up and as she scanned the tree line a second time, she saw a rabbit hopping between two trees.

"Jesus Christ, I'm getting really getting paranoid." Marina shook her head and got in the car.

Danny was wiggling in his car seat as they pulled into Stephanie and John's driveway, no doubt excited because he was about to play with his favorite uncle. He really loved spending time with them, and of course they loved to spoil him. Sometimes to the point it was almost impossible to settle him down once she got him back home again. No matter how many times she asked them not to hype him up before they dropped him off, or she picked him up, Danny would still come home talking a mile a minute and jumping around like a cat on a hot rock.

Her sister's home was a large white duplex with dark green shutters that they'd bought just after they got married, mostly because they wanted kids right away. It wasn't fair that two people who loved kids so much were having issues but maybe their little vacation would give them exactly what they wanted. A child.

Danny's feet hit the driveway and he bolted right to the house. Marina closed her car door. Again, that nagging tingle in the back of her neck. She whipped her head around and walked down to the end of the driveway. Was someone watching her or was she just losing her mind?

Chapter 4

James watched her from inside the glass door of the daycare as she hurried to her car. He couldn't help it. Her dark blonde hair was tied back into a neat ponytail that swung back and forth when she walked. He wanted to tangle his hands into that mane of hair while he devoured her plump lips. He wanted so bad to taste her lips and feel her naked skin next to his.

It was getting more difficult to hide his attraction to Marina, and his emotions made him tremble whenever she was close. If the truth be told, James was apprehensive, because losing Sarah was the worst thing he'd ever been through, and he knew he'd never survive that pain again. He didn't know how he'd done it the first time.

His attraction to Marina was unsettling, because it had hit so suddenly. That first night when her ex-husband showed up at John's house and he saw her on the couch trembling with pure terror in her eyes, every protective instinct he had kicked into gear. Knowing some of what that ass did to her made him angrier than he'd ever been in his life. He'd never understand how a man could treat a woman with anything but reverence.

Then there was John and Stephanie's wedding. That day was so hard, or at least made him hard, because Marina looked sexy as hell in the dress she wore as her sister's maid of honor. It also didn't help that he was John's best man and ended up paired off with her at the church. Then there was the bridal party dance where he was required to dance with her. Holding her in his arms was heaven, but the guilt was overwhelming. It had been almost three years after Sarah died, and lusting after another woman seemed a betrayal of his late wife.

Now Marina was invading his thoughts and his dreams. He couldn't get her out of his head, and he still struggled with the thought of moving on with his life. Plus, Marina's previous relationship was pure hell, and Ms. Marina Kelly did not seem interested in a relationship with any man.

James thoughts were abruptly interrupted when two little arms wrapped around his leg. He looked down to see the smiling face of his son. Mason was so energetic and spontaneous, traits he got from his mother. As much as it hurt to lose Sarah, he remembered her words every day. *"You'll always have a piece of me with you in Mason."*

He wondered if she knew how right she was, because Mason resembled Sarah more and more every day with his dark brown hair and pert nose. He also had the O'Connor blue eyes, the dimples and the mischievous grin, but the grin made Mason look a lot like his youngest brother Aaron. He still wasn't sure if that was a good thing or a bad thing.

"Daddy!" Mason squealed as he started to jump up and down still clung tightly to James' leg.

"Hey there, buddy." James tousled his hair.

"Are we gonna go home now?" Mason picked up his backpack and struggled to get his small arms through the straps.

"Well, we're going to go see Uncle John and Aunt Stephanie before they go on vacation." The noise his son created had heads turning and James' ears ringing. It looked like it was a yes to the visit. "Let's go." James lifted Mason into his arms and walked through the door receiving nods and smiles from the other parents picking up their children.

On the way back to Hopedale, he knew it was time to have a serious talk with Mason about his abrupt question during breakfast. The last thing he needed was his son saying something about him dating Marina in front of Stephanie, or worse Danny.

"Mason, I need to talk to you about what you asked this morning." James glanced into the rearview mirror to make sure Mason was paying attention. "Do you know what I'm talking about, buddy?"

"Yep, what Nanny said, right?" Mason started to kick his feet as he bounced in his seat.

"That's right. I don't want you to say anything to anyone else about that, okay?" James turned onto the off ramp that headed into Hopedale.

"Why?" James should have known it wouldn't be that easy with Mason being so inquisitive, and he always needed to have a reason for everything.

"It's a secret, and nobody can know about it." The one thing he was sure about was Mason knew some secrets were meant to be kept quiet.

"Okay, Daddy, but when will it not be a secret?" James shook his head in frustration.

"I'll let you know, okay?" James held his breath until Mason nodded.

"Uncle John!" Mason yelled as he bolted through John's front door. Before James was able to get into the living room, Mason was scooped up in John's arms and thrown into the air. This was the reason it was so hard to get Mason to calm down after a trip to his brother's place.

"There's one of my best buddies." John chuckled. "I got a surprise for you."

James groaned, because John's surprises were either noisy or gave Mason a sugar rush that took hours to wear off. He couldn't wait for the day that he could return the favor to his brother.

"You're taking him with you if you give him anything with sugar," James shouted as John disappeared from view obviously not paying any attention. Stephanie's laugh made him turn to see her glide out of the dining room.

She reached up and kissed his cheek. "Don't worry, this surprise should knock him out." She linked her arm into his and pulled him towards the patio doors in the kitchen. It led to a back garden with an incredible view of Hopedale Beach.

"What the hell?" Standing in the center of the yard was the largest playset he'd ever seen in a private yard. It was probably bigger than the one in Hopedale Park. Four swings and a slide took up one side of the structure, and a large fort with an upper floor and a lower one took up the other side. Mason was squealing and running around it as if John had just given him a million dollars, or in Mason's case a chocolate bar.

"This is mine?" Mason said excitedly

"You've got to share it with Danny, but you can play with it any time you're here." John scooped him up and put him on top of the slide.

"This is so cool." Mason slid down and ran around the slide to climb up himself.

"Are you trying to make me look bad, bro?" James walked closer to investigate and clamped his hand down on John's shoulder.

"Well, I'm the cool uncle. You're just the dad," John boasted.

"I wonder what our younger brothers would say about that." James walked around the structure to check everything out.

"They already know I'm the cool uncle." John laughed as Stephanie tucked herself under his arm. They were so happy together, but they still wanted a baby. They were constantly asking James to bring Mason over for a playdate with Danny.

"I ran into your sister today." James tried to sound casual as he hoisted Mason up on top of the fort. "Well, actually I grabbed Danny before he got hit by a car." The wide eyes and gasps from John and Stephanie told James he needed to explain quickly.

James told them how Danny had gotten away from Marina and ran out into the parking lot. His own heart had almost stopped when Danny darted out in front of the oncoming car, which was why he'd run full speed towards him. Danny had become like a nephew to him since he spent so much time with John but in no way did he think of the boy's mother the same as a sister.

"He's a little bugger sometimes," Stephanie said. "Actually, I just invited Marina and Danny over for supper."

"That's nice." James kept his focus on Mason to try to hide how his heart went into overdrive at the mention of her name.

"Why don't you and Mason stay too?" Stephanie smiled and her green eyes sparkled. He knew what she was doing, but the smell of roast beef was making him drool so it was making it hard to say no, plus, he'd get to see Marina again.

"Sure, why not?" James said.

"Good. The boys can play for a bit, and we can spend some time together before John and I leave for the airport."

"What time do you have to be there?" James followed Stephanie back into the house, leaving John outside with Mason.

"We've got to be at the airport by nine tonight, but our flight doesn't leave until eleven." She grabbed a set of oven mitts off the counter and opened the oven door.

"Hopefully, you'll have a great time." James glanced out through the window and watched John push Mason on the swing.

"I'll be doing nothing but relaxing." Stephanie recovered the roaster she'd taken out of the oven and pushed it back into the oven. "It should be ready shortly." Stephanie wiped her hands with the cloth she pulled off the counter. While he and Stephanie were talking, Mason came rushing through the patio door squealing with John behind him growling like a fool.

"Unca John's a monster." Mason giggled and hid behind James.

"You're a big youngster." James rolled his eyes.

"I'm just a big kid at heart." John stood behind Stephanie and snaked his arms around her waist as he growled into her neck.

"If you don't let me go you're going for a time-out." Stephanie giggled.

"Gonna send me to my room?" John turned her around and pulled her into his arms.

"No that wouldn't exactly be a punishment for you." Stephanie smiled.

"Child in the room," James reminded the couple as they started to get a bit too intimate.

"Kissin' girls is gross, Unca John." Mason made a gagging sound.

"Oh is it now." Stephanie pulled away from John and chased Mason into the living room.

The love they had for each other was obvious to anyone who met them. Their relationship had been such a whirlwind, but there was no doubt they were meant for each other. The twinge of jealousy that hit him every time he saw them being affectionate made him feel like an ass. He was happy for John but James didn't have that anymore, and no matter how many times he was told he'd find it again; it was still hard to believe. The only woman to even draw his attention since Sarah passed was Marina, but it seemed nothing would ever happen between them.

"What's with the long face, bro?" John's voice pulled him from his depressing thoughts.

"Just a little tired," James lied, but as always John could read him better than anyone.

"You wanna have a chat?" John grabbed a couple of beers and handed one to James. Stephanie carried Mason back into the kitchen, kissing his cheeks while he wiggled and squealed. She gave James a nod, letting him know she'd keep Mason entertained while he took a moment with John.

"I guess." James followed John outside, and John closed the patio door behind them.

"So, what's up?" John leaned against the railing.

"Nothing, really." James sighed as he plopped down on one of the patio chairs. "I'm just a little lonely."

"It's been almost four years. That's a long time to be alone." John moved to the chair opposite James. "I know losing her was hard for you, but you've got to at least try and move on."

"I know, but I don't have time for anything anymore." A lump formed in his throat. "Between work and Mason, I don't have time for dating." Did it make him a terrible father even saying it? "I love Mason more than anything in this world, but I miss having someone in my life."

"Why don't you get a babysitter for a night and get out of the house," John suggested. "I'm sure Mom wouldn't hesitate to take Mason."

"I know, but I hate the fucking club scene." There were two in Hopedale, and most of the women who went there were either too drunk to talk, or close to jailbait. If he went into St. John's, he could go to George Street, but that was worse. He wanted someone he could sit down and have a conversation with. Someone who loved kids and would treat Mason like her own. Someone who would be just as content to spend an evening watching a kid's movie or have a glass of wine and listen to some music. Someone like... *Marina*.

"That scene is more our younger brothers' speed." John chuckled and James had to agree with that one hundred percent. The three youngest O'Connor brothers seemed to thrive on jumping from girl to girl at the bars. "What about Marina?"

"What about her?" James said casually or at least he thought he sounded that way.

"Aunt Cora seems to think you two are meant for each other." John raised an eyebrow and grinned.

"Yeah, I'm not getting into Aunt Cora's weird Cupid powers." James rolled his eyes.

"Maybe your first step should be to remove that." John pointed to James finger where his wedding band still remained. He'd tried to remove it the first year but could never bring himself to do it. Now it was part of him—or he was just too afraid to take it off because that meant he was ready to move on.

"I probably should." He twisted the ring on his finger.

"I know you still miss her, James, but I also know she didn't want you to be alone. What was it she said, she was supposed to be with you for a short time but there was someone out there for the rest of your life."

John paraphrased part of the conversation James had with Sarah shortly before she passed away. James really didn't need it repeated to him, because he remembered it like she'd said it to him yesterday.

"I know what she told me, and I'm trying." James let out a ragged breath. "Thanks for being there for me, bro."

"From conception, bro." That was their catch phrase, since they were twins, they'd been together since day one. They may not be identical, but he always felt a stronger connection with John than any of his other brothers. Not that he wouldn't do anything for the other five, but it was always as if he and John could read each other without even speaking.

When they stood John pulled him in for their typical man hug and handshake. It was so good to finally get things off his chest. Things always seemed better after a chat with John, and he was right. James needed to move on.

While they waited for Marina and Danny, Stephanie gave Mason her iPad to play a game. He climbed up on James' lap and became engrossed in the device. At least until a squeal floated in from the hallway. Mason dropped the iPad on the table, and jumped down from his lap. He rambled excitedly about the new play set.

Stephanie and Marina were talking in the foyer, but he couldn't make out everything they were saying. They seemed to be having an argument, but he couldn't be sure.

"Steph!" Marina raised her voice, and he knew he shouldn't be listening but he couldn't help it.

"James and Mason are here and they're staying for supper." Stephanie had a huge grin on her face when they walked into the living room. Marina didn't look happy but she was beautiful.

"Hi, James." Marina greeted him with her soft quiet voice as she glared at Stephanie.

"Nice to see you again." He tried to sound casual, but it was hard to do when he was around her.

"I see John and Steph are still spoiling the boys." She glanced through the patio door as James moved next to her. Danny and Mason were running around with John chasing them, and he could hear the muffled laughing from inside the house.

"At least this one will probably knock them out not hype them up." He was way too close to her because her scent filled his senses. He hadn't quite figured out what it was but probably strawberry or raspberry or something but it made him instantly hard.

"That's a bonus." She laughed as he turned to head outside, but she turned at the same time and tripped. James caught her around the waist to keep her from falling, and she grabbed the front of his shirt. Probably to balance herself, but it brought her so close that his lips brushed against her forehead. He lowered his eyes to meet hers as his heart thudded in his chest. His gaze moved to her lips just as her tongue flicked across her bottom lip, and his cock jerked. Before he had a chance to do anything stupid, Marina pushed against his chest and stepped back.

"Sorry." Her voice sounded as if she was having trouble breathing.

"That's okay." James mumbled as he stepped back and almost tripped trying to get outside with John and the kids. He came too damn close to completely embarrassing himself and devouring her mouth. It had been a long time since he'd wanted anyone so desperately. Even with Sarah he hadn't felt that type of desperation to be close to someone, and that scared him.

James glanced down at his hand, and the ring reflected the sun. Did he really need any more signs to remove his last tie to his late wife? He needed to be sure before he pursued anything with anyone, especially Marina.

Chapter 5

James was so close to her, and much to her dismay it affected
her in a way she didn't want it to. It was so hard to breathe around
him and she wasn't comfortable with her attraction to him. For some
reason he seemed spooked when she met his eyes. Hopefully, the
desperation didn't show in her expression, but the way he bolted
outside she had a feeling it did. She really needed to steady her
nerves which was why she was standing in the middle of the room
taking long, slow breaths. It always worked whenever she felt
anxious and although this wasn't the same as her anxiety attacks, the
breathing exercise helped.

She found her sister in the kitchen scurrying around as
always. Stephanie always seemed to have a huge bundle of energy,
probably because she could sleep through the night without
nightmares.

"James dropped in just after I was talking to you and I asked
him to stay for supper." Her sister seemed to be trying to justify why

James was there, but he had every right. After all, John was his brother.

"You don't need to explain anything to me." Marina didn't want Stephanie to be uncomfortable with James being there. It wasn't her sister's fault that James O'Connor had taken up way too much time in her thoughts and dreams. At least the dreams that didn't have her waking drenched in sweat and her heart pounding in her chest.

"James told me he ran into you today at the daycare." Stephanie pulled a roaster out of the oven, and the smell of the succulent beef filled the air and almost made Marina's discomfort disappear. Almost.

"It was more like Danny ran into him." Marina forced a chuckle.

"That kid needs to be on a harness." Stephanie laughed. "It's a good thing James was there. Kind of a white knight."

And there it is.

Marina leaned her hip against the counter, crossed her arms over her chest and glared at Stephanie. Her sister was anything but subtle.

"What?" Stephanie turned as if she sensed Marina's mood.

"What are you up to, Steph?" Marina didn't really need to ask because she knew.

"Nothing!" Stephanie held her hands in the air.

"Why don't I believe you?" Marina narrowed her eyes.

"I told you the truth. I'd already called you when James showed up to see us before we left. No motive at all. I swear, Rina." Maybe she was being paranoid so she tried to give Stephanie the benefit of the doubt.

Marina peered out through the window as John rolled around the grass with the two little boys, but as if she had no control, her gaze moved to James. His hip was propped against the railing as he watched John and the boys. A shiver of need surged through her body as she drank in every sexy inch of him. It had been a long time since a man made her feel so wanton, and the last man to do it ended up breaking her heart as well as most of her spirit.

"Have you heard from Mom and Dad since they went to Fredericton?" Stephanie's question gave her the distraction she needed to look away from James and shake the memories of Marc out of her thoughts.

"Yeah." God, she hoped Stephanie didn't hear how breathy her voice sounded as she glanced out the window again.

"She called me this morning and said they were having a time." Stephanie stepped next to her. "He really is a terrific guy, Rina."

"I know he is." Marina spun away from the window and snatched a plate from the counter. "You want to call them in before the food gets cold or this conversation gets hot?" She didn't turn around when she heard Stephanie groan, she just proceeded to scoop food onto a plate for Danny. She really wasn't trying to irritate her sister or upset her in any way. She just didn't need to be constantly reminded of how great James was. It was obvious but it didn't matter if he was a saint, Marina didn't know if she could ever open her heart to anyone ever again.

Danny and Mason practically inhaled their food. She didn't even have to negotiate with Danny to finish a meal. Maybe she should get one of those playsets to have at home. He was so anxious to get back outside; Danny barely gave her enough time to wipe his hands before he was out through the door behind Mason.

It was nice he had someone his age to play with, and James lived two houses away, so by the time summer rolled around, they'd be old enough to run back and forth to each other's houses. For now, they only got together at Stephanie's or when one of the O'Connors took them out together. It seemed whenever any of the family brought Mason to something they'd always magically have an extra ticket or they would use the excuse that Mason asked if Danny could go. She didn't mind really because it made her feel like part of their family.

While the boys played outside, she enjoyed sitting around the table with the other adults chatting. She'd even forgotten her annoyance with her sister, but that was because she couldn't keep herself from constantly glancing at James. She tried to do it subtly so her sister wouldn't gloat. There was nothing wrong with enjoying the view.

James was incredibly handsome, with light brown, wavy hair that showed auburn highlights when the light hit it a certain way. He kept it slightly shorter than John and it always had that sexy, tousled appearance. He was a little shorter than his twin around six foot but still a lot taller than her five foot one inches.

Marina smiled at the memory of the first time she'd seen John. He'd pulled her sister over for running a red light but the only reason Stephanie did was because Marina was in labour and screaming bloody murder. She'd nicknamed him Officer Hunky, but she didn't know he had a brother. Officer Sexy as Sin.

James' career in law enforcement obviously required him to be in good physical condition and boy was he. The white T-shirt he wore stretched across his broad chest, and the sleeves strained over his biceps almost to the point it could possibly rip. Black jeans hung low on his hips and cupped his amazing ass in just the right way. She'd managed to take a quick peek when he'd bent over to pick up a spoon he'd dropped. How could she not? The man oozed sex appeal and didn't even know it.

As if her hormones weren't already in overdrive, James raised his arms over his head and cupped his hands behind his head as he listened to John tell them about their plans. His shirt rose up over his stomach, revealing a very happy trail that made Marina's mouth drop open. It was all she could do to quickly snap it shut and prayed nobody noticed, but her sister's snort assured her Stephanie didn't miss a thing. Marina glared at her older sister but a scream from the back yard had all four of them jumping to their feet.

Danny ran through the door his eyes wide and yelling, "Mason falled down and he got blood comin' out his knee." James didn't say a word as he bolted outside and returned with a crying Mason in his arms. John appeared with a first-aid kit and Stephanie with a couple of cloths. James kept his attention totally on his son. He spoke to Mason in a soft, soothing voice to calm the squealing boy as he gently cleaned Mason's knee. The whole scene only made her more attracted to him. *I'm so pathetic.*

"You okay, Mason?" Danny's brows furrowed while James crouched to examine Mason's injury.

"He'll be okay, buddy. It's just a scratch but they can hurt a lot sometimes." James turned to Danny and gave him a smile. *Those damn dimples.* Then he had to go and let Danny put the Band-Aid on Mason's knee. *Oh dear Jesus.* Did he have to be so sweet with her son? It was making it difficult to rein in her fascination with him, especially when he did something so sweet. She smiled when he helped Danny open the second Band-Aid because the first one somehow got twisted. What else could she do when he was being so attentive to her child? At that point Stephanie walked up next to her and nudged her shoulder. *Damn it. Caught again.*

"Don't start, Steph," Marina whispered and made a quick exit from the kitchen with Stephanie close on her tail.

"Start what, Rina?" Stephanie was obviously gloating.

"I know what you're thinking and it's nothing." Hopefully her voice sounded as firm as she meant it to be.

"For your information, I wasn't thinking anything, but I can see very well and you're captivated by him." God she wanted to smack the grin off her sister's face.

"Yes, he's handsome and he's a great dad, but you can forget whatever devious plan you've got in that brain of yours." Marina flopped down on the couch and Stephanie stood in front of her.

"I don't have any devious plans but I do think Cora is right about you two." With that statement she turned and left Marina to roll her eyes.

The infamous Cora Nightingale otherwise known as Cora the Cupid. The story she'd been told was, when Cora met people, she had a gift of knowing who they were meant to be with and she made no bones about telling them. The first time Marina met the woman was at Stephanie's wedding shower. She'd been invited because not only was she Stephanie's boss but also John's aunt. The woman walked right up to Marina, wrapped her arms around her and asked if she'd met John's twin brother James. So now whenever Marina was in the company of any of the women in the O'Connor family, they'd never fail to remind her that Cora was never wrong. As if the woman had some magical power to know the future.

This was not a conversation Marina was in the mood for at the moment. Especially, with James only a few feet away. She knew her sister meant well, but Marina just wasn't sure she was ready to jump into anything with someone that caused her to have such intense emotion. She'd promised herself that she'd never let her emotions dictate her again.

She'd almost completely relaxed when the front door burst open and in floated Nanny Betty. This was not what she needed at the moment. The O'Connor matriarch was a sweetheart, but she didn't seem to have the buffer that made you think before you spoke. Marina knew before she could get a chance to leave that Nanny Betty was going to have her flustered, especially if she said anything in front of James.

"How are ya, ducky?" Nanny Betty's sweet Irish lilt echoed through the room. Marina knew Nanny Betty was from the Southern Shore of Newfoundland but even if she didn't know she'd have figured it out pretty quickly from her accent. For a tiny woman she certainly knew how to make her presence known.

"I'm good, Mrs. O'Connor. How are you?" Marina asked.

"Mrs. O'Connor was me mudder-in-law and I was taught not ta speak ill of da dead, or I'd tell ya she was a contrary old bat. Ya call me Nan or Nanny Betty." She pulled off her coat, and Marina jumped up to help her but she quickly backed off when Nanny Betty held up her hand. "I've been taking off me coat fer over seventy years."

"Nan, what are you doing here?" John walked into the living room followed by Stephanie and James.

"Why does everyone ask me dat? I came ta see ye two before ya go." John and James both bent to kiss her cheeks as did all the O'Connor men whenever she entered the house. It was as if she was the queen and they all treated her that way.

"You know we love to see you, Nan." Stephanie hugged the tiny woman and linked into her arm.

"It's nice ta see ye two here together." Nanny Betty glanced between Marina and James. Marina could feel her cheeks burn as James smiled at her.

"They were both here for supper, Nan." John chuckled.

"Hmmmm…" Nanny Betty sat next to her and Marina knew what was coming next. "My Cora is never wrong."

Stephanie stifled a giggle as she tucked herself into John's side.

James seemed to be as uncomfortable with the statement as she was. Obviously, the family had kept him in the loop of Cora's conclusion. This was going to make things even more awkward. If that was possible.

"How did you get here, Nan?" James asked, and Marina didn't miss the quick glance he gave her. Thank God her brother-in-law could see how uncomfortable his grandmother was making her.

"I walked a'course," Nanny Betty said.

"It's pretty dark out there—you shouldn't be out walking by yourself," John said.

"Johnny, I've been walking around dis town since ya parents moved here and I'm not about ta stop now." Nanny Betty pointed her boney finger at him and turned to Marina. "They'd have me in a wheelchair and locked in a room if I let them."

Marina couldn't help but laugh as the older woman glared at John. In the times she'd been around the family, she'd seen Nanny Betty give one of the family members 'the look' as they called it. It always worked, even on all the large men in the family. Marina wondered if she should take lessons from the older woman to make sure she kept Danny in line.

Marina was ready to go home. She was wound up tighter than a drum from being around James and dodging Stephanie's subtle hints as well as Nanny Betty's not so subtle ones. She was in the foyer helping Danny with his jacket as the front door opened and she stared into the face of yet another gorgeous O'Connor brother. Nick smiled at her but his smile didn't give her the same intense reaction she got when James smiled at her.

"Hi, Unca Nick." Danny bolted right to him and jumped into Nick's arms. He truly loved John's brothers.

"Hey there, Dan the man." Nick tossed him into the air. "Are you here to spend time with Uncle John and Aunt Stephanie before they go on vacation?"

"Yep, and they gonna bring me back a surprise," he boasted.

"Lucky you." Nick chuckled as he put Danny down and before Marina could catch him Danny ran back into the living room.

"Danny!" Marina groaned and glanced at Nick.

"I'm guessing he doesn't want to go because Mason is here. I saw James' truck outside." Nick smiled again. He really was a great-looking guy with the same blue eyes and dimples but he didn't give her the butterflies in her stomach or make her pulse race. Not that she wanted to have that reaction, but it just forced her to admit that the way James made her feel was not because she'd been celibate for so long.

"Yeah, and your grandmother." She sighed and followed Nick into the living room.

"Let me guess, she walked from home?" Nick rolled his eyes.

"You know her very well." Marina chuckled.

She finally managed to drag Danny out through the front door once he finished hugging everyone for the fourth time and promised Nanny Betty he would come help her make cookies soon. He started to whine as she buckled him into his car seat, proving that her son was up way past bedtime. As she settled herself in the car she glanced up to see Nick and John lugging suitcases out to Nick's truck.

She pulled on her seatbelt and then put the key in the ignition. She turned it and nothing happened. She tried again but the car growled a bit and then nothing. She tried once more just to be sure, but still nothing. *This is just what I need right now*. Marina got out of the car and pulled Danny out of his car seat. Marina walked back into the house as Stephanie was putting on her coat.

"My car won't start," Marina explained when Stephanie stared at her.

"What's wrong with it?" Stephanie asked.

"I just said it won't start. It thinks about it, but then nothing." Marina didn't mean to sound nasty but she was tired and sexually frustrated.

She followed Stephanie into the living room where James was helping Mason with his coat and talking to John and Nick. All three men glanced in her direction.

"Rina's car won't start," Stephanie explained.

"I'll take a look at it," John replied. Marina tossed him the keys as he passed her.

"Let me give you a hand." James followed him.

"Yeah, 'cause two cops know how to fix a car." Nick chuckled as he trailed behind them.

"Don't ya worry, ducky. Jimmy will figure it out," Nanny Betty said as she pulled on her coat.

A few minutes later, they walked back into the house. Their diagnosis, a problem with the starter. Marina had no idea what that meant, but she did know it meant she had to call a cab for a two-minute drive. There was no way Danny was going to walk home.

"I'll call the garage tomorrow to pick it up." Marina put her phone to her ear, "I need a cab..." Nanny Betty snatched her phone from her hand.

"Never mind, we don't need a cab. Thanks anyway." She handed her back the phone. "Jimmy can drop you and Danny off." Of course it made sense. They lived on the same street.

"I can't ask him to do that." Marina's heart thumped in her chest. Stephanie's house was only two minutes away from hers by car but being in the close confines of his truck was going to drive her hormones into overdrive.

"It's not like I'm going out of my way and besides, I'm not arguing with Nan, but you can go ahead and try." He smiled as he lifted Mason into his arms. The man had to stop smiling or she was going to melt into a puddle on the floor.

"No thanks," Marina said and besides Nanny Betty had already told Danny he was going for a ride in James' truck. Danny would have a fit if she said no and besides she was just too tired to argue with anyone right now. She pulled the car seat out of the back seat and James took it out of her hands.

For two little boys who seemed to be so tired a few minutes earlier, Mason and Danny were making it difficult to buckle them into their seats. They enjoyed spending time together and got along really well.

Once Marina was buckled in herself, James pulled out of the driveway with a honk to his brother. Stephanie and Nanny Betty waved from the doorway with huge grins on their faces. Marina rolled her eyes because she knew exactly what was going through both of their minds.

"I've got to drop into the store on the way home. I hope you don't mind." James made a left-hand turn off Sunset Street, down Sandcastle Road and on to Beach Street. It was the only road in Hopedale that didn't have any homes on it. Probably because Hopedale Beach ran the entire length of the street. It was one of the prettiest places she'd ever seen, and during the summer she spent a lot of time there with Danny.

It wasn't a sandy beach like those you see in the tropical places she read about because it was covered in beach rocks. Danny enjoyed going there to search through the rocks to find the perfect one to add to his collection. Something he started right after his first trip to the beach and now he kept them in a large box under his bed. It didn't matter to her if he brought home one rock or a hundred because it was relaxing to sit there and listen to the roar of the ocean, but now that winter was around the corner, the beach wasn't the best place to go. The breeze that blew in off the water was bitterly cold.

James pulled onto Harbour Drive where all the main businesses lined the harbour front. There was one small grocery store, a fine dining restaurant that belonged to James' cousin Isabelle, two night clubs or at least Hopedale's version of nightclubs, an Irish pub called Jack's place that was owned by another member of the O'Connor family. The rest of the businesses were an ice cream shop, theater, a coffee shop, drug store and a gas station. There were also a few buildings that were vacant. That was the extent of Hopedale's business district.

"I'll be right back." James stepped out of the truck. "Did you need anything while I'm inside?" Marina shook her head and James closed the door. Her gaze followed him as he dashed across the parking lot and disappeared into the grocery store. Marina leaned her head back against the seat and watched the people walk down the street, most of them with smiles and looks of contentment on their faces. As if they didn't have a worry in the world, and it was one of the things she loved about the small community, because although each one of them could be going through some bad times, it didn't matter, most of the population of Hopedale were friendly and stood by each other. It was probably why the O'Connors were so close, since they were born and raised in the town.

James walked out of the grocery store and back to the truck. As he settled into his seat, she studied his profile. His full lips seemed to get most of her attention, and she wondered what it would be like to kiss him, just once. Her attention moved to his hands as they gripped the steering wheel. They appeared strong, and she ached so badly to feel him touch her that she had to squeeze her legs together. She really needed to stop before she drove herself crazy, because being with James O'Connor was an impossible fantasy. Her past was still too fresh in her mind, and giving herself freely to anyone seemed impossible. That wouldn't be fair to him. "Marina?" James waved his hand in front of her face.

"Huh." She glanced up to see the only traffic light in Hopedale was red.

"I asked if you want to take the boys for some ice cream before you go home." The light turned green and James proceeded through the intersection.

"It's getting kinda late." She needed to get home and away from him, because he muddled her brain to the point she was pretty close to completely embarrassing herself.

"Maybe another time." He sounded disappointed but she was probably reading more into it.

The rest of the way home was relatively quiet since the boys had dozed off. The soft sound of country music floated from the radio through the cab of the truck and she felt her own eyes getting heavy as they turned onto Hart Street.

"What the hell?" James pulled his truck in behind a police cruiser parked in front of her house.

"What's going on?" Marina leaned forward as James pulled his truck across the street.

"Stay there and let me find out." James was out of the truck before she could respond. His command kind of took her off guard but to her surprise it didn't give her that sick feeling in the pit of her stomach. The one she got whenever Marc gave her a demand.

She watched as he ran across the road and was met by one of the officers standing in her driveway as another walked out of the house and stood next to James. He towered over the first one, but the second was about the same height. Marina realized the shorter one was female and when the woman touched James on the arm, Marina's whole body tensed. Being jealous over a woman touching James was ridiculous. He was single and the burning sensation in her stomach had nothing to do with the thought of someone making a play for James.

She was worried since police were in front of her house and not because that woman could possibly be interested in James. When Danny spoke Marina forced herself to turn around. Anything so she wouldn't have to watch the way the female officer was gazing up at James.

She was entertaining the boys by singing with them when the truck door opened. James stood with Aaron or A.J. as everyone called him. Aaron was also a police officer and another ridiculously gorgeous O'Connor brother. What the hell did their parents have in their genes?

"Marina, I need you to come out here for a minute." James' expression was unreadable and Aaron wasn't giving anything away either. Talk about having a poker face. She encouraged the boys to keep singing so she could hear them outside when the door was closed. The muffled sounds of the boys singing the alphabet song wasn't making her feel any better.

"What's wrong?" Marina glanced at her house as another cop walked into her home.

"Someone broke into your house. A.J's been trying to get in touch with you," James explained as her knees wobbled and she fell back against the truck. He caught her around the waist and helped to steady her.

"My phone is dead. Who…who would break into my house?" She could barely get the words out she was shaking so badly.

"Sandy got home about an hour ago and saw your front door open," Aaron started to explain. Sandy was her neighbor and one of her sister's close friends. "She noticed your car wasn't in the driveway and went to check it out." Sandy worked for the Newfoundland Police Department, but her main job was with Keith O'Connor's security firm. Marina didn't know a lot about his business but she did know the men that worked for Keith were highly trained for security.

"Sandy called the station and A.J. heard the call go out over the radio. He got here a few minutes ago." James was still holding her and she was glad because she wasn't sure if she'd be able to stand on her own.

"Marina, the house has been cleared, but you need to go inside to see if anything is missing," Aaron said. It was strange to see him so serious, because any time she'd been in his company, he was usually clowning around and flirting with her. She knew he didn't mean anything by it because she'd been told a long time ago Aaron, Nick and Mike were habitual flirts.

"I can't take Danny in there." She didn't know what she had to face and if it was as bad as she was expecting, it would probably scare her son.

"I'll stay with the boys, and James can take you through the house." Aaron opened the door to the truck and had the boys laughing in seconds. James wrapped his arm around her and guided her towards the house. She had a feeling if he wasn't supporting her, she would be flat on her face.

Her heart raced as she peered through the front door. The house looked like a tornado had blown through it. Things were thrown everywhere and all she wanted to do was break down in tears. She glanced up at James and he tightened his arm around her.

"Marina, I know this is hard but you've got to see if anything is missing. Just try not to touch anything."

She nodded because she couldn't do anything else.

In the living room, all her ornaments and trinkets littered the floor with most of them smashed to pieces. Her couch and loveseat were sliced open with the stuffing pulled out and thrown all over the floor. Her television lay on the floor with the screen shattered. Tears filled her eyes and she blinked them back before they spilled over. James must have sensed her distress because he wrapped both arms around her and it gave her the strength she needed to continue through the house.

She stepped over the mess on the way to her bedroom. Her dressers smashed to pieces and her clothes were everywhere. The picture of Danny she had on her nightstand was face down on the floor and her lamp was in pieces. She didn't know when the tears started to fall, but they were streaming down her cheeks.

"I… I… d… don't think anything is missing but everything is destroyed." She sobbed as she turned into James' strong embrace and buried her face into his chest. "W…Why would someone do this?"

"People are cruel, honey." James soft voice vibrated into her ear. "Are you sure nothing's missing?"

"I can't be sure, but I don't think so." She turned out of his arms and picked up the picture frame that held Danny's picture. The pieces of glass hit the floor when she turned it over but the picture was not in it. She scanned the floor but it was impossible to tell where it was especially with the mess.

"Marina, grab some of your things." She nodded. "I'll bring you back to John's." She picked up some of her clothes from the floor and threw them in an overnight bag. She was afraid to touch anything but took another minute to find Danny's picture.

"What are you looking for?" James asked.

"The picture of Danny that was in this frame. It's gone." Marina held up the broken frame.

"Honey, it's probably under this mess. We'll find it when we can get back here and clean everything up." James took the bag from her hand and wrapped his arm around her shoulder.

"I know it was there this morning because I knocked it over when I turned off the alarm." For some reason it gave her an uneasy feeling that she couldn't find it. It was just a picture but she couldn't let it go.

"We'll find it, but we just can't touch too much right now." James guided her out of the room and the tears formed in her eyes again.

James led her into Danny's bedroom to grab some things for him as well. His room was not touched. Everything looked the same as it did when she left that morning. She assumed the person that broke in figured they wouldn't find anything of value in a child's room. Although nothing seemed to be missing.

"Shit!" James groaned and Marina's head snapped up from where she was putting Danny's things into a bag.

"What's wrong?" She glanced around for what had caused his outburst.

"I just remembered John and Stephanie are gone to the airport." James picked up a teddy bear that was laying on Danny's bed and held it up to her. Marina nodded because they needed to take it since it was Danny's favorite.

"That's okay, I can stay at the motel on Harbor Street until tomorrow. I should be able to get back in here by tomorrow afternoon, right?" She wasn't comfortable staying at a motel, but what other option did she have? Stephanie and John were probably on the plane by now and her parents were out of the province, not that it mattered because her car wasn't working, so she wouldn't be able to get into town anyway.

"You're not staying at the Harbour Inn by yourself with Danny. For one Stephanie would kill me for letting you. Second, I've seen your dad and I don't want to piss him off. Third my mother and grandmother would string me up. So for my safety you're coming to my house tonight. The boys will enjoy it and I'd feel better knowing you're not alone."

"James, thanks but I can't impose on you." Marina closed Danny's overnight bag and followed James out of the room.

"You're not imposing. You're keeping me from getting my ass kicked, and besides you're part of my family. That's the end of it. You're coming to my house and no arguments." James gently grasped her hand and led her from the house.

"I guess you're not giving me a choice." Marina sighed as James guided her to his truck.

"You've met Nan, right? She'd kill me. So no, I'm not giving you a choice." James chuckled.

"Yes, I've met her and since your life would probably be in danger, I won't argue." Marina laid her head back against the seat once she climbed into the truck. James closed her door and spoke to Aaron for a few minutes. "I'm too scared to argue," she whispered to herself.

James hopped into the truck and glanced at her. She forced a smile but he seemed to sense it wasn't real and reached for her hand. The odd thing was, it was comforting and unnerving at the same time. She turned her head to look at him. It would be so easy to fall in love with him. That was something she had to shake from her thoughts, because falling in love was the last thing she needed. Besides, James was a friend helping another friend. That was all.

She glanced back at her house and it suddenly seemed eerie with the red and blue lights from the police cars flashing across the front of it. How could the little house that she loved now strike fear in her heart? Probably because something was telling her that this break in had a whole lot more to it than just someone trying to steal something.

Chapter 6

James led Marina into his house as Mason and Danny darted past them and right into the living room. They didn't seem to be affected by the night's events but Marina was quiet. He had a feeling she was keeping her composure for Danny's sake.

When he dropped Marina and Danny's bags at the bottom of the stairs, he motioned for her to follow him into the living room. He was somewhat embarrassed since he hadn't had a chance to tidy up before he'd left that morning.

"Sorry about the mess." James hurried around the room picking up Mason's toys that were scattered around the room. Hopefully, she didn't think he lived with the mess all the time.

"Toys aren't a mess." Marina smiled as she handed him a small Matchbox car and sat down. "My mom says if you walk into a house with kids and it's neat, the kids aren't happy."

"If that's true, Mason must be damn near delirious." James chuckled. "I'm just going to bring your things up to the spare room."

Marina nodded and turned her gaze towards the window. James stood in the doorway for a moment as he studied her. She always sat with her back rigid and her shoulders hunched. Always as if she was expecting something to happen, but at that moment she looked about ready to jump out of her skin.

James made his way up the stairs two at a time with Mason and Danny behind him. He wasn't surprised in the least that Danny knew exactly where Mason's bedroom was. John had brought Marina's son over several times to play with Mason and he'd even slept over a couple of times.

James dropped the bags on the bed in the spare room and then headed to Mason's room. The boys were head and arms into the toy box. James grabbed a couple of pajamas from Mason's dresser as they pulled out the huge box of Legos.

"Why don't you boys get on these PJs and then you can play for a little while before bed." They quickly stripped down and pulled on the Spiderman pajamas with each of them needing some help getting their arms into the sleeves. The next thing James saw was Lego blocks being tipped onto the floor. He reminded Mason to pick them up when they were finished, but he knew he was going to be stepping on at least one of the damn blocks before the night was over. The damn things hurt like a son of a bitch too.

When he got back downstairs, he entered the living room but Marina wasn't on the couch. James scanned the room and spotted her next to the mantel staring at the pictures lining the shelf over the fireplace. She turned, smiled at him and his heart felt like it flipped in his chest. The way she affected him was still so unsettling.

"You've got a really nice place." She glanced around the room.

"It's nothing fancy but thanks." He flopped down on the couch. "I forgot you've never been here." Marina sat next to him with a sigh but the nervous silence between them was almost deafening. James sat forward with his elbows resting on his knees.

"The boys are playing in Mason's room." She nodded. "Would you like a cup of tea or something?" James really needed to break the silence before he went crazy. She nodded again as he stood up.

Marina followed behind him and sat at the kitchen table with her hands folded in front of her. Once he'd flicked on the kettle and pulled two cups from the cupboard, he turned around to see her staring at him. He'd never been so aware of a woman in his life and it was as if her presence enveloped him.

"Are you okay?" Her beautiful face was pale and her eyes glistened with unshed tears he knew she'd been holding back.

"A bit confused and worried, I guess." She dropped her gaze to her hands. He wanted to wrap her in his arms and tell her everything was going to be okay, but if he touched her right now he wouldn't be able to let her go. Touching her earlier had taken every ounce of strength he had not to keep her tight in his arms.

"Marina, you'll be fine here, and we'll get to the bottom of all this." Comforting her from a distance was the only option because touching her again was a no-no.

"I've never had anything like that happen to me. I feel violated." Her eyes filled with tears and his heart thudded in his chest. *Shit, if she cries I'm so screwed.*

"That's understandable." A change of subject was needed quickly. "Hey, it's getting late, why don't we get the boys settled for the night and we can chat a bit afterwards?" The distraction worked because she smiled and followed him upstairs. The tears stopped, at least for the moment.

Mason and Danny were still excited about having a sleepover and it took quite a while to settle them down. Marina read them a story and then they negotiated a second story from James. Hopefully, Mason was distracted enough to forget their nightly ritual.

Every night before Mason went to sleep James sang to him, a song Mason called 'the tough boy song.' James was uncomfortable singing in front of anyone outside his family. His brothers, with the exception of him, Ian and Keith sang in a band they'd formed to help raise money for different charities around the province. James hated the spotlight so he only sang to Mason and his grandmother on her birthday.

James kissed Mason's forehead and was almost out of the room when Mason sat up in the bed.

"Daddy, you forgot the tough boy's song." The word forgot sounded more like *fordot*. James groaned inwardly because the kid wasn't going to settle down until he heard the song. James glanced at Marina and she was staring at him with a raised eyebrow. His face heated because by the cute grin forming on her face, she had no intention of leaving the room.

"It's a Gary Allan song, *Tough Little Boys*." James sat on the bed next to Mason and tried to act as if it was no big deal. "I sing it to him every night."

"I see." Marina's smirk said she definitely wasn't going to leave.

"Okay buddy, lay down." James took a deep breath and began to sing. He could feel the heat of her gaze on the back of his head. As usual, halfway through the song Mason was out like a light. He glanced at Danny and it seemed the song worked on both of them.

It took everything he had to turn around. Marina had her back propped against the doorjamb and her arms wrapped around herself. The soft glow of the nightlight made her green eyes sparkle and then she smiled. *So God damn beautiful.* He wanted her so badly, but he still felt guilty wanting another woman.

"You've got an amazing voice," Marina whispered as they left the room.

"Thank you." He closed the door and turned.

"Why don't you sing with the band?" James was already halfway down the stairs and desperately hoping she wouldn't ask that question. Why wasn't he in the band with his brothers? Probably because the thought of singing in front of people made his stomach churn.

He'd had stage fright since high school when he was given a solo with the school choir, but that day he hadn't been feeling well. When he walked to the front of the stage one of the popular girls in school was sitting in the front row and he had a huge crush on her. He started to sing and when he glanced down at her, she was laughing. It was at that point his stomach revolted and he threw up all over the stage with some of it hitting the girl. He hadn't been able to sing in front of a crowd since.

"I just don't like the spotlight." He turned when he got to the bottom of the stairs. "How about that tea?" She nodded. "Make yourself at home and I'll bring it into the living room."

In the kitchen he tried to slow his racing heart. Just knowing she'd heard him sing made him feel that way. The only other person besides his family that heard him sing was Sarah. His grandmother called it stage fright, but he called it not wanting to relive the most embarrassing moment of his life. After all, he was a big strong cop who wasn't supposed to be afraid of anything or at least Mason seemed to think that. The truth was James was terrified when it came to being around Marina, or maybe it was the overwhelming guilt for betraying Sarah.

James brought the tea into the living room and handed one cup to Marina. He wasn't a big tea drinker himself, but he poured himself one. She smiled when he glanced at her but it wasn't hard to tell her mind was still reeling from her house being trashed. If he was being honest, he was concerned about it himself. People just don't break into people's homes and destroy everything for no reason and especially not in Hopedale. Not unless it's personal, and that's what worried him the most.

Marina's ex-husband, Marc O'Reilly, put her through more than any woman should have to go through. Just before John and Stephanie got married, Marc tried to break down John's front door to get to her. Now Marina lived in that same house. Something told him her ex-husband was written all over this.

"Oh my goodness." Marina covered her mouth to stifle a yawn. "I'm sorry, I haven't been getting a lot of sleep lately."

"Well, you can sleep in tomorrow." James had a feeling her lack of sleep had to do with the nightmare last night. "It's been a rough evening. I'll show you to the guest room." He reached out and touched her hand. *That was a mistake.* James gazed into her eyes and as if a string was pulling him, he leaned forward. The doorbell rang, breaking the spell. James jumped up and almost tripped over the coffee table on the way to the door. *Saved by the bell.*

"Hey, bro." Aaron sauntered in with his cocky smile and attitude to match.

"What's up?" James closed the door.

"I just wanted to let you know there's a cruiser watching Marina's place." Aaron followed him into the living room. "I don't know when she's going to be able to get back into the house. The place is a mess, but they did get some fingerprints so we should know more tomorrow." Marina stood up when they entered the room.

"A.J. dropped by with an update." James nodded at his brother.

"Hi A.J.." Her voice was shaky as she sat back on the sofa.

Aaron filled her in on what he knew and her face drained of all its color. James was about to go to her but Aaron was faster and gently grasped her hand as he sat next to her. In his head James knew Aaron was just trying to comfort the woman, but it made James want to punch his youngest brother in the face.

"We'll find out who did this, Marina." Aaron kissed her hand before he released it and stood up.

"You said it's going to be a while before I can move back, but you don't have any idea how long?" Her voice was barely above a whisper.

"It'll probably be a couple of days before we're finished with our investigation, but it's a real mess," Aaron said as James walked up next to him still controlling the urge to slap his brother.

"We'll help you clean it up." James nudged Aaron with his elbow and thank God he got the hint, because James really would have punched him if he hadn't.

"Of course we will. There's enough of us O'Connors in Hopedale to have it cleaned up in no time." Marina smiled but it was obvious she was forcing it.

Aaron left after a quick cup of coffee and assured James he'd keep them up to date on the investigation since James was off for a week. A few inappropriate jokes and comments later and James was almost shoving Aaron out the front door.

"Jesus Christ, bro, if you wanted to be alone with her all you had to do was ask," Aaron whispered when James pushed him through the door.

"Fuck off, A.J," James growled. He was really going to kick the bastard down over the steps. How Aaron made it to the ripe old age of twenty-six without one of them pounding the shit out of him was beyond James. Not that they didn't give him his fair share of sly pokes during their younger years, but as the baby of the family his youngest brother always seemed to know which buttons to push with all the brothers and right now he was pushing a major one with James.

"It's been way to long for you, bro. You should probably do something about that." Aaron jumped into the cruiser.

"I swear to God, A.J, one of these days…" James never got a chance to finish the statement because Aaron was pulling out of the driveway and he could see the bastard laughing behind the wheel.

He closed the door and turned his attention to the one person that really needed it. Marina was going to need a place to stay until her house was cleaned up, and she was going to argue if he suggested she stay with him until then. With her sister and John out of town as well as her parents, he didn't see any other options or at least he didn't want to see one. It was obvious from his quick glance around her house she was going to need new furniture as well. Most of what she owned was destroyed. He was sure between all of his family, they'd manage to come up with enough furniture for her so she wouldn't have to go out and purchase all new.

As he was running through how to get Marina to agree to stay, James remembered Ian was supposed to be staying with him for a few days. He'd have to call Ian to fill him in on the situation and let him know he could still stay, but he'd have to crash on the couch since James had given Marina the guest room.

As he reached in his pocket to grab his phone, it began to vibrate in his hand. He tapped the screen to see Ian's number flashing.

"Hey, bro, I was just about to call you." James slid into the kitchen so Marina wouldn't hear the conversation. The last thing he needed was for her to feel she was pushing Ian out.

"I guess I saved you the trouble of tapping in the phone number." Ian chuckled. James heard a muffled giggle in the background and smiled.

"Who's that?" James asked.

"An old friend. I just wanted to let you know I'm going to stay in St. John's so I won't need to stay at your place." Ian didn't sound like himself.

"That works out great because Marina and Danny are staying with me for a bit. Her house was broken into and everything is trashed," James explained.

"What the fuck is with that damn house? When John was there, something was always happening to it." Ian was referring to the numerous attempts on Stephanie's life when she and John lived in the house.

"I don't know. You're still welcome to stay but you'd have to crash on the sofa." James told him.

"Thanks, bro, but I'm good." Another giggle. "Gotta go." James chuckled when he hung up the phone. Seemed like Ian was getting lucky and he wondered if he'd finally made a move on Sandy. The thought had no sooner entered his head, when a knock sounded.

James opened the door and quickly realized the giggling he'd heard on the phone wasn't Sandy since she was standing on the other side of the door. Now he was confused, because he knew Ian was crazy about Sandy and it wasn't typical for him to run off with some random woman.

"Hi, James," Sandy said as he motioned her inside.

"Hi." It was odd for her to drop by his house.

"I wanted to see if Marina needed anything."

"She's in the living room." James motioned for her to go ahead of him.

Marina was on the edge of the sofa with her elbows resting on her knees and her hands over her face. It didn't take long for Sandy to hurry next to her and wrap her arm around Marina's shoulder. When she lifted her head, James felt a squeeze in his chest. Tears ran down her cheeks and she swiped them away with her fingers. It broke his heart to see her like that and all he wanted to do was pull her into his arms to make her forget all of it.

"Marina, everything will be okay," Sandy told her as she reached for the box of tissues he always kept on the table.

"I'm okay, really." Marina took a deep breath and let it out slowly.

"Of course you are." Sandy nudged her with her shoulder. "You're a tough cookie."

Marina smiled at the woman sitting next to her. Sandy had become part of his family over the last few years. She worked for Keith and his quiet brother seemed quite protective of her. For a while James thought Keith might have had a thing for the perky woman, but at one of their monthly brother bonding nights it had been brought up about Keith and Sandy. Ian's face had turned completely red and James remembered expecting steam to come out of his ears. Keith must have noticed it too and made a point of saying Sandy was like a sister to him nothing more. Ian relaxed and it was forgotten but James still wondered why Keith seem to be more protective over Sandy than any of his other employees.

"Sandy's right, you need a good night's sleep, and we'll figure everything out in the morning." Hopefully they'd know more by then.

"Everything always seems better after a good night's sleep. I'm going to head home but if you need anything call me." Sandy gave Marina another hug.

"Thank you, Sandy." Marina said.

"No thanks necessary, plus I know you're safe with James and Ian." Sandy stood up and turned towards James.

"Ian's gone back to St. John's." James wanted to take the statement back right away when Sandy's face fell.

"Oh. Well… I should go. I'll talk to you later." Sandy hurried past James and was out through the door before James could say anything. She was obviously upset, but James didn't really have time to deal with his brother's shit right now. He needed to make sure Marina was okay.

"That was odd." Marina nodded towards Sandy's hasty exit.

"I guess Ian didn't mention he was going back home." James sat next to her.

"She's head over heels for your brother." Marina smiled.

"I've no doubt the feelings are mutual." James chuckled. "But right now I'm more concerned about you."

"I'm fine, really. Just tired." Her tone didn't convince him.

"I'll show you where you'll be sleeping." James stood and wrapped his arm around her shoulders. He'd meant it as a friendly, supportive gesture but touching her turned his thoughts more than friendly. It pissed him off that his brain was going there at the moment because it was the last thing she needed, and the way her body tensed let him know that she wasn't comfortable with the gesture. He dropped his arm and motioned to the stairs.

At the top of the stairs James turned and headed down the short hallway to the spare room. She stopped and glanced towards Mason's room. As a parent, it was automatic to check your child before turning in for the night. James didn't even need to ask because he did it without even thinking about it anymore.

"Do you want to check on Danny before you turn in?" James knew the answer before he asked the question.

"He tends to kick off the blankets."

"I think it's a kid thing. Mason does the same thing."

Marina opened the bedroom door quietly and as usual, Mason's blankets were in a pile on the floor. James smiled and shook his head. *Every single night.* He picked up the blankets and tucked them around Mason. The youngster didn't stir. He was one of those kids that slept through anything, which was why it was a struggle to get him up in the mornings if he wasn't ready to get up. James turned to see Marina kissing Danny's forehead as she pulled the blanket up over him, and it looked as if Danny was a deep sleeper as well.

"I love you, Danny," Marina whispered before she backed away from the bed. James was standing in the doorway waiting for her. "I know it's weird to tell him I love him while he's sleeping but I believe he can hear it even in his dreams."

"I've no doubt." James smiled when she stifled another yawn. "I think I better show you to your room before you fall asleep standing up."

"I guess the rush is wearing off." Marina walked behind him down the hall and he could feel her eyes on him.

"This room is small but it serves the purpose." James switched on the light. "There's a bathroom right there." James pointed to the closed door on the other side of the room.

"Right now I think I could sleep on a clothes' line." She stretched her arms over her head and he had to hold back the groan at the sight of her bare stomach. He turned away before he really embarrassed himself, because at the sight, his dick twitched. Seeing Marina's curves in clothes was bad enough, but getting a glimpse of her milky white skin was not good for his hormones. Aaron was right. It had been a long while since he'd been with anyone, and that didn't help his urges.

"Goodnight and sleep well. If you need anything, I'm just down the hall," James rambled as he made a quick exit. The last thing he wanted was for her to notice the growing issue in his pants. *Fucking ridiculous.*

James rushed into his bedroom, closed the door and leaned his forehead against it. There was no way in hell he was going to get a good night's sleep. No woman ever affected him so easily besides Sarah, and it was as if his own body was betraying his late wife.

When he'd met Sarah Mason, he'd fallen so hard he thought he'd never recover from it. Sarah's grey eyes always sparkled with mischief, and she constantly kept James on his toes. She brought him out of his conservative shell because before Sarah, he was always the level-headed one. The one who thought everything out before he acted on anything. That's why when he proposed to Sarah, she hadn't seen it coming. Her eyes had filled with tears when she screamed 'yes.' The day she'd told him she was pregnant, he was scared to death because they'd agreed to put off having kids for a few years. Sarah being a fly-by-the-seat-of-her-pants kind of person, just told him that the baby was a wonderful surprise.

They were so happy when Mason was born and then they were given a cruel dose of reality when three months later, Sarah was diagnosed with breast cancer. It was like someone had thrown a bucket of ice over him because his blood had run cold. From that moment it was a nightmare to watch the woman he loved slowly fade away. She'd been so brave, even up until the end.

The first year after Sarah passed was incredibly hard. Trying to raise a little boy by himself with his hours at the station was rough. His parents and brothers helped as well as his neighbor, Mrs. Ray, but every night he still went to bed alone thinking of Sarah. Now he was in his bed thinking of another woman and it made him feel guilty. In his head he knew he needed to move on, but it wasn't easy.

"Sarah, I still miss you," James whispered as he lay back on his bed. "I know you want me to live my life and I'm trying, baby, but it's not easy."

The attraction to Marina was there and nothing could be done about that. She was beautiful with her wavy, honey-blonde hair that hung in soft waves most of the time unless she had it pulled back. Her green eyes were always so expressive and he could tell her every emotion just from gazing into them. Marina was curvier than her sister, probably because she'd had a child, but to him, it made her even sexier. Thinking about her body was a mistake because his cock twitched at the thought and the ache returned. If he didn't stop thinking about her he was going to go out of his mind and he definitely wasn't going to be able to sleep. *Shower time.*

After a relatively cold shower, James felt a little better. As he pulled on a pair of lounge pants and a T-shirt, his gaze landed on the picture of Sarah on their wedding day perched on his dresser. He thought he'd put the picture away. He didn't remember putting it back on his dresser, but it reminded him he was still wearing his ring. He glanced at his hand where it encircled his finger.

"Is this a sign you want me to take this off, or am I losing my mind?" He knew the answer and slowly slid the ring from his finger. It felt strange with it gone, but if he was going to keep his promise to Sarah, he had to say goodbye. It was time.

James placed the picture in the top drawer of his dresser and lay the ring on top of it. "Goodbye, my love. You'll always have a piece of my heart, but I'm going to keep my promise." James closed the drawer and flopped down on his bed. He glanced at his hand and the faint tan line from his ring, still a reminder of his late wife. His hand felt naked without it, but he had to get adjusted.

Everyone told him to get on with his life and it used to piss him off. Mostly because he couldn't see it happening. Then he met Marina and of course there was Aunt Cora. She made a point of telling him every time she saw him that his future was with Marina.

Even if he was ready to pursue something, it didn't mean she was. She had a rough marriage, and it was hard for people who were in abusive relationships to trust again. He could show her that not all men were like Marc. He put his hand behind his head and closed his eyes.

"Time will tell." Maybe Marina would give him some sign that she was ready to move on from her past and find a new future—hopefully with him.

Chapter 7

Marina stared at the closed door. It was beyond her how James could be so sweet to someone who was not exactly family. She shouldn't be surprised since the entire family had stepped up to help her when she first moved to Hopedale. Sometimes it was overwhelming with so many of them, but she also felt secure with them around.

She'd grown to care about the family over the last four years. James' parents were a lot like her own parents and would drop by from time to time to check on her and Danny. Danny loved them and would get just as excited to see them as when her own parents would come visit. James' cousins Isabelle, Jess and Kristy would drop by as well. Isabelle lived in Hopedale but the other girls lived in St. John's. They were all single and would try to talk her into going clubbing in town, but she'd always decline. Mostly because she hated the small strip of clubs in St. John's known as George Street. She hated the crowded clubs or how guys would cop a feel and then pretend it was an accident.

She did join them a couple of times at Jack's Place for a girls' night with her sister and Sandy, but she always felt guilty when she left Danny with a sitter to go out. Of course the conversations during those times would always lead to James and how she needed to make a move on him. She'd never been the aggressive type when it came to men, and she wasn't about to start with a man like James.

She really couldn't think about him anymore. She was emotionally exhausted and every muscle in her body was so tense she didn't know if she'd be able to relax. She grabbed her bag from the bed and slipped into the bathroom. When she flicked on the light, a new toothbrush and tube of toothpaste were sitting next to the sink. She'd forgotten she didn't have any of her toiletries. Luckily she kept her hairbrush in her purse so she didn't look as if she'd stuck her finger into a socket once she got up, but he'd saved her from having the breath from hell in the morning.

After brushing her teeth and shoving her hair up into a messy ponytail, Marina crawled onto the bed and pulled the covers over her. It had been such a long day, and with everything spinning around in her mind, she didn't know if sleep was going to be her friend tonight. She turned onto her side and curled her hands under her cheek.

As always, her brain was going a mile a minute as she ran through the events of the day. Someone broke into her home and touched her things, but not just touched them—destroyed them. She didn't have a lot, but her television and computer could be sold if someone needed money. Why break in and beat up things? It didn't make any sense. As if someone had poured ice water down her back, she shivered. If her car hadn't refused to start, she would have ended up going home to face everything alone.

Her mother believed things happened for a reason. Maybe the reason her car had died was the universe trying to keep her from dealing with the whole situation by herself or was trying to tell her something else. Maybe it was giving her a chance to get to know James in a way she'd been avoiding.

She'd been telling everyone she'd moved on from Marc and she wasn't going to let him run the rest of her life. The truth was, he was still running parts of her life. The part that opened her heart to another man and not just James, even though he was the only one she wanted, but any man. She'd turned down invites to dinner from a couple of guys from work and even a guy she'd met in Ottawa when she lived there. The thought of opening her heart to anyone again made her anxious, but for some reason she didn't feel that type of emotion with James. Probably because he hadn't asked her out or maybe it was because she was ready to move on.

She had to stop thinking about the man. She turned over and gazed out through the small bedroom window. It looked like it was going to rain, but that wasn't uncommon for October. At least it wasn't snowing yet and with that thought, James popped into her head again.

He'd kept her driveway cleared the winter before without her even asking. She thought Stephanie or John had put him up to it, but they'd denied it. Then she'd seen him a couple of days later clearing all the driveways on the street. Not that it was a lot because Hart Street only had four homes. He seemed to take it on himself to make sure nobody got stuck in their driveway during the winter.

He was such a considerate person, and she felt such a connection to him. In the beginning she'd thought it was because he was John's brother, but since she didn't feel the same draw to any of the other O'Connor brothers, she knew that wasn't it. Something about James was drawing her to him, and it was confusing.

Marc had been her last relationship. In the beginning it was wonderful, but the end was hell. Nobody knew everything Marc put her through. Not even her family.

She told Stephanie about the day she kicked him out of the house. The day Marina found the drugs, but Stephanie didn't know he'd almost killed her that night. To this day, she didn't know what stopped him. He pinned her against the wall with his hands around her throat and she remembered not being able to get any air as everything around her went fuzzy. She didn't know where the strength came from, but the next thing she knew he was on the other side of the room with her crumpled on the floor. It had been almost a week before she called her family because the bruises on her neck would have had them asking too many questions.

Part of her knew James was different from Marc, and it was hard to keep that part of herself from falling for the guy. Then there was the part of her that remembered how great Marc was in the beginning, and how he'd turned into a monster almost overnight. It made it hard to trust that what she saw with James was real.

The thing that terrified her the most was what James could do to her body with a single smile, or the scent of pine that always seemed to surround him. It was the same as an aphrodisiac to her, but someone's scent had never affected her before. When he'd wrapped his arms around her earlier, she'd almost bolted but something came over her. Almost as if his touch had some magical way of calming her frayed nerves. She felt safe. Nobody, besides her father, ever made her feel safe since all the crap with Marc but he did.

"I really need to get a grip," she whispered as she grabbed her cell phone. It was after midnight and she was exhausted, but sleep just wouldn't come. Why hadn't she taken a book from her house? *Oh yeah*. Probably because she wouldn't be able to find a book in the mess the intruder left behind. She'd seen a bookcase in James' living room,—maybe she could find something to read and help her relax.

It was dark downstairs with the exception of the light from the front lawn shining through the living room window. She found a lamp and switched it on because it was still too dark for her to see. The shelf didn't contain a huge variety of books; at least not the kind she would read. Most of them were on criminal codes, true crime, world wars, and police procedures. She raised her gaze to the top shelf and saw a small collection of old classic books. Most of them she hadn't read since she was a teenager. She ran her fingers across the binding of each one and stopped. Jane Eyre was her favorite of all time, and she'd fallen in love with it in high school. Jane had gone through such a difficult time, but in the end she found happiness. It was every woman's wish to find a happily ever after. She pulled it down off the shelf and settled herself on the sofa.

It was well worn, and she carefully opened the cover. The name inside made her eyes fill with tears. *Sarah Mason.* James' late wife obviously had read it numerous times and for some reason, a warm feeling flowed through her body. Almost as if someone was holding her hand and telling her she didn't have to be scared anymore. Something told her she would have liked Sarah, but she had no idea why since she didn't really know much about the woman except she'd died way too young.

She was floating, but secure and safe with warmth surrounding her. She was going higher and higher then, the floating stopped and she was eased into a cool fluffy cloud, but even though the warmth was gone, she knew she was in a place where she was protected. Her eyes fluttered open and a white knight stood over her, keeping her safe from all the evil in the world.

"Shhh… Go back to sleep, Marina." His soothing voice willed her to close her eyes again, and she sighed as she settled comfortably into the cloud.

Marina opened her eyes and sat straight up in the bed. How the hell was she in bed? The last thing she remembered was reading on the couch and then the wonderful dream of being wrapped in warm comfort as she floated. *Floated?*

"For the love of God, Marina. You're really losing your mind. That's the only explanation." She flopped back on the pillow. "And now you're talking to yourself." Marina grabbed her phone and cursed as the time glowed on the screen.

"Five a.m.? Are you kidding me?" Her internal clock never failed. Even if she went to bed late, her eyes opened at five. Now the desperation for coffee was kicking in, and she wasn't sure how James would feel about her rummaging around in his kitchen. She tried to distract herself by scrolling through social media, but it was no use.

After a few minutes, her craving took the lead and she crawled out of bed. After she pulled on a pair of jeans and tank top, she fixed her hair back into a neat ponytail. On her way out of the room she grabbed an outfit for Danny. Standing at the top of the stairs, she noticed James' bedroom door was still closed and the house was completely quiet. That meant the boys were still sleeping as well. She really needed some dark, liquid energy to get started. She tiptoed down the stairs and into the kitchen.

It was odd poking around someone else's kitchen, but surprisingly it was well organized. She found the coffee in a container right next to the coffee pot, the same as she kept it at home. Things for her in the morning needed to be as easy to find as possible because even though her internal clock woke her in the morning, she wasn't a morning person without her coffee. She couldn't even form a coherent thought until her first couple of sips.

She leaned against the counter and sipped the steaming coffee with her eyes closed. It was heaven. James was so kind to let her stay with him, she needed to find a way to repay him. She knew as a single parent, nobody ever cooked breakfast for her and she was pretty sure James hadn't had someone cook him breakfast in a long time. She searched around the cupboards and managed to find the ingredients for pancakes. This would be her way of saying thanks for being a friend. It didn't seem much, but it was the only thing she could think of.

She poured a second cup of coffee for herself and realized it was still relatively early, so she'd grab a quick shower to kill some time before the boys woke. Danny never slept past six, so she had about thirty minutes before chaos ensued. She was pretty sure even if Mason didn't normally wake up at six that Danny would ensure that his friend would be waking up.

She was digging through her overnight bag when she noticed the plastic bag stuffed inside it. When she opened it she found her body wash, shampoo and all the rest of her shower things along with

Danny's bubble bath. James must have grabbed it while she was getting the rest of the things together. How he managed to do it without her noticing she didn't know but she was more than thankful.

She stood in the shower and let the hot water flow over her for a few minutes. Her body was so tense from a combination of everything. Lack of sleep, worry about what had happened with her house and James. He made her body tense in a whole different way and since her vibrating helper was somewhere in the mess at her house and she didn't have time to relieve it manually.

"Oh, shit." She remembered James saying that he and his brothers would clean her house for her so she could move back in. She'd have to insist she be there because the last thing she needed was for one of them to find that little helper of hers. Especially A.J. because knowing him, he'd never let her live it down. He was a sweetheart like the rest of his brothers but he was the biggest flirt she'd ever met.

Reluctantly, she turned off the shower and quickly dressed in some fresh clothes because she was right on the money. As she got to the top of the stairs, the two boys came charging out of Mason's bedroom. She put her finger to her lips to quiet them down so they wouldn't wake James. That was if they hadn't already woken him.

"We're going to cook breakfast and surprise your Daddy," Marina whispered to Mason. She shook her head as the boys tiptoed downstairs behind her doing their best to whisper, but it was anything but quiet. If James didn't wake at this point he would sleep through anything. The thought of how James' parents dealt with seven boys made her chuckle. The noise from two was bad enough.

Mason was a big help as he showed her where James kept everything. He pulled the maple syrup out of the fridge and placed it on the table. He showed Danny where to get the forks, and Marina handed them plates to put on the table. They were bouncing around waiting for her to give them the cue to wake James. She'd lost count at how many times they'd asked if everything was ready.

"Can we wake Unca James now, Mommy?" Danny asked as she piled the large platter with the last of the pancakes. She only had one more batch to grill and they were so anxious, she couldn't make them wait anymore.

"Okay. Go." Marina laughed as they ran up the stairs sounding like a heard of elephants. James was going to be awake before they even got to the top of the stairs.

A picture of him sleeping on a bed flashed through her head, but it wasn't the boys waking him. It was her. In her mind he was naked and sexy as hell. She was getting lost in the daydream but the smell of burning pancakes snapped her back to reality.

"Damn it." She sighed as she turned them over to see they weren't too bad. She'd make sure that these ones were on her plate so at least James wouldn't think she was a terrible cook. Hopefully the smell of burned pancakes didn't linger. She poured the last of the batter onto the grill and made sure she kept her thoughts on the pancakes. Not on the beefcake upstairs.

Chapter 8

James didn't even know what time he'd eventually fallen asleep, but the aroma of coffee woke him. He couldn't remember setting the coffee machine but he did remember going downstairs the night before to see Marina curled up on the couch asleep holding Sarah's favorite book. It was not the most comfortable thing to sleep on and he didn't want to wake her, so he lifted her into his arms. Marina snuggled into him, making him aware he wasn't wearing a shirt.

Her warm breath brushed across his chest, causing him to sink his teeth into his bottom lip to keep from groaning. When he placed her on the bed, it took everything he had not to lay next to her and pull her into his arms. For a moment he thought she was going to wake up, but she just mumbled something about a white knight. When he told her to go back to sleep, he held his breath for the seconds her eyes were open, but they fluttered closed again and he quickly left the room.

He'd lay in his bed for hours after trying to force himself to sleep. It didn't work. He wondered if the reason she was on the couch was because of another nightmare. She didn't really admit that she was having them frequently but anybody with eyes could see she looked exhausted. He knew that anyone who'd been through the type of abuse Marina went through usually ended up seeing a therapist but he wasn't aware if she did. Maybe that was why she was having the bad dreams. It really was none of his business and he was sure she'd at least talked to someone in her family about it.

Mason and Danny burst into the room distracting his thoughts. He stretched to ease the stiffness in his muscles. His lack of sleep was playing havoc on his body and although the boys seemed to think they were surprising him; he'd heard them long before they came running into his room. They both started talking at the same time and it took a moment to figure out what they were trying to tell him.

"Auntie Marina says to tell you breakfast's ready." Mason jumped on the bed.

"Mommy made pancakes." Danny stood next to the bed jumping up and down.

"Okay, guys. You both go on down and I'll be right there." He gave his son a big hug and ruffled Danny's hair. They ran out of the room and he chuckled at how two little boys could make such a racket. He couldn't imagine the noise he and his six brothers must have made. His poor parents must have worn earplugs.

Marina was serving the pancakes onto the boys' plates when James entered the kitchen. Danny and Mason were digging in before she even finished pouring the syrup. She nodded towards the cup of steaming coffee as she piled another plate across from the boys.

"Here you go." She'd showered and her hair was still damp. The scent of some sort of berries filled his senses. It seemed she'd found the things he'd grabbed from her bathroom. That scent had been making him hard since the day he met her. Hell, it was at the point anytime he smelled something with berries he'd get aroused.

James pulled out the chair and sat quickly before she noticed. It was insane he was getting hard all because he smelled her shampoo or body wash. He still didn't know where the scent was actually coming from because he'd never been that close to find out. Even when he'd carried her to bed he was afraid to breathe too deeply.

"You didn't have to do this." He poured cream into his coffee as he watched her ease into the chair next to Danny.

"It's the least I could do after what you did for us." She covered her pancakes with syrup, and all he could think was the damn things were going to start floating on the plate.

"I didn't do anything." James smiled at Mason devouring his food, not because his son didn't eat, but he seemed to be really enjoying the pancakes.

"You did more than you think. I don't know what I would've done if I'd gone home alone." Her voice cracked.

"But you didn't, so don't mention it. I'm glad I was there." He met her eyes and had to quickly look away. "You should probably stay here until Stephanie and John get back home." Hopefully the statement sounded casual and not a plea for her to stay.

"I can't impose on you for three weeks, James. It wouldn't be right." She'd placed her fork on her plate and was shaking her head.

"Don't start that again." James sighed as Marina opened her mouth to speak. He put his finger to her lip. "I'd feel better and the boys will love it."

"Fine, but I'm hoping it won't take that long to get my place cleaned. Will it?" Her hopeful expression had him flinching since he didn't want to lie to her. The place was a disaster from what he'd seen, and it was going to take a while to repaint the walls and fix the front door. He wasn't sure if Marina had actually seen all the damage that was done.

"We'll have to take a better look at it, but it's pretty bad." He didn't want to upset her, especially in front of the kids. If she wanted to get back into her home as quickly as possible, he'd do everything he could to make that happen. He'd do anything to make her smile.

The rest of breakfast was pretty quiet except for the forks clinking against the plates. He'd glanced up several times to see

Marina wasn't actually eating much. She just seemed to be moving her food around her plate but Mason and Danny quickly cleaned their plates. Then Mason put James in a state of shock when he instructed Danny to put the plates in the dishwasher. James was constantly reminding him about clearing his dishes away. Guess it was another positive of having Marina at his house.

Marina began fixing the dishes in the dishwasher and wiping down the counter but when James tried to help, she waved him off. He liked how at home she was in his kitchen. Maybe a little too much because he knew she would be leaving as soon as her house was ready. His heart clenched when he thought about her going.

"You cooked breakfast, I'll clean up." James placed his cup into the dishwasher.

"Nope! You go do whatever you need to do. I got this." Marina turned him and pushed him out of the room and even though it was his kitchen, he knew better than to argue with a woman. His grandfather and father taught him that. He chuckled as he made his way upstairs thinking about all the times he'd heard his grandfather tell him he never argued with Nanny Betty because there was just no way to win an argument when a woman had a rolling pin in her hand.

James shaved, had a quick shower and got dressed. It was the fastest time he ever got ready in the morning because Mason wasn't running in every five minutes to ask him something. He also wanted to spend as much time with Marina as possible before she went back to her own house.

He raced back downstairs and heard the bouncy hip-hop music float out of the kitchen. It wasn't his favorite type of music, but it had a good beat. The lyrics said something about hearing the singer roar and an eye of the tiger.

He stepped into the doorway and stopped. Marina had her hands in the sink, but what drew his attention was the swing of her hips as she danced to the music with her slightly off-key singing. James leaned against the door-jamb and crossed his arms over his chest. He smiled as she sang louder to the chorus of the song. He chuckled as she raised her hand in the air at part of the chorus, causing her to turn around. Her face flushed beautifully as she scrambled to turn off the iPod and then turn back to the sink.

"Don't stop on my account." James casually moved to the counter and poured another cup of coffee. "Do you always do dishes that way?" he teased and hopped up onto the counter next to the sink.

"Okay, you caught me." Marina sighed. "I like to sing badly and dance when I clean." She tossed the cloth into the sink, and the soap splashed up on her cheek. James reached out without thinking and brushed it away with his thumb. Her tongue darted out and flicked across her lower lip as her gaze met his.

He cupped her cheek and it was as if a magnet was pulling him closer to her. His eyes moved to her lips and his thumb grazed the edge of her mouth. A soft gasp escaped her as her lips parted. His eyes moved back to hers and they drew him in as if they were talking to him, telling him to do the thing he'd been aching to do. James brushed his lips against her mouth and she whimpered but she didn't pull away. So he pressed his lips full against hers and slid his hand behind her head.

When she kissed him back, his body came alive for the first time in a long time, and he completely devoured her mouth with his. Her lips were soft and his tongue glided across the seam, begging to let him enter. She opened with a whimper and he plunged his tongue inside. She tasted of maple syrup, coffee and heaven. Marina fisted his shirt as he slid off the counter and plowed his fingers through her silky hair. Their kiss came to an abrupt halt when Mason and Danny thundered down the stairs. James stepped back just as the boys ran into the kitchen.

"Can we go to the park, Daddy?" Mason held his hands together as if he was praying.

"Sure, bud. You guys go grab your coats. It's probably a little chilly outside." They raced out of the kitchen chattering about slides and swings and who was going to climb the highest on the jungle gym.

Marina had turned back to the sink and her hands were in the water, but he couldn't see anything left to wash. She just stood there gazing down into the water. James put his finger under her chin and tipped it up so she had to look at him. She met his gaze and he could see the confusion and fear in them.

"I'm sorry, Marina. I shouldn't have kissed you." James pushed a stray piece of her hair away from her cheek.

"It's okay, it didn't mean anything." She pulled back from him and turned back to the sink. James put his hands on her shoulders and turned her to face him.

"I didn't say it didn't mean anything. I just don't know if either of us are ready for this but it isn't because I don't want it."

"What do you mean?" She was leaning into him, and he couldn't think with her so close. He stepped back and dropped his head.

"I don't know what I mean, Marina. I'm confused and I can't explain it but as much as I want to kiss you again, I just feel like it would be the wrong time to start something, or maybe I'm just scared." James plowed his fingers through his hair.

"It's probably better if we go to a hotel until my house is ready." She turned away and started to walk out of the kitchen. James caught her hand and turned her back around.

"You're not spending the night in any hotel. You're staying here." He hadn't meant to raise his voice but when she pulled back from him as if she was afraid he was going to hit her, he wanted to kick his own ass. *Shit!* With her history he should know better than to grab her or raise his voice. "I'm so sorry."

"James…" she started, but he held up his hands to stop her.

"You're staying here. That won't happen again." The boys ran back into the kitchen. They grabbed Marina's hands and dragged her out of the kitchen. "At least not until I'm sure we're both ready for something more," James whispered to himself.

The drive to the park was anything but quiet with the boys chattering away in the back seat. It was hard to get a word in with them talking. Marina hadn't said a word since they left the house, but the wheels in his head were spinning. The only person he felt comfortable talking to about his feelings for Marina was John, and since that wasn't possible at the moment, he had to work through this on his own.

It seemed lazy to be driving to a park he could see from his front step but he figured once the boys were tired of playing at the park, they could take a drive to Harbour Street for a treat. Plus, it was easier to wrangle two boys in a truck than walking down the road to the park.

It was probably going to be the last trip to the park for the year. It was the end of October and the weather was getting cooler. There was still a warm breeze in the air which was unusual for the time of year. When he glanced at Marina she had her hands clasped in front of her resting on her knees, and she sat with her back rigid.

A sure sign that she was tense. He cursed himself since he was more than likely the reason she was uncomfortable. He didn't regret kissing her, but he could have handled it better especially if she wasn't ready. Hell, he was questioning if he was ready himself. He'd jumped the gun, but he'd gone with his instinct.

James pulled into the parking lot and scanned the park. It was second nature for him to search the area before exiting his truck. There were only three other vehicles in the parking lot because most people were within walking distance. He stepped out of the truck and the hair on the back of his neck stood up. He spun to check behind him, but nothing was out of the ordinary. He walked around the truck the whole time keeping his eyes sharp because there was something giving him a bad feeling.

He couldn't let Marina see his uneasiness so when he opened her door, he held out his hand and smiled. For a moment she just stared and then hesitantly placed her hand in his. The boys were yelling in the back seat as they wiggled in their car seats impatiently waiting to be set loose.

They were hardly free from the truck when they darted to the playground. James glanced at Marina and she smiled but it wasn't her normal bright smile, the one that made his heart skip a beat. This one was a shy, and hesitant one, almost as if she was nervous to be with him.

They walked silently towards the playground with James keeping his eyes locked on the boys. He'd spent time working with the department that dealt with missing children, and he was always overly cautious when it came to Mason. He'd seen a lot of the missing children cases not end well and someone taking his son was his biggest fear. Although Hopedale was probably the safest place in the world.

Marina sat on one of the benches and James sat next to her. He leaned his elbows on his knees and did a quick scan of the other benches since he still had an uneasy feeling. Most of the adults were women, with a few men but none of them seemed out of place. That didn't make him feel any less edgy. It was as if he was being watched. He turned in the direction of the parking lot but again nothing. He turned back to the boys and they were climbing up to the top of the slide. Mason suddenly stopped in the middle of the ladder and jumped down.

"Daddy, can you come push me and Danny on the swings?" Mason begged as he and Danny ran up to him. James glanced at Marina. She nodded and he took it as a sign she was okay with him leaving her alone, although, he wasn't sure if she should be. He chased the boys to the swing set and helped them climb in. His gaze met Marina's and he wondered what was going through that beautiful head of hers. She still seemed extremely tense and with the way she was scanning the park, he had a feeling she was getting the same uneasy feeling. What the hell was going on? Most of the people here were obviously from Hopedale and the ones that he didn't recognize were talking to people from the area.

"Daddy, push me higher," Mason yelled.

"I wanna go up to the sky." Danny giggled.

"Okay, hold on tight guys." James said as he pushed both boys harder making them squeal, but something out of the corner of his eye had him spinning around to see a shadow disappear behind a tree.

Chapter 9

James tossed Mason into the air, and her son squealed with glee. When he did the same with Danny, her heart melted. James treating Danny the same as his own son only drove home what a great father figure he could be for Danny, and her son could see how a father should be. He'd never know how it felt to be with his own father, but she was glad Marc was not in their life anymore. She sometimes wondered how to explain what happened to his father when she didn't really know what happened to him herself. At some point Danny was going to ask, and all she could do is tell him about the man she'd fallen in love with. Nobody would know how to explain the evil man he turned into.

It was getting hard to swallow, and her eyes blurred with tears. She didn't want the boys or James to see her about to lose it, yet again. She made her way to the lake at the side of the park.

Over the past four years she'd managed to keep her tears hidden from Danny, and she wasn't going to let him see it now. James wasn't going to see them either. In her mind, she knew Danny was better off without Marc in her life. The drugs had turned him into a cruel and violent monster, and her son didn't need that. He needed a man like her own father or James. It hurt to know Danny would never have what Mason had, but then again Mason didn't have a mom. Maybe it was why the boys seemed to get along so well—they were each missing a parent.

Danny had only asked once why he didn't have a daddy. She'd explained that his daddy had gone away, but it wasn't because he didn't love him, it was just that he and mommy didn't get along. She told him that his daddy loved him and always would. It was a lie, but what else could she tell him? The explanation appeased him and he told her it was okay because he still had Uncle John and Poppy.

A cool breeze blew off the lake making her shiver. The threat of winter was in the wind even if it was a nice day. She tried to control the tears streaming down her cheeks but it was no use. She'd opened the flood-gates again, and she wiped the drops away angrily. She was so tired of crying because of Marc O'Reilly. It was all so overwhelming, and being near a man that made her body come alive with want wasn't helping. Then there was that kiss. It was so tender and she'd felt it right to the depths of her soul so much so that she probably would have let him take things much further had the boys not interrupted. That would have been a bad idea. Especially since she still didn't know if her head was on straight.

An icy chill skittered down her spine, and it felt as if someone was watching her. She glanced at James but he was busy pushing the boys on the swings. Marina glanced around the park, but there were only a few other families and they all seemed oblivious to her. She pulled the collar of her jacket around her neck as she tried to control the tears that were refusing to stop. To make it worse, the creepy feeling of being watched wasn't subsiding.

She took a deep breath and let it out slowly. The park was probably the most beautiful place she'd ever seen. It was a piece of heaven in the middle of Hopedale and she loved spending time there. Although, all of Hopedale was paradise. People could actually let their children play outside without worrying about them being run down by a speeding vehicle or being taken by some crazy person. One of the reasons she'd moved there was because she'd always been afraid of something happening to Danny, and for a while the fear had subsided, but over the last few hours, the feeling was becoming overwhelming.

Then there was James. She'd done a lot to make sure they weren't around each other often, but her sister was making that difficult. Now she was staying in his house and she didn't want to be anywhere else. That was a problem, because the more time she spent with him, the more time she wanted to spend with him. He'd stepped up when his wife died and was raising his son by himself the way a father should.

She'd been holding back on her growing attraction to him because she was afraid of falling in love again. She could fall in love with James O'Connor way too easily. Maybe she was already in love with him. She had all the signs. When he was around, her heart pounded, her pulse raced, and he was always the lead of her dreams, well at least the dreams that didn't include Marc trying to kill her. What was she going to do? The kiss they shared gave her hope that he was attracted to her, but was he really ready to move on? Was she?

She was sure that Marc had killed the part of her that allowed her to trust a man, but there was no way of denying it, James was bringing that part of her back to life. She trusted him more than she ever thought she could.

She turned and James was scanning the line of trees as if he was searching for something. When he turned around, she saw him glance towards the playground and a sudden look of panic came over his face. What the hell did he see? She spun to see and tripped over a rock sending her sprawling on the ground.

Chapter 10

James glanced at the bench. Marina was gone. He frantically scanned the park for her. Whatever he thought he saw was giving him a weird feeling. He lifted the boys off the swings and they ran to the slide. He quickly searched the park, and his heart finally slowed when he spotted her next to the lake. With a sigh of relief, he made his way towards her, but the boys tackled him, knocking him to his knees. He'd been so wrapped up in getting to Marina, he didn't hear them run up behind him. He laughed as they both knocked him over and landed on top of him. He glanced at Marina again and saw her wipe her hand across her cheek. Something was wrong.

"Okay guys, I need a break. You two go play for a bit but stay where I can see you." The two boys ran back to the slide. James turned around just as Marina fell to the ground. He sprinted across the park and fell to his knees. She was sitting up with her forehead resting against her knees and he could hear her sobbing.

"Marina, why are you crying? Are you hurt?" James helped her to her feet. She kept her back to the boys and he could still keep an eye on them.

"It's nothing, I'm fine." She was avoiding his eyes.

"People don't cry over nothing. How did you fall?" He wiped a tear from her cheek.

"I tripped on a rock and I think everything's hitting me all at once. I just don't know why someone would break into my house and destroy my things." She sobbed and tears spilled down the side of her face. James pulled her into his arms and tucked her head under his chin. How could he answer her question? None of it made any sense to him.

"I don't know why people do these things, but we'll find out what happened, Marina. Please, don't worry." He kissed the top of her head, and his heart was breaking to see her so distraught. He knew firsthand people did terrible things for no reason, or at least no good reason. Hell, he arrested them on a daily basis and it was hard to stay disconnected from the victims of these crimes, but with Marina, it was impossible.

When her sobs subsided he pulled back, but fear and sadness still filled her eyes. If he only knew how to make all of it go away. Maybe there was one thing he could do at the moment. Distraction.

"Let's go get some ice cream." James held her hands, and Marina smiled. He gave her a moment to get herself together and reluctantly released her hands. She took a couple of deep breaths. "Are you ready?" She nodded, and James linked his hand with hers.

Danny and Mason were not happy about leaving the park. Well not until James used the secret word. Ice cream. Suddenly, they were more than ready to go and bolted for the parking lot. James held Marina's hand in his until they were in front of his truck. He gave it a gentle squeeze before letting go, and she mouthed the words, 'Thank you.' James nodded and turned to help Danny and Mason into their car seats. She didn't have to thank him, because no matter what he would do anything for her.

"How about we make an afternoon of it and go into town for lunch?" James asked once he had himself buckled in.

"Sounds good." She smiled but it certainly didn't reach her eyes.

"All right, boys, we are going to get lunch before ice cream," James announced as he pulled out of the park

"Awww… You said we were getting ice cream," Mason whined and James didn't need to look in the rearview mirror to know he was pouting.

"It's okay, Mason, we're gonna have ice cream after lunch. Right, Unca James?" Danny reminded him of Keith. Growing up, Keith always tried to be the mediator between any brothers who were having a fight. It seemed Danny had that same type of personality.

"That's right, buddy." James glanced back at Mason. His son still had his I-don't-like-this face but at least he wasn't whining anymore.

"Can we go to Dairy Queen?" Mason asked. "They have burgers and ice cream." Obviously Mason was going to make sure they didn't miss out on the ice cream.

"Great idea." James chuckled as they pulled out of Hopedale and headed to St. John's. He didn't miss the fact that Marina wasn't saying anything. All she did was stare out through the window. He couldn't stop himself and reached across the seat to cover her hand with his. She didn't look at him, but she covered his hand with her free one. The gentle squeeze she gave it told him she really needed the contact. They stayed this way the entire way to town without saying a word. The kids had dozed off, so the only sound was the soft music playing from the radio.

Burgers and ice cream were apparently the best thing in the world according to Mason and Danny. Marina didn't eat much, but she did manage to join in the conversation with the boys. James was glad they didn't seem to notice her distraction.

"Why doesn't Mason have a mommy?" Danny asked out of the blue, and Marina almost knocked over her drink at the question. James glanced down at Mason, and he was staring up at James.

"Do you want to tell him or will I?" Mason asked and James chuckled. James had made sure Mason knew about Sarah and answered any questions he had over his short life.

"You can answer him, if you want?" James glanced at Marina. She seemed surprised by Mason's reaction.

"My mommy had to go to heaven when I was a little baby," Mason started. "She was real special and couldn't stay here for a very long time." James shook his head for a moment since he had never said anything like that to his son. He didn't know where on earth Mason came up with what he was telling Danny. "She's my angel mommy, and Nanny Betty says she'll always keep me and Daddy safe." It all made sense now. It seemed Mason had been talking to Nanny Betty and as always, his grandmother explained people's deaths with being needed in heaven. It was probably the better way to explain to a child.

"Do ya miss her?" Danny asked.

"I don't remember her but I know Daddy misses her. Don'cha, Daddy." Mason looked up at him.

"Every day, buddy." James felt odd talking about Sarah with Marina at the table.

"My daddy went away," Danny said and Marina instantly stiffened.

"Sometimes that happens, buddy." James wanted to help, but he didn't know exactly what Danny knew about his dad.

"Yeah, but I have Poppy, Unca John and you." Danny grinned as he scooped the last of his ice cream into his mouth.

"You have lots of unca's, Danny." Mason stood up on his chair.

"I know." Danny smiled.

"Could you excuse me for a moment?" Marina stood, and he watched her quickly disappear into the bathroom.

"I think Mommy misses my daddy," Danny said when Marina made her quick exit.

"Why do you think that, buddy?" James needed to know what was going on in Danny's head to think Marina missed the asshole.

"She's always telling him to stop when she's sleeping." Danny sighed. "She gets real scared in her dreams."

James knew Marina might have been having bad dreams because of the night that Danny had called him but if what Danny was saying was true, she was having them more often than he first thought.

"They're just dreams, buddy." He didn't know what else to say to the kid. "Mommy will be fine."

Danny nodded though something told him that the little boy had a lot more questions about his father but he didn't want to ask. He probably thought it would upset Marina and if there was one thing James' knew about Danny it was, he didn't like to see his mother upset.

James rerouted the conversation by helping the boys assemble the small toy they got with their meals. Marina seemed to be gone a long while, and he was constantly glancing towards the bathroom area. He saw a couple of men and women enter and exit but Marina hadn't returned. He checked the time on his phone. He was giving her one more minute and he was going to check on her.

Almost as if she'd sensed his panic, Marina opened the bathroom door. James tensed when a grungy-looking man stopped her. She spoke to him for a moment and although she didn't seem afraid of him, she didn't seem comfortable talking to him. He was about to go see what the guy was saying, but Marina smiled at the man and continued towards them.

She sat at the table and ruffled Danny's hair. She seemed more relaxed but when the man that had stopped her kept staring on his way out of the restaurant, James had to ask.

"What did that guy want?" James cringed at the way he blurted out the question, but she turned and met his eyes.

"He told me I had a cute kid and I was a very lucky woman." Marina told him.

"That you are." James glanced at Danny, who seemed to be oblivious to their conversation since he and Mason were now completely concentrating on their new toys. "He's a pretty lucky little boy too."

Marina smiled and lowered her eyes as her cheeks flushed. It was nice to see the color back in her cheeks. It didn't matter to him either way because to him she was absolutely beautiful. He couldn't help watching her help Danny on with his coat. Her ponytail was hung over one shoulder, and the memory of how her hair felt between his fingers that morning when he tangled his hand in it made his body react the way it always did around her, and he was the biggest ass in the world. Here they were at a restaurant with their kids and all he could think about was how much he wanted to strip her naked and bury himself inside her.

"Daddy, are you okay?" Mason was standing in front of him with his head tilted to the side. He glanced up from where he was still sitting to make sure his ridiculous reaction was hidden from view.

"I'm fine, Mason." James turned himself in the chair and zipped up Mason's jacket but as he glanced out the window he caught a glimpse of the man that had stopped Marina, sitting in a car just outside the window. He was leering at Marina and it sent chills through his entire body. The good thing was it helped his previous situation because now he was more concerned with the way the guy seemed focused on Marina.

"You see him too," Mason whispered.

"Who?" James noticed Mason had seemed to pick up on the man as well.

"That creepy guy is staring at us." Mason pointed towards the guy and when the man saw Mason point, he backed away from the window and sped out of the lot.

"Okay, so that wasn't creepy at all." Marina glanced at him, the concern was clear on her face.

"He's gone now, and there is no way he'd get near any of you." James motioned for her to stay behind him and he held tightly to both boy's hands. "Just stay next to me in case." Something about the whole incident gave James a bad feeling but he wasn't going to let Marina know that or the kids. He just wanted to get them out to the truck and home safe. Maybe he was over reacting but his instincts were usually pretty good.

They walked out of the restaurant, and he scanned the lot as they walked to the truck. He opened the door for Marina and the boys to pile in. He'd worry about getting the boys buckled in when they were all safely in the truck. He ran around to his side and scanned the lot as well as the road. The guy was gone and James puffed out a breath as he climbed into the truck.

"Well that was fun." Marina tilted her head to the side and stared at him.

"Do we have to sit in our seats?" Danny asked.

"I'm afraid so, buddy." James said as he twisted around and help each of the boys into their seats. It was awkward, but he managed to buckle them in and turn back around in his own seat.

"You know it would have been easier if you'd let me do that," Marina said.

"Why is that?" James buckled himself in and glanced at her. She was grinning at him.

"Well you aren't exactly a small man." She moved her hand up and down. He knew she meant his height.

"Are you calling me fat?" James feigned outrage and she laughed.

"You are anything but fat, but you are tall and wide." She said.

"So you are calling me fat." James held his hand over his chest. "I'm so wounded."

"Oh God, and you talk about A.J. being over-dramatic." Marina rolled her eyes.

"Dear Lord, don't compare me to him." James chuckled as he started the truck.

"A.J. is sweet, but he doesn't even come close to his big brother," she said so low that he almost didn't hear it. He glanced over at her to see her staring at him.

"I'll let John know you think he's sweeter than A.J." James smiled.

"I wasn't talking about John, and before you list the long list of big brothers A.J. has, I'll narrow it down for you. I was talking about you." She gently slapped the back of her hand against his arm and he caught it before she pulled away. She raised her gaze to meet his and felt an odd tightness in his chest as he took in her true beauty. She seemed to be doing the same as her bright green eyes scanned his face.

"Are we gonna go anytime soon?" Mason whined.

Marina pulled her hand from his and turned her head to look out the side window. She rubbed her hands against her thighs and cleared her throat.

"We're going now." James put the truck into drive and pulled out of the parking lot. He knew what was happening to him and he was terrified to admit. The last time he'd felt this way about someone he'd lost her. Going through that again would probably kill him, but the draw to Marina was becoming stronger every day. He'd started falling in love with her the day he met her, but admitting it was his problem. Was he ready to admit it?

Chapter 11

James rushed to unlock the front door as the shrill ring of the land line could be heard from the front step. He ran to answer it as soon as he threw the door open while Marina helped Danny and Mason out of their coats. They clambered into the living room as she kept her focus on James. They'd had a moment in the truck and if Mason hadn't spoken she knew she would have kissed him but kissing him again wasn't going to be enough. She needed him so badly that she ached.

Her mind was so jumbled with the whole day. First her lack of sleep was making her an emotional basket-case, then the way it started, her break-down at the park, and then the creepy guy at the restaurant. Just thinking about him made her shudder. He'd seemed harmless when he told her she had a cute kid but when they'd noticed him staring, she was glad she was with James. Then again she was glad to be with James period.

James spoke quietly into the phone, and she couldn't read his expression. When his eyes met hers, he smiled, but there was tension in his jaw that said he was getting news she probably didn't want to hear. He hung up the phone and jerked his head towards the kitchen. Goose bumps popped up all over her body. This wasn't going to be good.

"What's wrong?" She asked.

"That was Greg Harris, the lead investigator looking into the break in at your house last night."

Marina nodded.

"They ran the fingerprints through the database." He stopped. "I think you better sit down, Marina." He pulled out the chair, and she lowered herself into it. James crouched in front of her and cupped both of her hands into his.

"What is it, James?"

"Marina, the fingerprints belong to Marc." She'd never felt so cold in her life and her stomach lurched, but she managed to keep down the contents. She gripped his hands so tightly that she was sure she was going to break his fingers.

"No." Her voice was a whisper.

"That's not all. They found an envelope in your mailbox. It was from Marc." James squeezed her hands. "He said he wants his son." *No!* "I think he may have that missing picture from your room."

"No… No… No!" With every time she said the word, her voice got louder.

"Marina, please, don't worry. I want you to stay here until we find Marc. If he does have that picture, then he knows what Danny looks like, and I'd feel better knowing you're where I can keep you both safe."

"James, you've got to work, and there is no way on God's green earth that he is getting Danny." She tried to keep her voice low so the kids wouldn't hear her.

"I'm off until next Friday." James passed her a napkin from the table. It wasn't until then that she realized she had tears running down her cheeks. "I'll help you keep Danny safe from him and keep you safe too."

"Mom and Dad will be home in a few days. When they come home, I'll go stay with them until Marc is found."

"No!" James' voice resembled a growl. "I mean; he'd expect you to go there. He wouldn't know you'd be here." That made sense, but why did he sound so desperate? She wanted to stay with James. God, did she want to stay, but the longer she did, the harder it was going to be to leave.

"James, I'll be fine with my parents. Trust me Dad will not let Marc near his house."

"You're not going to argue with me over this, Marina. You're staying here." His voice was stern. "No arguments. I'm going to call Mrs. Ray to come watch the boys for a bit. We'll go to your house and see what we can salvage for you and Danny." He stood.

"James, you don't have to do this, but I'm going to say this once and once only. Don't try and tell me what to do. I'll stay for now because honestly, I don't want to leave." Her gaze met his.

"I don't want you to leave either, Marina." He crouched again and cupped her cheek. "I need to make sure nothing happens to you or Danny. Just don't argue with me about this." He was such a good man, and Danny loved him. If she was being completely honest, she was falling in love with him too.

"I guess there's no sense in arguing with you, is there?" Marina sighed when he traced her lower lip with his thumb.

"No, there isn't. I do have my grandmother's stubborn streak." James smiled.

"I guess I'll never win an argument with you in that case. Maybe I need to take some lessons from that grandmother of yours." She smiled.

Marina stood in front of the kitchen window staring out at the waves crashing against the small islands in the distance, waiting while James called the babysitter. The back of James' house and all the houses on the street had a beautiful view of the Atlantic Ocean. James' view was even better than hers. Still, it was hard to enjoy at the moment. Why was Marc back, and why did he suddenly want Danny?

She had the documents he signed giving up his parental rights. She'd even changed Danny's last name to Kelly, so there was nothing of Marc connected with her son. The documents were one hundred percent legal. She knew this because another of the O'Connor brothers checked them for her. Mike specialized in family law and assured her Marc had willingly signed the papers and was fully aware of what he did.

There wasn't any way in hell Marc was getting Danny. She'd make sure of that even if she had to leave Newfoundland again. Her son wasn't going to have to be around his drug-addicted, abusive father. The day he left, she'd made a vow to her unborn baby that his father would never put a hand on him.

The day she kicked him out, Marc told her he wanted to forget she ever existed and Marina felt the same way. Only once since then did he try to see her and Danny but that ended with him being arrested without seeing either of them. Why he suddenly wanted Danny had nothing to do with him suddenly wanting to be a father.

Nobody knew what he put her through and she still wasn't sure what happened to the man she married. He'd become a completely different person two months after she found out she was pregnant. From the way he spoke to her to how distant he'd become unless he wanted to smack her around. It had been so humiliating and she was so ashamed to tell her family what was going on. She still didn't know what had come over her to allow him to treat her the way he did because she hadn't grown up with that type of man.

She hugged herself when the memories caused her to tremble and the lump in her throat she'd been trying to swallow was threatening to choke her. James walked up behind her, and wrapped his arms around her and pulled her back against him. Her body actually relaxed and she stopped shaking. Just that one simple gesture and she felt safe.

"It'll be okay, sweetheart." James whispered and pressed his lips against the top of her head. Something told her he'd do everything to protect her and her son. Not because he said it, not because Stephanie was his sister-in-law, it was a feeling deep inside her that made her trust him implicitly. There was a connection with him she couldn't explain and at that moment she knew Cora was right.

When the doorbell rang, James kissed the top of her head again and released her. She missed his body heat immediately. He returned with an older woman who seemed to be in her mid-sixties. She seemed familiar but Marina couldn't remember how she knew her but her warm friendly smile put her at ease.

"Marina, this is Mrs. Ray." James wrapped his arm around the older woman, making it obvious he knew her well.

"Nice to meet you, Mrs. Ray." Marina smiled, desperately trying to remember where she'd seen the woman before.

"You call me Mary, my dear." She said. "I've been telling Jimmy and his brothers that for years." She chuckled and Marina didn't miss the slight flush of James cheeks.

"I'm sorry, Mary. I'm trying to remember where I know you from," Marina said.

"Mary lives in the house between us." James chuckled. She was a complete idiot. She'd seen the woman a few times and even said hi to her from time to time.

"I feel like I should apologize for not recognizing you." She was so embarrassed.

"Don't you worry about that, my dear." Mary chuckled.

"I hope you don't mind watching Danny." Marina was apprehensive letting anyone outside the family babysit Danny especially since she knew Marc was stirring up trouble.

"Not at all. I raised nine children of my own and have twenty grandchildren. Two little boys are a holiday for me." Mary laughed.

When they got into the truck James just sat watching the road. She buckled up her seatbelt and turned back to him. He was tapping something into his phone and he kept glancing up at the road.

"Are we just going to sit in the truck?" Marina asked when it seemed he wasn't going to move.

"Just waiting for Keith to send one of his guys over to watch the house," James said without looking up from his phone. "Before you say anything. I'm just being cautious."

"I wasn't going to say anything but thanks for being cautious." It probably seemed a little over the top but she appreciated it.

A black car pulled into the driveway. James nodded to the guy in the driver's seat as he started the truck and pulled out of the driveway. Marina glanced behind her to see a very large man exit the car. He walked to the front door and turned around.

"Did you let Mrs. Ray know that there would be a mountain of a man in front of the house?"

"Keith called her to let her know Trunk would be watching the house while we were gone." James chuckled.

"Trunk?" Marina laughed.

"Yeah. His real name is Ben Murphy, but for some reason all the men that work with Keith go by nicknames. They call Keith, Rusty because of his hair color but his employees are the only ones that call him that."

Here they were again driving the two-minute walk between houses, but she had to see how much of her and Danny's belongings she could salvage. James pulled into her driveway and Marina turned to face him. She tried to stifle a giggle but the name Mary called him hit her funny. She'd heard his grandmother and Cora call him Jimmy but for some reason it struck her funny with Mary.

"Speaking of nicknames. Jimmy, huh?" She giggled.

"Don't start." James groaned.

"Start what? Jimmy." Marina put the emphasis on the name.

"You're amused by that, aren't you?" James turned to face her, and it was obvious he was trying to hide the smile.

"You just don't look like a Jimmy. It makes you sound like a little boy." But James was far from a boy, he was all man.

"I've known Mrs. Ray all my life, and besides Nan and Aunt Cora, she is the only other one to call me that." James pulled the keys out of the ignition. "And John is Johnny, Keith is Keithy, Mike is Mikey, Nick is Nicky but the funniest one is Ian. They used to call him Inky, and he's tried to make sure that name gets used as little as possible." Marina burst out laughing.

"You forgot A.J," She held her stomach because it hurt from laughing.

"Oh he got off easy. They call him plain old A.J. Imagine, he's the worst of us all, and he gets away with what everyone calls him anyway." James rolled his eyes.

"He's not that bad." Marina smiled.

"You really don't know him very well. First he hits on anything with a pulse, and he's the biggest practical joker in the family," James said. Marina turned her head and focused on her house. Her smiled disappeared, but James gently grasped her hand and kissed it.

"Don't worry, you're not alone." James released her hand and got out of the truck. She noticed whenever he walked out of the house or got out of his truck, he looked around. Almost as if he was checking for danger. It must be something ingrained in him because of his job.

He opened her door and held out his hand. She stared at the house and for a moment she just wanted to stay in the truck and go buy all new things. James grasped her hand as she drew a deep breath and let it out slowly. There were things in the house that just couldn't be bought again. She had to at least try and collect some of those special things.

She glanced around as they walked inside. Black spots were all around her living room and it was like something she'd seen in one of the one-hour crime shows. It sent a chill down her spine seeing so many of them because it would have been so much worse if she'd been home when it happened.

Mentally shaking the thought from her head, she released James' hand and hurried to Danny's bedroom. His room was the only one that hadn't been destroyed. Nothing was broken, nothing tipped over, and his bed was still made. The only thing that seemed to be moved was his favorite stuffed animal. A huge black Newfoundland dog that usually sat on the foot of Danny's bed was now on the floor next to his dresser. Besides the teddy bear Danny wouldn't sleep without, it was the only other stuffed toy he paid any attention. Probably because he was so infatuated with dogs.

"I brought a couple of duffle bags to pack your things." He dropped one on Danny's bed and she started to open the drawers in his dresser. "Why don't you go into your room and get your clothes. I'll get Danny's things." He handed her the other duffle bag.

"Okay, but make sure you take that dog. It's one of his favorites." Marina grabbed the other bag and left the room.

Her room was a disaster area. Clothes were tossed all over the floor and her bed. Her dresser drawers were splintered on the floor and the dressers were smashed. Marc had touched all her things, and it made her want to wash every last piece of it. She grabbed the clothes as quickly as she could, shaking the splinters of wood off of them right before she stuffed it all into the bag. When the bag was full she opened her closet and grabbed the suitcase from the top shelf.

The closet of course was completely emptied, except for her jewelry box that was neatly placed in the middle of the closet floor. She held her breath as she picked it up and glanced through it. Her breath blew out in a whoosh seeing that everything was still there. At least he hadn't taken any of her grandmother's jewelry. She packed it carefully into the middle of her suitcase with as much of the rest of her things as she could fit.

With one last quick scan of the room she made her way out dragging the two bags behind her. She dropped them in the foyer and made her way back to the living room. James stood in front of her fire-place, holding a picture frame in his hand and didn't seem to notice her entering as he stared at the photo.

Marina needed to distract herself from the disaster surrounding her, so she focused on the only thing of beauty. The only thing she'd found in the last four years that made her feel desirable. James. His white shirt fit snuggly against his body, showing every sexy muscle. His jeans hung low on his hips and hugged his backside. The man had the sexiest ass she'd ever seen. He reached up and placed the picture on the mantel making the muscle in his bicep flex and she wanted to swoon but he turned around and his eyes met hers. She met his gaze as he moved towards her.

"I'm ready," she managed to say but couldn't look away, and then he was in front of her. Close enough that his scent surrounded her, making it hard to think. The way he gazed at her made her heart pound, and when he touched her cheek with his finger, she closed her eyes. His thumb glided across her lower lip just before his lips met hers. The fingers of one hand slid into her hair and the other cupped the back of her neck, and she rested her hands on his hips as she pressed against him. When his tongue entered her mouth she moaned but pulled back.

"James, we can't do this here." Marina rested her head against his chest.

"I'm sorry." He kissed the top of her head and wrapped his arms around her for a few minutes while they both steadied their breathing. He stepped back and plowed his hands through his thick hair. She'd come to notice it was something he did when he was frustrated.

"You said today it wasn't the right time, and maybe you're right." She cupped his face in her hands.

"It isn't but it will be someday soon, I promise." James stared into her eyes and she smiled.

"I'll hold you to that." She turned and scanned the living room.

"Let's pick up some burgers for dinner. Aunt Alice makes the best cheeseburgers in the province." James lifted the bags as if they weighted nothing and she took one last look around. She didn't know when she was going to get back, but she wasn't sure if she'd ever feel safe there again. At least not until Marc was caught.

Chapter 12

Marina was on the phone trying to convince Stephanie not to cut their vacation short, because of the break-in. From the way she rolled her eyes, it was going about as well as her conversation with her parents went. The only way her father was finally convinced to stay and finish out his vacation was when he spoke with James and made him promise to keep Marina and Danny safe from her ex-husband. Doug Kelly was almost as intimidating over the phone as he was in person. The man was huge and James didn't want to get on his bad side. Not that he'd seen the man angry, but he was sure it wouldn't be pleasant.

When the doorbell rang, James opened the door and was almost knocked over as his family swarmed into the house. Did it surprise him to have his entire family show up at his house when they found out who broke into Marina's house? Not in the least, because when there was a crisis they were an army ready to do battle. Obviously, his family considered Marina part of the family, but he didn't know whether she should feel blessed or if he should tell her to run like hell.

Nanny Betty, as usual, was the first one through the door, and as the matriarch of the family she'd be considered the Commander of their family army. She was respected by not only the family but the community as well but they also feared her. She was less than five feet tall and in her early seventies, but she was a force of nature when anyone pissed her off. James bent to kiss her cheek and she almost bowled him over on her way to the kitchen. James assumed the large containers she held were full of food.

Behind his grandmother was his mother, Kathleen and she kissed James' cheek as she hurried behind Nanny Betty with yet more containers. His father, Sean was next and gave him an apologetic look, but he wasn't sure if it was because of Marina's situation or because of the O'Connor invasion.

Before he had a chance to close the front door, his brothers arrived. Ian, Keith, Mike, Nick and Aaron filed in one after the other. Aaron held up his phone, and James read the text message showing on the screen. It was from Nanny Betty telling him to get to James' house right away. It wasn't a good thing that his grandmother had learned how to text, because now she could order them around from anywhere.

Mike waved him into the living room with the rest of his brothers. James didn't bother to close the front door, because Isabelle, Jess and Kristy were walking up his driveway.

"I brought over the papers, and I've read them over again." Mike held papers. "I even had one of the senior partners look at them, and there's nothing Marc can do. His parental rights have been dissolved."

"At least there's that, but I just get a feeling there's more to this." Aaron was peering over Mike's shoulder at the papers.

"Right now there's an APB out on him, and when I left the station there was still nothing." Kurt's voice boomed from the front door.

His father's younger brother was also the superintendent with Hopedale's division of the Newfoundland Police Department. He was also one of the best police officers in the province, and highly decorated. If anyone could help them figure this out, it was Kurt.

"Uncle Kurt, what do you think?" James had a feeling Marc had something planned, but he just didn't know what it was.

"I don't know, but if he's gotten back into the drug scene, he could be capable of anything." Kurt's comment made James blood run cold. He'd dealt with drug addicts and they would do anything for their next fix. He also knew about people selling women and children for cash and drugs, although he wasn't aware of anything like that going on in the province.

Marina sat on the stairs with her head in her hands with Isabelle next to her. Isabelle had her arm around Marina's shoulders while she spoke softly. Out of his Uncle's three daughters, she was probably the quietest and had the biggest heart of anyone he knew. His other cousins Jess and Kristy appeared from the kitchen.

"Marina, this should help with your headache." Jess dropped something into Marina's hand and sat on the step below Marina. Kristy gave her the glass, and he didn't miss how Marina's hand trembled when she took it. When Isabelle met his eyes, he knew she hadn't missed it either.

His cousins were the younger sisters he and his brothers never wanted, but he was so glad they were there right now. The majority of his family was male and she needed some female support especially since her sister and mother were away.

As he moved towards Marina and his cousins, the front door opened. His two aunts hurried in and gave him a quick wave before they hurried into the kitchen. It seemed in a crisis all the women in his family thought food fixed everything. Cora, put him a little on edge, since she'd made it clear James and Marina belonged together. She had no issues with telling him every chance she got too.

The sound of squealing drew his attention to the back garden. Nick and Ian had taken the boys outside to keep them occupied. It was probably better they didn't overhear any of the conversations going on around the house. The last thing Marina needed was for Danny to feel scared or asking questions. He was pretty sure Danny didn't know the truth about his father.

Marina finally raised her eyes to meet his and she seemed to relax. Isabelle stood up and motioned for him to take her place on the stairs as she followed her sisters into the living room. It wasn't subtle, but he knew they were giving him some privacy with Marina.

"Are you okay?" James covered her hand between his.

"I'm fine. It's not me I'm concerned with." Marina sighed. "Mike says Marc didn't have any legal rights when it comes to Danny, not that it would make a difference because there is no way in hell he is getting my son. I just don't know what he's capable of anymore. He's not the same man I married. His personality completely changed four years ago. I don't trust him."

"I don't trust him either and I don't even know him." James glanced up as Keith passed them on his way to the kitchen. "If having my family here is too much, I can ask them to leave."

"No. I love your family and so does Danny." She smiled at him and for a few minutes he just held her hand as they watched the bustle of the people he loved. They really were the best family in the world.

"This is so nice to see. I told you, didn't I?" Aunt Cora stood in the doorway of the kitchen holding her hand over her heart. "I'm never wrong." Before he or Marina could say a word, Cora disappeared into the kitchen again.

"I know she's your aunt and this Cupid thing is a little odd." Marina shook her head but James didn't think it was odd at all.

"She's odd, but she means well." James wasn't explaining Cora to Marina.

"Stephanie told me about it." Marina stared at him.

"Yeah, it's a running joke." James chuckled.

"Is it true she's always right?" Marina gazed into his eyes.

"As far as I know." James admitted because he'd never heard anything different.

"Hmmm." Marina stared down at where he held her hand as if she was contemplating something.

"Why? Has she said something to you?" Cora already told him Marina and him were meant to be together, but he wasn't aware of her telling Marina.

"A couple of times she's told me I'm the one." She wouldn't meet his eyes.

"The one for who?" James put his finger under her chin and tipped her head so she would meet his gaze.

"She never really said." Marina gazed into his eyes and he held his breath. "But the couple of times she said it, she always nodded towards..." She closed her eyes.

"Towards who, Marina?" He needed her to say it. She opened her eyes and met his.

"You." He smiled and released her hand to cup her face. He grazed his thumb across her lower lip and a small whimper came from her as her eyes closed. "James." His name on her lips sent a wave of desire through his body right to his groin, and everything around them disappeared as his lips brushed against hers. It was just the two of them and he was so completely lost in the kiss he barely heard the sound.

"Ahem." James pulled away and slowly turned his head. His father was staring at them with a raised eyebrow but there was no hiding the grin he was trying to keep from appearing. "Sorry to interrupt, but your mother said the food is ready, but if you two need a moment…"

"Thanks, Dad." Sean nodded and moved back into the kitchen. James grasped Marina's hand and led her upstairs out of sight of his family. "Sorry about that. I just need to say something before I lose the courage to say it." Her grip on his hand tightened. "I know we really don't know each other well but if I'm being honest, the first time I saw you I felt it. I was still grieving, and fought it because I felt guilty. Then at John and Stephanie's wedding, the feeling was stronger especially when I was dancing with you. Again, I ran from it. In the last couple of days, it's been so hard to keep my feelings under control and Marina I don't want to run from this anymore. The more time I spend with you the harder it is to fight this. I know things are stressful right now, and I know your last relationship was awful, but I just need to know if you feel it or am I imagining it." He took a deep breath. He was talking nonstop because he was terrified she'd tell him it was all in his head.

"I feel it too." She stepped closer to him and his heart pounded in his chest.

"So it's not just me?" She shook her head but her eyes never left his. He rested his hands on her hips as her hands lay against his chest. He swept his lips against hers and her breath caught. "We really should go back down before someone comes looking for us. When everyone leaves, and the boys are in bed, I'd like to pick up from here."

James pressed his lips against hers again. He tried to keep the kiss simple, but the minute their lips met that thought went out the window. She opened her mouth, and his tongue slipped into hers. The sweet taste of her mouth had him about to lose all rational thought as he backed her against the wall and pressed against her. He really needed to get his head together before he dragged her into the bedroom and said the hell with everyone downstairs. He pulled back and rested his forehead against hers.

"Well that almost got away from us." Marina sighed. "Do we really need to go downstairs?"

"Yeah." James pressed his lips against her forehead. "If we don't they'll come looking like a bunch of bloodhounds." Marina giggled as they headed downstairs.

On the bottom of the stairs, Aaron and Nick were near the foyer and glanced up when James and Marina descended the stairs. She smiled and released his hand then headed straight to the kitchen. When a whistle came from Aaron's direction, James turned and narrowed his eyes.

"What were you two doing upstairs, bro." Aaron wiggled his eyebrows.

"Talking." James snapped because he knew what was coming next. The two youngest O'Connor brothers teased the older brothers when it came to women. One of these days, payback was going to be a bitch and James wanted a front row seat when the two of them were knocked on their asses by a woman.

"I never took you for the dirty-talking type." Nick nudged Aaron with his elbow.

"Get your minds out of the gutter," James warned. "We were just talking. She's going through a lot, and this family can be overwhelming for someone not used to it." It was a lie, and the grin on their faces told him they didn't believe a word. He wasn't in the mood for their needling nor was he going to explain himself to them.

"Why do you, John, Ian and Keith get so defensive?" Aaron chuckled. "I mean she's hot and she's definitely got eyes for you, bro."

"You, little brother, are just one big walking hormone." James pushed him playfully, but he had to admit Aaron seemed to never let things get to him. Maybe they would all be better off taking a lesson or two from him. Not that he would ever admit that to him.

"You know; this little brother crap really has to stop. I'm bigger than most of you." Aaron flexed his arms and James had to admit he was getting pretty ripped.

"You'll always be little brother no matter how big you get." James said.

"I'm still bigger in more ways than one." Aaron winked.

"You wish, asshole." James chuckled.

"Maybe we should get Marina to compare." Aaron teased and quickly stepped out of James' reach.

"You really want to get your ass kicked." Nick managed to slap the back of Aaron's head as he ducked by James. "How's she handling all this shit with her ex?" At least Nick asked. As much as he could be as big of an ass as Aaron, Nick had a big heart.

"She's worried he's up to something, other than wanting to see Danny." James leaned against the wall.

"I'm thinking the same thing. I mean the guy's a fucking dickhead, and look what he did to her house," Aaron said. "Plus they had trouble with him a few years back."

"I know, but he was supposed to have gotten himself cleaned up," James said.

"At least she's safe here with Danny," Nick said. "He wouldn't have guts enough to come here."

"Yeah." James sighed.

"You know we're here for you too, bro. I like to fuck with you, but you know I always got your back." Aaron dropped his hand on James' shoulder.

"I know and I appreciate it." James knew even with all the teasing the O'Connor brothers would always be there for one another.

James chuckled as Danny and Mason knocked Keith down on the grass and climbed on top of him. It must have been like knocking down a giant to the boys. The middle O'Connor brother was not only the mildest of the seven, but he was also the biggest. Keith was a solid wall of muscle and stood about six feet four. He was also a genius, although not many people outside the family knew of his off-the-charts IQ. It was ironic to see such a tough guy letting two little boys get the better of him, but that was Keith.

The patio door opened behind him, and his father walked through the door. After he closed the door, he stood next to James and for a few minutes they stood in silence watching the boys and Keith.

The temperature had dropped drastically from earlier in the day. However, the boys didn't seem to notice as they ran away from Keith, who was now chasing them like an overgrown child himself. The sun had gone down, and they were playing by the light from the deck.

"I enjoyed watching you boys play when you were youngsters." His father chuckled when Mason ran between Keith's legs and knocked him over.

"We did more fighting than playing, Dad." All the times his brothers used to play in their yard there would always be someone who got upset and a fight would break out.

"I guess so, but it was always worked out in a few minutes."

"Only because you made us sit in the room together until we stopped fighting." James laughed and his dad just smiled. There were a few more minutes of silence.

"I like her."

"Yeah." James sighed.

"I'm guessing you do, too." His father turned to James and put his hand on James' shoulder.

"I do."

"I know she had a hard time with that Marc fella." His father's voice was quiet. "Why a man would treat a woman so bad, I'll never understand."

"Me either." Just knowing Marina had been hurt by that ass made him physically ill.

"Can I give you some advice?" His dad would give James the advice whether he wanted it or not so he just nodded. "She may be skittish. From what John says, she hasn't dated since the divorce, so don't rush her, son. I'm not saying I don't think you shouldn't pursue this. Just be patient."

"Nothing's happened between us, Dad." James felt the need to make that clear to his father.

"I don't doubt that, but I also know living in such close quarters with someone you're attracted to can send your hormones into overdrive."

James rolled his eyes and shook his head. His father was talking to him as if he were sixteen years old again. "I'm not A.J, Dad." James chuckled.

"I know, but you're a man and she's a beautiful woman. I also know it's been a while for you too, son."

"Dad, really, I can handle this." He was not comfortable with his father knowing about his sex life or his lack of it.

"I'm just making a point. Don't go getting all prudish on me. Take things at her pace." His dad squeezed his shoulder. "Oh I thought you should know; Cora has your mother all excited because she saw you holding Marina's hand." Then he walked back into the house.

Just what he needed. His mother tended to go over board when her sister gave her the Cupid information. She was probably planning a wedding in her head by now. His father was right though; he hadn't been with anyone since Sarah and being with someone had never entered his mind until he met Marina.

After what seemed like hours, his family slowly trickled out of his house. When the last of them left, James let out a huge sigh and leaned against the door. He loved them, but when they were all together it was loud. Marina had gone upstairs to get the boys settled in bed, but it was probably to escape the chaos that was his family. He didn't blame her.

James walked into the kitchen and it was as if nobody had ever been in there. Nanny Betty was wiping down the counter as she hummed along with the radio. James was surprised to see her because he thought she'd left with his parents. She folded the cloth and hung it over the tap and turned around.

"Nan, you didn't have to stay and clean up." James walked over to her and gave her a huge hug. She really was one of the best people in the world.

"I didn't clean dis up, yar mudder and aunts did most of it." She handed her coat to him and he held it up for her to put it on. His grandmother expected a gentleman to help a lady with her coat and it was something she'd made sure all the men in the family remembered.

"I'll give you a run home, Nan." James grabbed his keys from the counter and started to head out of the kitchen to grab his jacket.

"Now doncha be so foolish." Nanny Betty hung her ever-present black purse over her shoulder and pulled on her wool hat. "I'll walk home faster den it'll take ya ta start dat truck."

"Nan, it's dark out." James didn't agree with her walking home by herself.

"Jimmy, ya need ta look after dat girl upstairs. She needs ya." Nanny Betty was already on the front step. "I'm not so old dat I can't walk five minutes down da road."

"Let me call Dad to come get you." James knew he was fighting a losing battle since his grandmother was as independent as they came. She didn't appreciate when anyone treated her like she was old.

"I'll be at da house before he gets outta da driveway." Nanny Betty waved as she scurried down the road. James pulled his phone out of his pocket and called his father. Nanny Betty was going to be pissed that he called him, but he'd never forgive himself if something happened to her.

James couldn't hold back the laugher as his father cursed Nanny Betty's stubborn streak, but what really made him burst out laughing was when his mother reminded his father that he was just as pig-headed. He ended the call to his mother's laughter.

"Everyone gone?" There was no mistaking the relief in her voice.

"Yeah, Nan was the last of them and she just left." James met her at the bottom of the stairs and gently grasped her hands in his. "Do you want to talk?"

"Yeah." James held her hand as they moved into the living room and settled on the sofa. Where did he start?

"I had a chat with my dad today." It seemed the best place to start.

"That seems serious." Marina tensed when he kissed her hand.

"He told me I should take things slow."

"I see." She glanced down to their joined hands.

"Marina, I need to be honest. I haven't been with anyone since Sarah." Marina peeked up under her eye lashes.

"I haven't been with anyone since Marc." She seemed to choke on her ex-husband's name.

"I told you when I first met you I felt something and the truth is, it terrified me. I felt as if I was betraying Sarah. I know it's stupid to feel that way, but you've got to understand I thought Sarah and I would be together forever. Then I remembered something she said before she died. She said she was only meant to be with me for a short time and there was someone out there for me for the rest of my life." James swallowed hard when he noticed her eyes fill with tears. "According to Aunt Cora, it's you and I don't know if she's right, but I'd like to find out." Why did he always ramble when he was nervous? "Can you please say something because if you don't I'm going to keep rambling."

"Stephanie does that too. I was just going to let you go on until you ran out of breath." She giggled.

"Thanks a lot." James smiled.

"James, losing Sarah must have been heart-wrenching, because although what I went through with Marc wasn't close, it was still hard. My relationship with him was great in the beginning but during the end it was…" She stopped and he squeezed her hand. "Terrifying."

"You don't have to talk about it if you're not ready." James was sure she hadn't told the full story to anyone. Stephanie said she knew there was a lot more to what happened than Marina was admitting.

"I know, but I need to be completely honest if this is going to work." Marina gripped his hand tighter. "I'm not going to bore you with the details of how we met because it was nothing special. We met at a party and exchanged numbers. I fell for him right away and he said he did too. We married a year later." He didn't miss her shaky intake of breath.

"Marina, you don't have to do this." James didn't like the way she'd started to tremble.

"It's time I told someone the whole story. My family doesn't know how bad it really was and maybe it'll help with the dreams." She released his hand and walked to the window. James didn't want to hear it all because this was going to be horrible. What was he supposed to do? She obviously needed to get this out. If this helped he'd sit there and listen.

"Take your time, sweetheart," James said. "We've got all night." Marina turned to face him and smiled, but her eyes were filled with tears. She turned back to the window.

"After we were married the first few months was incredible. We'd moved into an apartment close to the university because I was still trying to finish my degree. Marc had just started working at the hospital as a chef. That turned out to only last a few months, but I didn't know until everything went downhill."

"He wasn't working at the hospital?" James said.

"He did for a couple of months, but after he came back from the training seminar, his boss let him go because Marc was screwing things up. His boss said it was like he didn't know what he was doing. Apparently selling drugs was more lucrative," Marina said. "He'd leave every day in his white chef's jacket and his hat. I was so proud of him. I'd go to school and when I'd offer to meet him for lunch, he'd tell me that he didn't have time." When she reached up and wiped a tear from her cheek, James brought her a box of tissues and stood next to her.

"Do you want to take a break?"

Marina shook her head as she wiped her eyes. "I found out I was pregnant about two months after we were married. It was before he went away. We hadn't planned it, but I was so excited. Marc was too, at first."

"That changed?" James couldn't understand why Marc wouldn't be happy about having a child or at least change how he felt.

"I was a little over three months pregnant when he was sent on that training seminar. He said it was for some new health standards that the hospital was trying to implement with their food service. When he came back a week later, he was like a different person. He'd gotten a tattoo and there was something about his eyes that changed. That night was the first time he…" Marina took a shuddering breath. "The first time he hit me."

"I'm sorry he did that to you." James really didn't know what else to say.

"I was in such shock, I didn't know what to do, but he apologized right away and said he was just stressed at work." Marina wiped her cheek. "The only time he touched me when he returned from that trip was to hit me, and after that night it got worse. He was really careful to not leave any visible marks and if he did, I was careful to cover them up. My family were constantly asking what was wrong, but I'd brush it off as pregnancy stuff. My dad called one day and asked him what was wrong with me, and that's when Marc started to put distance between them and me. He'd monitor my calls and make excuses why we couldn't visit."

"That's not unusual for abusers." James had heard the story too many times.

"I found the drugs under our bed about a month later, and I don't know why I'd never seen it there before, but when I opened the box I almost passed out. He came home that night and I confronted him. I was so tired of being afraid. He shoved me against the wall and slapped me so hard my ears rang. Told me I had no right to be digging around in his stuff. He wrapped his hands around my throat and I was pretty close to passing out, but something came over me and I pushed him so hard he fell over a chair. I told him to leave or I was calling the police."

"He lunged at me but something stopped him before he grabbed me again. He just grinned and it was so sadistic. I thought he was going to kill me, but he backed away and told me he never loved me and he didn't want the baby. He packed some stuff and left. I sat on the floor and cried and I don't know how long I was there before I got up. It was a week before I called my family. I had to wait for the marks on my neck and my face to fade. I guess I was ashamed that I'd let him do those things to me because I never grew up with a man like that. My dad is the gentlest man in the world and he treats my mom with so much love and respect. You know if someone had asked me what I would do if a man abused me seven or eight years ago, I'd probably tell them he wouldn't do it a second time but honestly the only thing that gave me the courage to finally kick him out was I wasn't going to let him ever do that to my child. I'll kill Marc before I'll let him get his hands on Danny."

"Marina, I wish I could take away everything Marc did to you, but I know it happens more times than it should." James wrapped his arms around her and kissed the top of her head. He ignored the comment about killing Marc because he wasn't really thinking as a cop at the moment and he understood the protection instinct as a father. She rested her cheek against his chest.

"He wasn't the man I fell in love with. The Marc I married was sweet, gentle and I don't know what happened but I blame the drugs."

James could feel the dampness of her tears on his T-shirt, but he didn't care if she soaked him. Marina obviously needed to get all of her emotions out because she'd been keeping this all to herself because she didn't want to upset her family.

"There's no excuse for what he did, sweetheart." James rubbed his hand up and down her back. "No man should treat any woman that way."

"You're the first person I've told the whole story." Marina pulled back and gazed into his eyes. "I didn't even tell my therapist all of that. I don't want my family to know. They had a hard enough time dealing with what I did tell them."

"I understand but I'm honored you felt comfortable enough to tell me." James kissed her forehead. "I'm really surprised, though."

"Surprised? Why?" Marina stared up at him.

"I've met your dad and I'm surprised he didn't beat Marc to a pulp." James caressed her cheek with his index finger.

"It wasn't because he didn't want to." Marina smiled as she leaned into his touch. "It took my mom, my sister and two of the men that work for him to keep him from leaving the house when I told them some of what happened. If I'd told them everything, he'd probably be in jail."

"Probably a good thing. I don't think Marc is worth your dad going to jail." James smiled down at her and she stood up on her toes and kissed his cheek.

"Thank you." She tucked her head under his chin and he held her in his arms. He didn't know how long they stood there but he could feel her tension ease.

"So, I guess we can talk about you and me now." Marina's voice was just above a whisper.

"We take things at your pace, and until we find out what Marc is up to, you'll stay here. I need to know you and Danny are safe." He rested his cheek against the top of her head and held her tightly.

"Okay," was all she said while she wrapped her arms around his waist. He prayed it wouldn't take long to find Marc because he didn't want the asshole to have her living in fear of when he would pop up out of nowhere or create havoc in her life. He'd screwed with her life long enough.

Chapter 13

A week had passed since the break in and Marc was still 'in the wind' as James called it. It wasn't any trouble to tell he was concerned because he'd requested another week off so he could be home with her. Although, she had no idea why he would need to stay home because of the two men that Keith had permanently stationed in front of James' house.

One of them would be there during the day and the other during the night. Danny and Mason had started referring to the two men as 'the superheroes.' Probably because the one she'd come to know as Trunk had worn a T-shirt with Superman on it and the boys dubbed him Superman. The other guy who'd been introduced as Hulk had the boys a little confused because he wasn't green, but the mountain of a man explained he only turns green when he was chasing bad guys. It appeased the boys.

Marina's boss insisted she work from home because he was worried about her driving back and forth by herself. David Molloy was one of the best bosses a person could ask for, and she thanked her lucky stars to be working for him. Still, the guilt of having everyone go out of their way for her was starting to take its toll.

She was starting to settle into James' house and the thought of leaving made her stomach clench and not because she was afraid to go home. No, the reason she wanted to puke when she thought of going home was because she wouldn't see James every day. She loved to spend time with him, but it was frustrating at the same time. Being around the man would send anyone's hormones into overdrive, but his care and concern for her son was making her fall so fast it was terrifying.

Stephanie had called a few times over the course of the last week, and her sister was relieved Marina agreed to stay with James. Not only to make sure she and Danny were safe, but it would give her and James more time to get to know each other. Marina didn't tell her about the kisses.

James said he was going go at her pace and there were moments when she wanted to double the pace, but then she'd remember her situation. It wasn't fair to start anything with James until everything with Marc was resolved.

James seemed to sense her seesaw of emotions because the only time he'd touched her since the night she opened up to him, was a quick kiss on the cheek goodnight or a hug when she seemed to be having a rough moment. She appreciated the support so much but she really wanted more. She just wasn't sure how much more she was ready for.

James was doing everything to make her comfortable and had gone as far as setting up a desk in the corner of his living room for her to work. When she was working, he kept the boys busy so they wouldn't disturb her. Mason would go to school in the morning and Marina would entertain Danny until Mason got home. Neither of them had been to daycare since the break-in mainly because Keith had said it would be safer.

The O'Connors were bending over backwards for her with the brothers constantly stopping by to entertain the boys. At least one of the women dropped in every day for a little girl time—and to ogle Keith's security guys. She had to admit they were pretty hot, but James was the only one to get her blood pumping.

She hadn't seen Sandy since that first night of the break-in but Keith said something about her needing to get out of town for a couple of weeks. It was strange, because Ian had been in the room when Keith told everyone and there was some obvious tension in both brothers at the mention of Sandy. Marina wasn't sure what was going on, but she was sure Sandy would fill her in when she got back home.

Then there was Nanny Betty, the comic relief in her otherwise tense life. The woman showed up every day with some sort of baked goods demanding Hulk and Trunk to come inside and eat. Marina could almost tell the time when the older woman breezed through. It was always after lunch when Hulk and Trunk would be switching out. The minute she walked in, James jumped at her commands. He wasn't the only one. Marina found herself jumping for the woman's orders as well as anyone else who was there. Nanny Betty definitely knew how to crack the whip. Marina had grown to adore her and looked forward to her visits.

It had been a pretty quiet day, and she answered the last of her emails. She'd also sent off the last of her editing to David with an email telling him she was hoping to be back in the office soon. She glanced up from her laptop to see James' tall, muscular frame propped against the doorjamb with his arms folded across his chest. Her stomach fluttered, and it was everything she could do not to sigh at the sight of him. Then he had to go and smile. *Oh dear God!*

"I think it's time to leave the office, Ms. Kelly." He was yummy in his white dress shirt, sleeves rolled up to expose his strong forearms and the top three buttons open, revealing the light dusting of dark hair on his chest. The worn blue jeans hung low on his hips and fit him so right. She finally knew what it meant for someone to take her breath away, because every time she saw him, James did that.

She smiled and stretched her arms over her head to work out the kinks. His eyes moved to her exposed midsection where her shirt slipped over her stomach, and his blue eyes sparkled. His intense stare sent a shiver of desire through her body, and that craving for him to touch her hit her like a freight train. She wanted him and she wasn't going to be able to hold back much longer.

"I guess you're right. It's almost bath time for the boys anyway." She stood up and walked around the desk.

"Already done." He looked proud of himself. "They're waiting for a story from you." She could really get used to this, but she was worried Danny was getting way to comfortable. He hadn't even asked when they were going back home and he loved sharing a room with Mason so much they had ceased calling it Mason's room. Both boys now said 'their room.'

Then there was all the pent-up sexual feelings she had. She wanted James so damn bad and he seemed intent on letting her set the pace. She didn't know what to do because she'd never been the one to make the first move on anyone and she was too embarrassed to tell him she was going to combust. She walked by him and he grabbed her hand.

"Are you okay?" She wasn't keeping her emotions hidden as well as she thought, because he'd obviously seen the frustration on her face and what was she supposed to say—'I'm so damn horny I need you to do me now?' That wouldn't be awkward at all.

"I'm fine, but do you know what would make me feel a whole lot better?" She knew he was probably going to hate her for it, but she couldn't help it.

"What?" His hand tightened on hers.

"To hear you sing the tough boys song to Mason and Danny." She burst out laughing at the look of mortification on his face.

"That's not fair." He narrowed his eyes.

"Sorry, but it's the only thing that will help." She exaggerated a sigh, turned, and ran upstairs. She knew he'd be behind her any second because Mason would not sleep without the song, but she always seemed to miss him singing it. Why he tried to hide it was beyond her. His voice was amazing. She grinned when he walked into the room while she was sitting on Danny's bed reading to both boys.

"Marina said it's time for the tough guy song," James said as he met her gaze.

She felt guilty, because he seemed to be so uncomfortable, but not to the point that she was going to miss him singing. She wondered why he was so intent on not singing in front of anyone. His brothers didn't seem to have an issue with it or at least most of them.

"Yay!" The boys cheered and scrambled into their separate beds. Marina walked to the door, and James glanced at her. She smiled as he shook his head just before his soft, soothing voice filled the room. She closed her eyes and let the sound flow over her. She'd always loved the song, but the way he sang it made her love it even more.

Mason and Danny were asleep before the song ended, and instead of waiting until he finished she went to her room and showered. Once she'd dried herself and changed into some comfortable yoga pants and a tank top, she headed downstairs.

James was on the back deck sitting on the railing. She grabbed a sweater she'd hung up earlier in the foyer and then hurried to the kitchen. With a beer for James and a glass of wine for herself, she headed outside to join him.

"Thought you might want this." She held out the bottle.

"Thanks." His voice seemed strange, but she didn't say anything because she was distracted by the view of the ocean. It really was relaxing to watch the waves rolling, but it didn't distract her from the feeling of James' gaze.

"Is something wrong?" She couldn't read his expression.

"I'm fine." He didn't sound okay, but she didn't push it.

"Marina, how long has it been since you've seen Marc?" He didn't look at her and she'd answered this question already.

"I told you the last time was when he was beating on John's door." Did he not believe her?

"I don't mean to pry, but it seems strange that he'd come back after all this time. He's wants something. Think about it. He didn't take anything from your house, except that picture of Danny, but the way your house looked, it was as if he was tearing everything apart to find something." James turned towards her.

"I don't know what it could be. I don't have anything at my house that belongs to him." She'd made sure there was nothing left of Marc, and what he didn't take, her father kept stored in his shed in case Marc wanted it. She wasn't even sure if the stuff was still there.

"Maybe I'm just overthinking things. How about we watch a movie or something. It's still early and I'm not tired." He pushed a lock of her hair behind her ear. "Unless you're tired, I understand if you want to call it a night." Marina stood on her toes and kissed his cheek.

"A movie sounds great." She was tired, but there was no way she was saying no to spending an evening with James.

"Great! I need to run to the store and pick up some milk for the morning." James walked into the house. "You can make some popcorn while I'm gone. I won't be long and Bull is outside keeping an eye on things."

"Doesn't he get cold out there?" Marina felt safer with Keith's guys outside but the weather was starting to get cold.

"I've told him to come inside and stay but he insists on staying in his truck." James pulled on his coat.

Marina watched through the window as James walked up to the truck at the end of the driveway and stood there for a moment talking to Bull. As James walked away Bull exited his vehicle and headed up the driveway. Both he and Truck did that when James was out of the house. They would stand on the front deck until he returned even if someone else was inside with her. Although it seemed a little excessive to have the security, she was relieved they were there. Not that she'd let Marc get close to Danny because she'd die first.

Marina had popcorn ready as she flicked through the on demand movies. There were a few she wanted to see, but it had to be something James would want to watch. She glanced at her watch and realized he'd been gone a while. Hopedale wasn't really big and the store wasn't that far. She walked to the window and looked up and down the street. There was no sign of James' truck and she began to feel a wave of panic. What if something happened to him? She grabbed her phone off the coffee table and was about to push his cell number when the lights of a vehicle lit up the living room. She ran back to the window to see him heading up the driveway. Now she felt like a complete idiot.

He stood outside talking to Bull for quite a while and it made her tense when Bull jogged back to his truck with his phone to his ear. James walked into the house and headed to the kitchen.

"I thought you got lost." Marina tried to keep the comment light though her heart was pounding. She had panic attacks but it was the first time she had one in a long time. Now she knew why James had been making sure she always had company. He probably knew she'd feel anxious when she was alone for the first time after the break-in.

"Wishful thinking." He sauntered into the living room. The last thing she wanted was for him to get lost. Her wishes for him required him to be in full attendance, minus the clothes. He plopped down on the couch next to her, and he turned towards her.

"I had a little trouble at the store. My tire was flat when I came out, and it looked like it was slashed. I had to change it," James said.

"Slashed?" The word sent a shiver down her spine.

"I can't be sure until I get a better look at it." He didn't seem overly concerned but she was.

"You think it was Marc, don't you?" Marina didn't need him to answer.

"I'm not worrying about it tonight because I'm looking forward to having a nice night watching a movie with you." He smiled at her. Nothing could be done until morning and he was home safe but if Marc did this, it meant he was in Hopedale and that was way too close, but James was right. They needed to forget about Marc for the night and just enjoy each other's company.

After a serious discussion on the romance and heartbreak of love stories, Marina using the romance argument, and James arguing the heartbreak part. They agreed to watch only one so each of them could prove their argument. Plus, she loved them.

She enjoyed the movie, but she was hyperaware of him sitting so close. James teased her about crying over one part, and she swatted him on the leg. He grabbed her hand and laced his fingers with hers. That was the way they sat for the rest of the movie. She was relaxed and content as the movie credits rolled up on the screen and hadn't even noticed she'd had her head resting on James shoulder. A sudden crack from outside made her bolt upright and practically jump into James lap.

"What the hell was that?" she almost screamed.

"I think it's the beginning of a thunderstorm."

She turned towards him when she felt his body shake. He was laughing, and she wanted to smack him again. A bright flash of light and the heavy rain began to beat against the window. She was doing her best to stay calm, but she was nervous of thunderstorms. James' grin told her she wasn't doing a great job of hiding that fear.

"I won't let the big bad storm get you." He was teasing her and she wanted to slap him.

Marina pushed him playfully, and he let out a full belly laugh. She did snuggle into his side, but mostly because she wanted to be close to him. He wrapped his arms around her and held her tightly. She'd never been so glad for a thunderstorm in her life.

James picked another movie, but she really didn't care what he picked. She was so content sitting next to him and having his warmth envelope her. The movie was about four guys who went on a trip for a bachelor party and ended up in all kinds of trouble. It was funny, and she laughed so hard her stomach hurt. She'd adjusted her position so that she was lying against James' chest, and every time he laughed the vibration rumbled through her. When the credits started to roll, she was disappointed. It meant she'd have to move.

When she tried to sit up he held her tightly, and she glanced at him. His eyes were hooded and his lips slightly parted. James ran his finger down her jawline and his eyes locked with hers. She couldn't look away.

"Marina, I want to kiss you so bad." His voice seemed strained, and her heart begin to flutter. They'd kissed before, but something about the way he was gazing into her eyes told her this kiss was going to be different.

He leaned in slowly, and keeping his gaze locked with hers. He slipped his hand around the back of her neck, and he grasped her hair in his hand as he tilted her head and brushed his lips against hers. His lips were soft and gentle at first, but he increased the pressure and she moaned. It was intoxicating and she couldn't get enough of his taste. When his tongue entered her mouth, she met it with her own. He groaned into her mouth as he lowered her back on the sofa. James hovered above her, never breaking the kiss, but she could feel his growing arousal against her leg, and moisture pooled between her legs. Things were getting out of control quickly and even though she really wanted this, with everything going on in her life, maybe starting something before Marc was locked away and Danny was safe would only put a strain on their relationship. She pulled her lips from his.

"James, wait… this is… oh God." Marina panted as he started to move his hand under her shirt. James was breathing so heavy she wasn't sure if he'd heard her, but when she pressed her hand against his chest, she could feel his heart thudding.

"Damn, that kiss kind of got away from me. I didn't mean to get carried away, but when I kiss you it's hard to think." He stared into her eyes.

"I think we both got a little lost there for a minute." She touched his cheek, and he closed his eyes.

"So what are we gonna do about this?" he asked, and she cupped his cheeks in her hands.

"What do you want to do about it?" She needed to know where he stood. "I mean this is going somewhere? Right?"

"I kinda liked where it was going a few seconds ago." He grinned.

"I could tell." She pressed her thigh against his erection, and he groaned as he sat up and pulled her with him.

"He invited himself to the party." James chuckled.

"Maybe we should call it a night." Marina smiled when he held her hand as he led her upstairs, stopping in front of what he now called her room. "Sleep well, sweetheart," he whispered as he kissed her softly.

"Goodnight." She pulled away reluctantly and entered the room. Marina pressed her head against the closed door for a moment and tried to slow her racing heartbeat. The man had her hormones raging but she couldn't blame it all on him. She flopped down on the bed and closed her eyes. Maybe it wouldn't be too long before she could get back to her life and possibly start one with James.

The sun peeped through the heavy drapes and Marina squinted her eyes to adjust to the brightness. Another week and she was still no closer to going home or finding out what the hell Marc was up to. Sleep wasn't her friend, but all the shit with Marc wasn't the only reason she wasn't getting a good night's sleep. Every night she'd toss and turn until she'd fall asleep only to dream about James doing really hot and naughty things to her body. She didn't know how much longer she could take this sexual frustration. At least they weren't nightmares about Marc anymore.

Stephanie and John would be home in a few days, and it would probably be a good idea for her to go stay with them until she could go home. It was getting really hard to keep things G-rated in such close proximity to James. Of course her frustration was her own fault. She and James had done more kissing and a little petting, but they'd always stop before things went too far. She didn't know why for sure. Fear of what Marc was up to was part of it, but she cared for James probably more than she ever expected. She wanted to take things further and he seemed ready to move on as well. What was she waiting for? A soft knock brought her out of her head.

"Come in." She leaned up on one elbow. James opened the door and sauntered in with a tray in one hand. The grin he was sporting said he was pretty impressed with himself, and it was so damn sexy. He moved next to the bed and set the tray next to her.

"Good morning." He sat on the foot of the bed.

"Good morning." Marina glanced at the tray and then back to him.

"Sleep well?" Her heart jumped in her chest when his eyes dropped to her breasts. She knew the top was probably too snug but it was only meant to sleep in. She did enjoy the hot look in his eyes when he moved his gaze back to hers.

"Yes." She smiled even though it was far from the truth.

"That's good." It almost sounded like a small growl.

"So what's this?" Marina motioned to the tray that contained a cup of steaming coffee, a bowl of fruit, and two slices of toast. Her normal breakfast.

"Thought I'd spoil you a bit this morning."

She smiled and his eyes moved to her lips. When he did that her stomach clenched with need and she had to squeeze her legs together to ease the ache there.

"Mrs. Ray took Mason and Danny to the park. She was taking her dogs for a walk and thought they'd enjoy it. So I figured I'd let you sleep in a bit and then I made breakfast."

"Are you sure it's safe?" Nothing had happened in a while but Marc was still out there and until he was caught Danny was still in danger.

"Trunk is gone with them. Although, Mrs. Ray's dogs would probably eat someone who went near her or the boys. She has two Bullmastiffs. They're great dogs and very friendly but protective." Marina had seen the dogs in the yard a few times and thought they looked kind of scary.

"So you thought you'd treat me to breakfast in bed." She sat up and the blankets slipped down, revealing the tank she was wearing. James almost jumped off the bed after he handed her the napkin from the tray. He shoved his hand into his front pockets, and her heart rate increased when she noticed the slight bulge he seemed to be trying to hide.

Marina started to eat as James moved to the other side of the room and leaned against the dresser. He was focused on her mouth as she put the last piece of fruit into her mouth.

"What's wrong?" She met his eyes and a shiver of desire ran through her.

"Nothing. Just watching you."

Why did those words make her panties wet? It wasn't only what he said, but it was the husky vibration of his voice. She placed the tray on the night stand, but didn't look away from him. When he pushed off the dresser and moved to the bed, her heart raced. He sat next to her and linked his fingers with hers. There was no more fighting what she wanted. She wanted James. She leaned towards him, and he tensed. Marina brushed her lips against his and cupped his cheek with her other hand.

His face was freshly shaven and the scent of his cologne she knew instantly because it was her favorite. Stetson. She brushed her lips against his again and inhaled. James seemed almost afraid to move, but his lips responded to her kiss when her tongue touched his lower lip. He moaned as her tongue entered his mouth and the kiss increased in intensity. She kissed him like someone starved and his lips were the only thing that would sustain her life. Her hands plowed into his hair, but he began to pull away. She only held tighter and tried to pull him down onto the bed next to her. She was done worrying about what the hell Marc was up to. She'd let him interfere in her happiness for too long.

"Marina, if you keep kissing me that way, I'm not gonna be able to control myself," he whispered against her mouth as he held his body as far away from hers as she would allow him.

"Then don't control yourself. I don't want to wait anymore. I need you. Now." She glided her hands down the front of his shirt and she frantically pulled it free from his jeans.

"Are you sure?" His warm breath blew against her ear and made her tremble, but she found his lips and answered with a deep, desperate kiss. His hand moved under her shirt and the gentle caress of his hand against her naked flesh sent an electric current through her body.

He cupped her breast, and she didn't think the sensation of his touch could become any more intense, but his thumb slowly circled her hard nipple, making her gasp and moan at the same time. He rolled it between his fingers as his mouth worked every nerve ending down the side of her neck. She slowly dragged her nails lightly against the skin of his naked chest under his shirt. His muscles bunched and she pulled back to meet his eyes.

"James, I guess I should ask if you're ready for this too?" She'd never even thought he may not be. When he smiled and moved her hand to the erection straining against his zipper, she knew the answer.

"Does that answer your question? I've never been more sure of anything in my life." James clenched his teeth when she squeezed him through his jeans. Her shirt disappeared with a quick flick over her head, and his jeans were shucked quicker than she'd ever seen a man undress.

James slid under the blankets and pulled her against his warm naked body. The heat of his skin against hers was scorching and making her hotter than she'd ever expected. His lips teased down her neck in small sensual kisses as he covered her breast again. Then his hot mouth covered her pebbled nipple and he sucked and licked one than the other. She gasped with pleasure. His hand seemed to have an agenda of its own as it slid down her body slowly making its way to where she needed him to touch her the most.

He continued to explore her body until he reached the aching flesh between her legs. His lips had found hers again as he slid his thick finger between her folds and pressed the heel of his hand against her sensitive clit.

"Ah, yes. James." She moaned into his mouth when he slid one thick digit inside her and continued to increase the pressure on her nub. His mouth moved back to her breast, and he scraped his teeth over the hard nipple. She was going to go up in flames and when her body started to quiver, she was sure of it. He thrust another finger into her and curved them inside her. A wave of pleasure began to flow through her, and squeezed her legs together around his hand as she embraced the first orgasm. Probably the most intense one she'd had in her life.

"Marina, I want you so fucking bad." His voice was desperate as he moved over her. He positioned himself between her legs but stopped. "Condom." He gasped and started to move off the bed.

"I'm on the pill." Marina grabbed him and pulled him down on top of her. His lips captured hers in a fevered kiss as his throbbing cock pressed against her wet heat. Just a little more pressure and she would come again.

"Jesus, Marina, you're so wet." James growled against her lips and flexed his hips against her.

"I want you inside me, James. Just you. Nothing between us," she whispered. He groaned and slowly pressed into her. He seemed so big as he slowly filled her, but it felt so incredible. At first his thrusts were slow and deep. It was driving her crazy as he took his time making her climax build more and more. His body started to tremble as his hips began to pump faster.

"James." Marina screamed when he thrust deep into her and she exploded. The pleasure rushed through her body, and she arched off the bed, her body convulsing as her orgasm seemed to go on and on. James didn't stop and pumped into her frantically drawing out her climax. One more deep thrust and he roared her name. His body quivered and his jaw clenched.

For a few minutes, she was warmed by the weight of his body and his hot breath against her neck. He lifted his head and smiled as he rolled both of them on their side with him still inside her. He propped himself up with his elbow with his head resting on his fist. He took a deep breath and let it out slowly.

"Are you okay?" Marina giggled.

"I'm so relieved." He sighed.

"I know the feeling." James rolled onto his back, and he slipped from her body. Marina missed him instantly and quickly snuggled into his side. For a moment she studied the tattoo on the right side of his chest. Her sister told her about the O'Connor family crest that the entire family had inked themselves with, including her sister. She lay her head on his chest and listened to steady beat of his heart. It was calming. Thump, thump… Thump, thump.

She started to drift off to sleep but the distant ringing of the phone made both her and James jump. He cursed as he hopped out of the bed, and she couldn't help but watch his naked ass as he dashed from the room.

Marina stretched and then let her body relax. She grabbed a pillow and put it over her face as she let out a squeal of delight and stomped her feet into the mattress. Nothing could take away how happy she felt right now. Well at least that's what she thought until James returned with a solemn expression and grabbed his jeans from the floor. *Whoosh!* There went the happiness.

"What's wrong?" Marina sat up and pulled her knees up to her chest. She didn't know if she really wanted an answer, because the hairs on the back of her neck were telling her this wasn't going to be good.

"Marina, I need you to get up and get dressed, quickly." James wouldn't meet her eyes as he frantically pulled on his jeans.

"James, you're scaring me. What's wrong?" She grabbed his arm as he bent to pick up his T-shirt. When he took her hand, her blood ran cold.

"That was Uncle Kurt on the phone. The police were called to the park." His voice cracked before he finished. "Marina, Danny's missing."

She shook her head in disbelief and tried to speak but nothing would come out.

"We need to go." James knelt next to the bed.

How could Danny be missing he was at the park with Trunk and Mrs. Ray?

"This can't be happening. Please tell me it's a joke because if it is it's not funny." She pulled her hands from his. It was a stupid thing to say. James wouldn't joke about something as serious as her son missing. *Dear God.* The sobs started to wrack her body and she was suddenly wrapped in his arms as the tears spilled.

"I'd never joke about that. You need to get dressed because we need to hurry, Marina. Every second counts." James stood up and kissed the top of her head. She was trembling as she jumped out of the bed. She couldn't get her brain to think about anything but Danny. She sat on the bed trying to get her brain to function.

"Marina, sweetheart, you've got to get dressed." James grabbed clothes out of the suitcase that she still hadn't unpacked after almost three weeks. "We'll find him. I swear to you if it's the last thing I do; I'll find your son. I promise you."

Her heart raced as she pulled on her clothes as quickly as she could. The only thing she could think about was her baby was missing and she knew exactly who had him.

Chapter 14

The terror in her eyes was tearing him apart as he helped her out of the truck in front of the station. He wrapped his arm around her trembling body and it made him wonder if she was going to be able to handle the whole situation. Although, maybe it was his own shaking he was feeling. Danny wasn't his son, but he'd grown to love the kid and his stomach was in knots wondering where in the hell he was. He couldn't let Marina see it though, because she seemed ready to fall apart. He almost had to carry her through the doors of the reception area.

"Marina, if that bastard has Danny, we'll find him," he whispered.

A sob escaped but she quickly composed herself again. How could he tell her not to worry when he was sick with it? He had to keep himself together for her and make sure he got Danny home to her.

James spotted Mary sitting on one of the benches in the lobby of the station, her eyes still wet with tears. Mason was next to her and he seemed completely lost as he held Mary's hand. Marina practically ran to them and wrapped her arms around the sobbing woman.

"Marina, my dear girl, I'm so sorry. The boys were playing in that fort at the park. Even that nice young man Trunk was watching it. Then the dogs started to go crazy and we saw a man running out of the fort and Trunk chased him. Mason came running from behind the fort saying a man took Danny." Mary sobbed as Marina hugged her and rubbed her hand up and down on Mary's back.

After Marina sat next to Mary and held her hand, James crouched in front of Mason. Huge tears fell from his son's eyes as he practically leaped into James' arms. Mason had already been questioned to see if he'd seen anything, and Kurt made sure he was with Mason when he was questioned. With the way Mason was clinging to him, James was beginning to think he probably should have been there. His son was obviously frightened.

"I told him not to talk to the man, Daddy." Mason sobbed.

"It's okay, buddy. Everything will be okay," James whispered into Mason's ear as he hugged him tightly. He glanced at Marina, and she held up her hands.

"Mason, honey, come sit with me and Mrs. Ray while we wait." Marina seemed to need to hold Mason as much as Mason needed to be held. James put him down and Marina pulled him onto her lap and he clung tightly to her.

"Mary, are you okay?" James asked.

"I'm fine. I just feel sick about all this, and that young man is still out in the park searching." James regretted asking because the older woman began to sob again. Marina wrapped an arm around her and motioned for James to look behind him.

Kurt was headed towards them, and the tense way his jaw was set told James that Kurt was about ready to snap. His uncle made it pretty clear how frustrated he was because Marc was eluding them. James heard him call Marc some pretty out of character names over the last couple of weeks. Kurt didn't like not getting the bad guy.

"Do you want me to handle this, Marina?" James asked her because he didn't want her to think he was trying to take over. She nodded as she hugged Mason tighter.

Kurt motioned to his office and stomped off ahead of James. The man was pissed.

"I'll be right back." James told her as he followed his uncle.

"What's happening?" James closed the office door.

"I'm pretty sure the youngster's father has him." Kurt slammed a file down on his desk.

"I had a feeling you were going to say that." James knew in his heart it's what everyone suspected, including Marina.

"Mason told Greg Harris a man took Danny," Kurt explained.

"Fuck!" James growled through clenched teeth. "If that bastard hurts him, I swear Uncle Kurt, I'll beat him within an inch of his life." That probably wasn't a great thing for a police officer to say in the presence of the police superintendent.

"James, watch what you're saying," Kurt warned. "We'll find him."

Kurt's phone rang, and his uncle snatched it from the desk. As he fired off a series of questions to the caller, James left the office to check on Marina and Mason. His son was still wrapped in her arms as she held Mary's hand. She was slightly rocking Mason side to side and his eyes were closed. James couldn't believe she'd pulled herself together so quickly to soothe Mary and Mason. Her son was missing and she was trying to help them.

"Any news?" His father said from behind him. He hadn't seen them come in, but there his father stood with his mother next to him. As always, his parents were there to support him.

"Nothing yet. How did you guys find out?" Hopedale was small, and the tiny police station that worked both in and out of town. It had been Kurt who'd gotten the small department open in

Hopedale because the town was growing so fast. So it shouldn't have surprised him that his parents had found out so fast.

"Kurt called us. He thought with Marina's family out of town she needed the support," his father explained while his mother had already moved next to Marina. Marina lay her head on his mother's shoulder, but she didn't let go of Mason or Mary. His mother wrapped her arms around Marina's shoulder and kissed the top of Mason's head.

"They think Marc has him," James whispered so Marina wouldn't hear, although she probably knew. His father nodded and James plowed his hands through his hair in frustration.

"I know."

"This is all my fault." He swallowed to dislodge the lump that was beginning to choke him.

"Why would you say that? This isn't your fault." Sean grabbed his arm and pulled him to the side.

"I promised I'd protect her and Danny. How could I be so stupid?" He squeezed his eyes closed to stop the tears. Jesus, he needed to get hold of himself.

"Don't be so hard on yourself. It's not like he was in the park alone." He needed to get it off his chest, and he knew his father wouldn't judge.

"What is it?" It was as if his dad read his mind.

"Marina and I… we were… we slept together while Danny was at the park." James stammered over his words as he avoided his father's eyes.

"I see," was all the man said.

"I let Mrs. Ray take Danny and Mason to the park instead of keeping Danny where Marc couldn't get him." He wasn't blaming Mrs. Ray because she didn't do anything wrong.

"It's not like you knew he was watching Danny, or whether he'd know Mrs. Ray would take him to the park. I've got to say the man is pretty cheeky to take him out from under the nose of that guy that works for Keith. We stopped by the park before we came here and he is ready to rip someone's head off."

He knew his father was right, but the guilt was killing him. "Dad, I'm falling in love with her. I haven't felt this in a long time. I should've been making sure her son was safe not…. well, you know."

"James Charles O'Connor, doncha dare blame yarself fer followin' yar heart. Danny'll be found. Den ya can tell dat lovely girl how ya feel."

Shit! Nanny Betty was behind him. *Fucking great!* Now he'd never be able to face his grandmother again.

"Now get over wit dat girl. Yar brudders are out lookin' fer dat angel. So are Kurt's girls along with de entire town and those overgrown goons that work for Keithy. It's already on de radio." She

- 192 -

walked around in front of him and reached up to cup his face in her tiny hands. "Now ya stop yar regrets 'bout bein' wit da first woman ta put light back in dem eyes since Sarah left us." His grandmother always had a way of putting things in perspective.

"Nan, you don't understand. I let this happen so how can anything happen between us after this?" He swallowed hard as he stared into his grandmother's blue eyes. "Her son is missing and it's my fault. I never should have let him out of the house. I promised to protect him."

"Lord, dine, Jesus, Jimmy. Dis is not yar fault," Nanny Betty snapped. "Ya stop blamin' yarself. Dere's nothin' ya did wrong."

"You're telling me not to blame myself, but Marina's going to blame me. I promised I wouldn't let anything happen to her son." The sting of tears burned his eyes. "I finally find someone I can see spending my life with, and I let some idiot take her son."

"Mudder." James glanced up to see his father looking behind him. He turned and Marina stood behind him with her hands clenched against her chest. Nanny Betty kissed James' cheek and hurried to where Mary, Mason and Kathleen were sitting.

"James." Marina moved towards him and he backed up until he was against the wall. "This isn't your fault." She stood in front of him and pressed her hands against his chest. The tears in her eyes were tearing at his heart. "I heard what you said to your grandmother, and you need to know I'm not blaming you for any of this or Mary or Trunk. It's Marc who did this." She wiped his cheek. It was the first time he realized the tears had started. "Just help me find Danny." James pulled her into his arms and buried his face into her neck as they both sobbed.

"I swear I'll make sure you have your son back if it's the last thing I do." He lifted his head and pressed his lips against her forehead. He loved her and the ache in his heart when he thought about Danny told him he'd fallen in love with her son, too.

"I'm going to get Mom and Dad to take Mary and Mason home." Mary had been through enough and Mason didn't need to be around all of this.

"That's a good idea. He's so confused." He held out his hand and she clasped it.

It seemed as if Danny had been gone for days, but in reality, it was only three hours. Time had seemed to come to a standstill. Kristy and Jess arrived at the station to support Marina and his coworkers were probably ready to string him up for harassing them. He'd called his brothers constantly for updates, but to his dismay they'd found nothing. His phone vibrated in his pocket and he answered it without even checking the caller id.

"Hello."

"Why in the fuck didn't you call us?" John snapped.

"I didn't want to upset you guys until we knew more." James really didn't want to upset Stephanie and there was really nothing they could do from Hawaii.

"We're boarding the plane now. We left Hawaii yesterday because we wanted to spend a few days in New York." John sounded pissed.

"I'm sorry you had to come home early." James' fuck up was screwing with everyone's lives.

"Fuck the vacation. We need to be there." John said. "Is there any news?"

"Nothing but everyone's still searching." James explained. "I want to get out there but I can't leave Marina. So you're in New York now?"

"Yes, and we're about to board. We'll see you in a few hours." The call ended before James could say anything else. He shoved his phone back in his pocket and turned as he heard a voice behind him yelling.

"They found him." Isabelle ran up behind him.

"What? Where?" James hurried over to Marina while they waited for Isabelle to catch her breath. She bent over and held her side while she gasped for air.

"A.J. was driving by your house and Danny was sitting on the step." Isabelle took another intake of breath. "He told A.J. the man dropped him off and told him to wait on the step until someone got home." James wrapped his arms around Marina and she sobbed into his chest. They'd found him, but James wasn't going to relax until Danny was in Marina's arms again.

Why the hell was it taking Aaron so long to get from Marina's house to the station? A person could drive around Hopedale twice in the time it was taking his fucking brother to get there. James yanked his phone out of his pocket and was about to tap Aaron's number when the doors of the station opened.

Aaron sauntered in with a grinning Danny in his arms. Marina ran to them and Danny jumped into her arms, giving James that familiar lump in his throat again. He scanned the lobby of the station and apparently he wasn't the only one getting emotional. His cousins were wiping tears from their eyes and even his youngest brother was getting misty. The only thing bothering him at the moment was separating Danny and Marina so he could be interviewed.

He walked behind Marina and Aaron met his eyes because as a police officer his brother knew what had to happen next. Marina was kissing Danny's head and his arms were wrapped around her neck. He didn't appear distressed, but nobody knew exactly what happened.

"What took you so long?" James asked Aaron.

"Danny said he had to go to the bathroom, so I let him in your house to use before we came here. He was taking forever so when I went to check on him he was in his bedroom kneeling by the bed. He said he was looking for his car," Aaron told him.

"Marina, I'm sorry to interrupt, but we need to ask Danny a few questions." Kurt said from behind them. Greg Harris was next to one of the interview rooms and it made James relax since Greg was one of the best with kids. Somehow he seemed to be able to gain a kid's trust faster than any other officer he knew. Marina didn't say a word. She just nodded as she followed Kurt and Greg. James met Kurt's eyes with a silent plea to let him stay with Marina and his uncle nodded but raised his eyebrow in a silent warning to keep his mouth closed, or at least that was what James assumed he was saying.

Inside the office, Greg sat across the table from Marina and Danny as James and Kurt stood next to the door. Greg introduced himself to Danny, and the little boy shook Greg's outstretched hand. For a few minutes Greg just asked him some of his favorite things and what he liked to do. Then got to the questions they really needed answers for.

"So, buddy, you gave your mom quite a scare," Greg said.

"I'm sorry." Danny glanced at James and then at Marina.

"We're just happy you're back." Marina hugged him.

"Danny, can you tell us where you were?" Greg asked but Danny seemed confused by the question.

"I went with my daddy, you 'member." Danny turned to Marina.

"Danny, mom didn't know where you were." Greg tried to keep Danny's attention. "What makes you think the man was your daddy?"

"'Cause he said mommy told him to pick me up because there was a bad man in the park and he was gonna bring me back to mommy." Danny jumped down from Marina's lap and reached into his pocket. He pulled out a folded piece of paper and gave it to Marina.

"What's this?" Marina asked.

"My daddy said to give it to you." Danny shrugged and climbed back into Marina's lap again. James was relieved Marc hadn't seemed to traumatize him, because Danny didn't think anything was wrong, but James was pissed the asshole pulled this shit. He watched Marina open up the paper and her face lost all color. He crouched down in front of her, and she tried to pass him the note. He knew he couldn't touch it because it was evidence and the less people that touched it the better. James motioned her to lay it out on the table. Marina dropped it like it was burning her fingers, and she pulled Danny into a tight hug.

James, Greg and Kurt bent over the table to examine it and when he read the words, he could actually feel his blood pressure rising as his temper started to rage.

If I could get him this easily, then it proves you're an unfit mother. I'm going to have my son and there's nothing you can do about it. Don't think you can stop me.

Marc

James clenched his jaw so hard that it was surprising he didn't crack his teeth. He had to keep his temper in check in front of Marina and Danny, especially when he noticed her shaking. Danny was squirming in her arms because she was holding him so tightly. James was going to kill the fucking prick if he ever got his hands on Marc O'Reilly.

He turned and walked out of the room closing the door behind him. He pressed his fists against the wall and took several deep breaths to calm himself. He felt a hand on his shoulder, and he turned his head. Keith, the calm level-headed brother stood behind him.

"You need to control this, bro," Keith said. "You don't want to scare Danny and the last thing Marina needs to see is your temper."

"That's why I left the room." He turned around and pressed his back against the wall. "I just want to beat that fucking bastard within an inch of his life. Not only did he put her through hell when they were married, now he's doing it again."

"He got lucky today, but he won't get that lucky again," Keith said with a calm, even tone, but there was something in the way the words came out that even made James shudder. Keith was even-tempered and he couldn't remember ever seeing the middle brother of the family lose his cool since they were kids. "Trunk thinks the guy that ran into the woods was a distraction and I'm thinking he is right. He said Mrs. Ray's dogs were going nuts and it was a good thing she had them secured to the post because she wouldn't have been able to hold them back. He's so pissed with himself."

"I fucking hate when these bastards get away with this shit then they hide away and we can't find them." James knew from experience when a criminal didn't want to be found they would do everything to keep themselves out of sight. Marc took a huge risk taking Danny and he was lucky he was able to drop him off without being seen.

"He can't hide forever and he wants something, so he's going to keep going until he gets what he wants and that's when we trap the prick," Keith said in a hushed tone. Although his brother had never been in trouble with the law, James had a feeling that the security company sometimes played with the lines of the law to keep his clients safe. James nodded and took one more deep breath before he reentered the interview room.

"It's been a long day, so I think we should get this boy home." James forced a smile but it was mostly for Danny's sake. He lifted Danny into his arms and Marina linked her hand into the crook of his arm. Danny was safe, but James wasn't going to relax until all this shit was over. He was going to do everything to make sure that man never got near Danny and Marina again. On the way out of the station he noticed Keith sitting in his truck with his phone to his ear. He nodded, and James knew it was a silent confirmation that he would be putting one of his guys on protection duty for Marina and Danny. If anyone could keep them safe when he wasn't around it was Keith's guys.

Chapter 15

It was the longest day of her life, and Marina was glad to see the end of it. Mason and Danny were exhausted, but neither of them seemed distraught over the day's events. Mason was glad to see Danny, and they quietly played in the living room while James had a pizza delivered for supper. The boys ate and were both bathed and in bed. Marina noticed James had been extremely quiet since they arrived home. He was blaming himself and she didn't know how to make him understand none of it was his fault.

The rain started just after the kids went to bed, and she stood in the kitchen staring out through the window. The fog had rolled in as well, and she could no longer see the ocean because it was so thick. She sensed him before he even touched her, and when he wrapped his arms around her she leaned against his body. His hug enveloped her like a blanket keeping her safe and warm. James rested his chin on her head as they watched the fog slowly swallow up the garden and the rain ease into a gentle mist.

"You must be exhausted." He pressed his lips to her temple.

"Not really. Relieved Danny is safe and in his bed and that he doesn't seem bothered by what happened today." Marina sighed when he squeezed her against him.

"I think I finally convinced Mrs. Ray none of this was her fault, and Keith is still trying to calm Trunk down," he said.

"I'm glad, but are you convinced it wasn't your fault either?" Marina asked.

She heard him swallow. "I'm trying and Mrs. Ray made me agree that it wasn't my fault either," he said. "She said, now Jimmy it's not your fault, so I'll believe it's not my fault, if you believe it's not yours." James tried to mimic Mary's voice.

Marina giggled because he sounded so weird but also the name Mary called him always struck her funny. "You know women are always right…Jimmy."

"Funny girl." James tickled her ribs, and she wiggled to escape his grasp. She managed to get away and ran out of the kitchen, but stopped short when Stephanie burst through the front door. Marina froze for a moment and then wrapped her arms around her sister.

"Are we playing tag?" Stephanie teased.

"No. She's running from her payback for calling me Jimmy." James stood in the entrance of the kitchen with his arms folded across his chest and that sexy grin lit up his face.

"Aww Jimmy, what's wrong with that?" John laughed.

"Nothing wrong with it, Johnny." Marina teased her brother-in-law.

"Cora calls him that too." Stephanie giggled. The names just didn't suit the two tall muscular men. Johnny and Jimmy reminded her of little boys and those two men were definitely not boys.

"Coffee, anyone?" James was obviously trying to change the subject and Marina nudged Stephanie with her elbow.

"Sounds great but I'll have tea… Jimmy." Marina said as Stephanie stifled a giggle.

"You're asking for it, little girl." James pointed his finger at her as he disappeared into the kitchen with John behind him. Marina linked her arm into Stephanie's and made their way to the living room. When Stephanie nodded towards the kitchen, Marina was expecting 'I knew I was right' from her sister.

"What?" Marina feigned innocence.

"You're just staying here so James can keep you safe, huh." Stephanie raised an eyebrow and crossed her arms over her chest.

"Don't start," Marina whispered but she knew her sister wasn't going to let it go.

"You couldn't find a better guy than James. Well, except for John but he's taken." Stephanie smiled.

"He's amazing, but part of me is still scared," Marina admitted.

"James isn't going to let Marc near Danny again," Stephanie said.

"I know but that's not the only thing that scares me, Steph," Marina said. "I'm afraid of my feelings for him. I'm falling for him so fast, and it terrifies me."

"He's not Marc, Rina." Stephanie hugged her but before Marina could respond, James and John entered the room.

It was so natural the way James sat next to her and rested his arms over the back of the couch behind her while John and Stephanie told them about their trip. Marina apologized for them having to miss the last couple of days, but John held up his hand and stopped her.

"I was ready to come home." John smiled. "She was wearing me out."

Marina giggled when Stephanie elbowed John in the ribs. "You're such a liar." Stephanie narrowed her eyes.

"I do not lie. Do you want me to show them the claw marks on my back? Little John was getting ready to crawl up inside me." John grinned as Stephanie gasped with embarrassment.

"Little John? Bro, you never name it anything with the word little." James laughed.

"It's one of those things like naming a fat guy skinny or a short guy stretch. What's it called?" John winked at Stephanie, and she rolled her eyes.

"You mean an oxymoron?" Marina chuckled.

"Yeah. Ask Steph there is nothing little…" Stephanie elbowed John in the ribs and her cheeks flushed.

"So Danny and Mason are okay." James cleared his throat and Marina could tell he was trying not to laugh at her sister's pink cheeks.

"That bastard's lucky he brought Danny back." John's teasing grin disappeared.

"I hope he doesn't try anything else." Marina shivered and instantly James arm wrapped around her shoulder.

"We'll get him, Marina," John said.

"I hope it's soon." James kissed the side of her head and she relaxed immediately.

Her sister and John stayed for a short while but it was obvious they were exhausted from their trip. They'd planned to stay in New York for a couple of days but as soon as they found out about Danny, they'd booked the first flight out. After they'd landed in St. John's, they'd rented a car and drove right to James' house as soon as they hit Hopedale.

"I think we're going to head home and get a good night's sleep. We'll drop back over tomorrow after we bring the rental car back," John said as they were getting ready to leave.

Before she left Stephanie pulled Marina aside. "I'm happy for you, Rina." Stephanie hugged her. "Don't overthink things."

James closed the door after they left and turned to her. "What was that all about?" James asked.

"What?"

"Why did Steph say she was happy for you and not to overthink things?" She'd hoped he hadn't heard any of that.

"She's happy Danny's home, and don't overthink things about Marc." She wasn't sure how he'd feel about her talking to her sister about her feelings before she even told him. Hell, she didn't even know if she was ready to tell herself.

"I see." James pushed himself off the door and stalked towards her with a sly grin and his sexy mouth.

"What are you doing?" Maybe he heard the whole conversation.

"I still owe you for calling me Jimmy." James moved closer, wiggling his fingers in front of him. She backed into the living room with her hands held in front of her.

"I'm sorry, James. Don't look at me that way and put those fingers away." She moved around the coffee table to keep him at a distance.

"I don't think so." He moved around the table and backed up farther until her back hit the wall. She'd backed herself into a corner and there was no way to get around him.

"James, please don't tickle me. I'm warning you." Before she could escape, he was in front of her and his hands were braced on either side of her body.

"Warning me, huh?" James raised an eyebrow.

"James, no tickling, please." Marina wrapped her arms around her torso but it probably wouldn't do much good.

"Hmmm, maybe I'll do this instead." James brushed his lips against hers and his hands moved to her hips. "Or maybe this." His lips grazed her cheek, and he pulled her hips to his. "Or this." He feathered kisses down the side of her face to her neck and she let her head fall to the side to give him better access. Her body was trembling again, but this time with anticipation of what he was going to do next.

"Oh. God." Marina gasped when James nipped the sensitive spot behind her ear and she could feel his erection against her stomach. Heat ignited in her core and she grabbed the bottom of his shirt and yanked it up to get it off him.

"Marina, slow down. We've got all night," James whispered in her ear when her hands smoothed against his tight abs and the muscles bunched under her touch.

"Yes, we do." Marina pushed him until his back was against the wall. "But I want you naked now." What was wrong with her? She'd never been this demanding, but God she loved it. She pulled his shirt over his head and pressed her lips against his chest. She inhaled and his scent filled her senses as she swirled her tongue around one flat nipple. His groan vibrated through his body and she sucked it into her mouth.

He reached for her but she pushed his hands against the wall and feathered kisses down his chest as she popped the button on his jeans. She wanted to be in control at the moment. It was empowering to hear his response to her. All thoughts of the terrible hours while Danny was missing disappeared, and all that remained was her and James.

She slid her tongue down the center of his stomach and he hissed when she circled his navel. She watched his reaction when she knelt and unzipped his jeans. Her hand grazed the silky skin of his erection, and she realized he wasn't wearing anything under his jeans. He'd been commando all day. His head hit the wall with a thump when her tongue flicked against the swollen head peeking out of his open jeans. She slid his jeans down and he sprang free, hard and ready. He gasped a string of curses when she sucked the head into her mouth.

"Jesus, woman, you're killing me here." James groaned and quivered when she wrapped her hand around his cock and circled it with her tongue again. He was too big to take all of him into her mouth, but she was going to take as much as she could. His breathing had become more of a pant as she slid her mouth over the length of him.

"Fuck, that feels so damn good." James panted. She started to move her hand and mouth together faster, but she was suddenly ripped away from it and lifted into his arms. How he made it up the stairs with his jeans hanging below his hips, she didn't know but he managed to get her upstairs and into his bedroom. He laid her on the bed and frantically started pulling her clothes off.

"Didn't someone say we had all night?" She giggled as he tossed her jeans to the side and grabbed the waist of her panties.

"Yes, someone did, but you've got way too many clothes on, woman." Her bra and panties disappeared with a rip, and he hovered over her his eyes ablaze with arousal. The intensity made goose bumps rise on her skin as she realized he was the one in control now and she wanted nothing more.

His warm skin pressed against hers and sent electric tingles through her body. His hand moved down her body caressing every inch while his lips devoured hers. She slid her hands around him and dragged her nails lightly down his back causing the muscles to flex under her hands. His lips brushed down the side of her jaw and between her breasts. He pulled her against his throbbing cock and his leg slipped between hers pushing them apart. His lips covered her hard nipple as his hand moved down to the heat between her legs. The man was going to drive her crazy.

The sucking sensation and his thumb teasing her sensitive nub was incredible, but then he inserted his long finger inside, and she arched off the bed. Her head was spinning with so many sensations at once. He tugged on her nipple lightly with his teeth and then nipped slowly down her trembling body. A second digit entered her and he sucked her clit into his hot mouth in one motion.

"Oh. My. God. Don't stop!" She thrust her hips up into his hand, and he swirled his tongue against her clit faster. The man knew how to use his tongue. She couldn't keep her eyes open when her body started to shudder with the most intense climax she'd ever felt. She almost screamed but pressed her lips together because the last thing they needed was to wake the boys. Then he continued his wonderful ministrations and another wave shot through her before she could come down from the first one. This time she couldn't hold back.

"James," she screamed and then clamped her teeth into her lower lip.

When she opened her eyes he was hovering over her and his lips were inches from hers still wet with her climax and she could smell herself. It was so arousing and surprised her how much it turned her on, then he pressed his lips to hers she pushed him to his back and straddled his hips. His cock throbbed against her wet heat and she flexed her hips grinding against him.

"Oh. Yes." James moaned and she knew he was more than ready to be inside her. He gripped her hips and she was pretty sure there would be marks there later, but at the moment it was so damn hot. She guided herself down his hard length until he was buried deep, she stilled and reveled in the feeling of him inside her. She began to move her hips, and he grabbed the cheeks of her ass as he thrust up to meet her motions. She felt more than heard the deep groan coming from him. It vibrated right through her entire body.

"Jesus sweetheart, I'm not gonna last much longer… ahhh." With one final thrust his body shuddered under her, and he pulled her down tight against his body as he jerked inside her. Marina kissed his lips as he wrapped his arms around her and then snuggled against his chest with him still inside feeling more content and happy then she'd been in a long, long time.

"I never thought I'd ever have you in my arms." James kissed her forehead.

"It's not something I do with everyone, ya know," Marina teased.

"It better not be." James smacked her bottom and she squeaked. She loved being in the warmth of his arms. Who was she fooling? She loved James, but was she ready to tell him or was he even ready to hear it? The voice in her head was screaming tell him. The man had taken her heart without her even realizing it.

"James?" Marina lifted her head from his chest so she could see his face.

"Hmm." His eyes were closed.

"There's something I need to tell you."

He opened his beautiful blue eyes, and she stared into them. "That's a serious face." He tucked a stray piece of hair behind her ear.

"I know this seems...well...crazy but..." She trailed off and closed her eyes. How did she do this and was he even ready to hear it?

"But what?" He brought her out of her thoughts.

"James... I love you," she whispered and stared into his eyes. He cupped her face and covered her lips with his in a soft and tender kiss. He pulled his lips from hers and smiled.

"It's not crazy. I love you too." His eyes glistened in the light of the lamp. "I knew there was something the night I met you, but for a while I was fighting it and then you seemed to be keeping your distance. The first time I kissed you I knew, but I didn't think it could happen so fast again."

She knew he was referring to his late wife and she wasn't ready to hear their love story, but even the thought of Sarah gave her a sick feeling. Not because she was jealous but because of all the pain James had gone through losing her. Part of James would always love Sarah just like part of her would always love Marc. No matter what he did she loved him once and that love gave her Danny. That was the part of her that would never stop loving Marc but the rest of her belonged to James. She kissed his lips and it was as if they read each other's thoughts because he rolled to his side and lay in each other's arms.

"James, I think I better sleep in the other room tonight." She didn't really want to go.

"What? Why?" James pulled back.

"Unless you want to explain why we're in the same bed to Mason and Danny." She giggled when James flopped onto his back and cursed.

"Fuck. I guess you're right." James sighed.

"You're like a kid getting his favorite toy taken away." Marina sat up.

"It hasn't been taken away yet." James pulled her back and pinned her to the mattress then claimed her with his lips.

After making love again, Marina eased out of bed and grabbed James' shirt next to the bed. If she couldn't sleep next to him, being wrapped in his shirt would have to do. She tried to sneak out of the room without waking him but when she got to the door he was behind her.

"Marina?" He wrapped his arms around her and his breath feathered against the side of her face.

"Yes?" She sighed.

"I love you," he whispered into her ear.

"I love you, too." Marina turned into his arms and gazed up at him. She brushed her lips against his, meaning to keep it a soft goodnight kiss, but James backed her against the wall and pressed his body against her as he deepened the kiss. Marina giggled and pushed against his chest.

"Oh no, you don't. I'll never get out of here if you keep this up." She moaned as he kissed the side of her neck.

"Marina…just one more kiss." She felt his erection against her stomach and looked down at his gloriously naked male form.

"Uh huh, and that looks like you just want one more kiss." She pointed to his groin.

"Little James got a mind of its own." James pulled her against him and nibbled her ear lobe, making her shiver.

"What am I gonna do with you?" Marina giggled.

"Come back to bed and I'll show you." James backed towards the bed, pulling her with him. She didn't need him to twist her arm. They didn't make it to the bed this time and made love on the floor. At the rate they were going, there wouldn't be much sleep for them, and she couldn't think of anything better.

Chapter 16

After four nights of Marina leaving his room to sleep in the spare room, James had enough. He wanted to wake up every morning with her in his arms, but she was refusing to stay all night because it might upset the boys. He'd suggested they talk to Mason and Danny about their situation, but Marina seemed apprehensive. Well, enough was enough. He loved her and it was time they told Mason and Danny.

The boys were playing in their bedroom. Mason no longer referred to the room as his, it was his and Danny's room. It made James feel the conversation would probably go well since the boys loved being together. He wasn't worried about telling them and hoped he wasn't being overconfident.

Marina was in the spare room folding clothes when he stomped into the room. He took the shirt she was folding out of her hand and tossed it on the bed as he grabbed her hand and pulled her out of the room. She didn't hesitate when he pulled her into his room and closed the door.

"You do realize Danny and Mason are here, right?" she asked when he grasped her hands and pulled her to the bed. He sat down and she tilted her head.

"I want to talk to Mason and Danny. Tonight," James blurted out.

"But…" Marina started to reject his plan and he raised his hand to stop her.

"I don't want you sleeping in the other room anymore. I want to go to sleep with you in my arms and wake up with you every morning. I hate when you go to the other room. I don't think the boys will have a problem with it and if they do, they'll learn to adjust. We'll see a therapist to help them adjust if we have to but Marina, I…"

Marina smiled and put her finger to his lip. "I know you mean business when you start rambling." Marina laughed, and he pulled her down on his lap.

"I love you, sweetheart, and I want the boys to know." He met her gaze and for a moment they just stared into each other's eyes.

"I love you, too, and… okay." She stood placed a soft kiss on his lips. "I hope you know what to say because I've got nothing." She stood up.

"I think I might have an idea." James cupped her cheeks and kissed her firm on the lips just before he grasped her hand as they made their way out of the room.

"Wait! I thought you said tonight," Marina tried to pull him back as he practically dragged her to the kids' room.

"No time like the present." James wasn't letting her back out now.

Mason and Danny were sitting on the floor surrounded by Lego blocks which James would probably be cursing later. It never failed but every damn night he'd step on one of the stupid things. At the moment, he just wanted the boys' attention.

"Boys, can we talk to you both for a few minutes?" Two tiny heads turned and looked up.

"Are we in trouble?" Mason asked. James chuckled and sat on one of the beds.

"No, buddy, you're not in trouble, but Marina and I need to talk to both of you. Can you come up here and sit next to us?" Marina sat on the other bed, and Danny quickly climbed on the bed next to her. Mason seemed more apprehensive about the talk, but eventually climbed on the bed next to James.

"Do you guys like sharing a room?" James asked, and Marina raised her eyebrow at him. He gave her a smile that said 'trust me.'

"Uh huh." Mason knelt on the bed and started to jump up and down. James quickly calmed him.

"I love this room. It's bigger than mine." Danny said quietly.

"Danny, would you rather stay in this room or go back to your own room?" James asked and Danny looked at Marina as if he didn't want to upset her.

"I want to stay here, but I miss my toys." Danny looked down at his hands.

"So if we brought your toys here, you'd rather stay here?" Marina asked. Danny nodded and smiled up at her.

"Mason, would you mind if we brought Danny's toys here?" James asked.

"No, we'd have lots more toys." Mason squealed.

"There's something else we need to tell you, and we hope you guys are okay with it." James held Marina's hand and the boys didn't miss the gesture. "Marina and I are in love with each other. Do you know what that means?" He wasn't sure if they really understood what two people being in love meant.

"Like Unca John and Aunt Stephanie?" Danny tilted his head and stared at Marina. She nodded but his face was unreadable. James couldn't read Mason's expression either, and his heart started to sink. It would be hard for them to be together if the boys weren't okay with it. As much as he loved Marina, he still had to consider Mason's feelings as well as Danny's.

"That's right," Marina said but the grip on his hand told him she was as unsure of all of this as he was. The boys weren't giving them any indication of how they were feeling about the news.

The boys stared at each other and when it seemed like they were never going to say anything else they both grinned and gave each other a high-five.

"I told you they were boyfriend and girlfriend," Mason said as he jumped off the bed and into Marina's arms. Danny did the same but jumped into James' arms.

"Can we get my toys today?" Danny peered up into James' face, and he didn't know what to say. The kid was more concerned about his toys than the fact his mother had a boyfriend.

"I'll get my brothers to pack up all your stuff at the old house and bring it here," James said and then realized Marina never agreed to move in with him. He was jumping the gun but when he looked at her, she was smiling. "If Mommy agrees to move in here with me and Mason."

"Please, please, Mommy." Danny held his hands together in front of him and Mason followed suit.

"Please, Auntie Marina, you'd have lots of fun livin' here." Mason begged her and James almost choked. His son's idea of fun wasn't exactly the fun James liked to have with her. She met James' eyes and he raised his eyebrow.

"I'd love to live here." Marina smiled.

"You could share Daddy's room but he'd have to get another bed for his room," Mason said. Marina pressed her lips together, and James covered his laugh with a cough.

"Maybe we can share my big bed. There's lots of room." James was finding it hard not to burst into laughter.

"If ya wanna but Mommy talks when she sleeps," Danny told him with a serious expression. He couldn't hold it in and completely lost it. Marina seemed to have the same problem. Danny and Mason seemed completely confused by their laughter and shrugged as they kept glancing between him and Marina.

His life was really looking so much better than it had in a long time. It had been a week since Danny was taken and there'd been no other communication from Marc. The police were still searching for him, and Kurt seemed more pissed about not finding him than anyone. His uncle didn't like to be made a fool of, and he seemed be taking it personally that Marc was evading them. James was frustrated with the whole thing himself. It pissed him off that Marina's ex-husband was outsmarting them.

Marina made arrangements to return to work and as much as it bothered him, James knew it was what she wanted. He'd gone back to work too, but there was always someone to stay with her and the boys when he was on shift. Keith had suggested having one of his guys drive her to work and Danny to daycare, but she refused. The only thing she did agree with was having one of them drop Danny off and they would even have Mason go with them.

The boys already knew two of the guys, Trunk and Hulk, so they were driving the boys most of the time. Since all of Keith's guys drove huge trucks it wouldn't be an issue to get the boys to go with any of them. Both boys had been also given the stranger talk by James and Keith. Trunk and Hulk would also quiz them on the drive to daycare. They weren't taking any chances again.

Another matter that had been cleared up was her house. Ian had agreed to buy it from her, because he said he was tired of living in town. There was also something going on with his attitude over the last few weeks. It was as if he was pissed at the world. James figured it was because Sandy had been gone out of town for quite a while. Although, when James mentioned her, Ian said he and Sandy were not on speaking terms. It was why he was surprised when Ian bought Marina's house.

Marina had mentioned a conversation with Stephanie in which the subject of Sandy had come up. Stephanie said Sandy was hurt over something Ian did but she wouldn't say what it was. Again when Ian was asked about it he brushed it off and said he didn't know what she was talking about.

Sunday was always his favorite day of the week, but he'd made this Sunday the day they'd get the rest of Danny's things from her old house. Of course, he used his brothers to make the lugging a whole lot easier. One advantage of having six heathy, strong, brothers was they were good for lifting and moving things.

Marina was loading the dishwasher when James brought in one of the last boxes. He placed it on the counter and pulled her into his arms, making her giggle as he buried his face in her hair and kissed it.

"The guys are bringing in the last of it now." He placed soft kisses across her jaw until he found her lips.

"Ewwww...they're kissing." Mason and Danny ran into the kitchen just as James pulled his lips from hers and turned to see the boys with their noses wrinkled.

"We're in love—that's why we're kissing." James told them. They still weren't big on girls and boys kissing.

"It's yucky, Daddy. You're gonna get girl germs," Mason said.

"Yeah, Daddy, girl germs are gross." Aaron crouched behind Danny and Mason as he wrinkled his nose. "Girls are yucky."

"Says the man that's kissed most of the single girls in Hopedale and probably some of the married ones." Mike sauntered in behind Aaron and put the box he was carrying on the floor next to the table. He ruffled the boy's hair as they ran out of the kitchen.

"Hey, I draw the line on married women." Aaron pointed his finger at Mike. "Only one was married and I didn't know until ... well afterward."

James shook his head. That was the youngest of the O'Connor brothers, the biggest Casanova in the province or at least one of the biggest because from what James knew Nick and Mike were not far behind him.

"You're one to talk." James grabbed a case of beer out of the fridge and put it on the table motioning for his brothers to help themselves. They didn't need to be asked twice.

"I'm not nearly as bad as A.J. or Nick." Mike chuckled and plopped down on one of the kitchen chairs.

"Why am I being compared to A.J.?" Nick entered the kitchen followed by John, Ian and Keith all carrying the last of the boxes from the back of James' truck. Without needing to be asked each one grabbed a beer.

"Being a whoremaster." Mike chuckled and ducked when John swiped at the back of his head.

"Watch your mouth. There are kids in the house." John warned, ever the big brother, even though he and James were the oldest and twins, John had taken on the oldest brother role.

"You guys are all terrible." Marina laughed as she tucked herself under James' arm and wrapped her arms around his waist.

"I'm wounded that you would think that about me." Aaron pressed his hand against his chest in mock hurt. "I think you're just jealous you missed out on all this." James narrowed his eyes at Aaron.

"Are we discussing A.J.'s over-inflated ego again?" Stephanie glided into the kitchen and as usual walked right up next to John.

"See, that's another jealous woman because she lost out." Aaron chuckled. "I think I should drop by Sandy's house on the way home and give her a chance to …" Before he could finish the statement, Ian put Aaron in a head lock and growled.

"You stay the fuck away from Sandy." Ian's voice could only be described as a deep, menacing growl.

"Why it's not like you're giving her what she needs?" Aaron choked and James was starting to worry Ian may really hurt the youngest of the brothers.

"Just leave her alone, asshole." Ian shoved him and stomped out of the kitchen.

"What the fuck is his issue?" Nick shook his head.

"Nanny's gonna put pepper on your tongue for sayin' bad words, Unca Nick." Mason stood in the kitchen doorway with his hands on his hips. James chuckled and Marina covered her mouth to hide her giggle.

"Sorry, buddy, I won't say it again." Nick did his best not to laugh.

"Okay, I won't tell her. This time." Mason pointed his finger at Nick. "Daddy can me and Danny watch a movie?"

"Sure." James started to follow, but Marina stopped him.

"I'll do it." She kissed his cheek before following Mason out of the kitchen.

"You know your kid is a rat, right?" Nick laughed.

"Shut up or I'll tell him to spill the beans to Nan." James grabbed a bottle of beer out of the box as he left the kitchen. Chances were Ian was on the front step trying to cool down. He opened the front door and sure enough, Ian was sitting on the step his head in his hands.

"So you want to get it off your chest, or do you want to keep being a dick to everyone?" James sat next to him and handed him the beer. Ian lifted his head and stared down the driveway. He didn't look at James and for a moment it didn't seem as if he was going to speak.

"I fucked up, big time, bro." Ian sighed.

"What did you do?" the distress on his brother's face was obvious. "Is it something with work?" Ian shook his head.

"No it's nothing with work. It's … fuck it… I screwed things up with Sandy because when it comes to my past I don't know how to let it go." Ian lifted the bottle to his lips and James watched him swallow half of its contents.

"What are you talking about?" He didn't know of anything in Ian's past that would screw things up with the one woman who turned his brother into a clumsy idiot. The only other girl James could remember Ian being interested in was Colleen Morgan.

She was Ian's best friend from the time she moved across the street from his parents. Ian was about seven and Colleen was the same age. The two were always joined at the hip. When they were in high school, they dated. Everybody assumed they'd eventually get married until Ian came home one night with a huge chip on his shoulder. Nick joked about there being trouble in paradise and Ian slugged him. It took John, Keith and James to separate them. Ian finally admitted Colleen ended things and was moving to Manitoba with her brother. To this day, that was all the family knew. Ian never talked about her after that, and nobody ever asked anything else.

James never knew what happened to her after that, but he did hear one of her brothers had killed himself after their mother passed away. That had been a couple of years ago but as far as he knew, Colleen had never come home.

"Do you remember the night I called and said I wouldn't be coming back to your house?" Ian still wouldn't meet his eyes.

"The night Marina's house was trashed." James remember that night vividly.

"I spent the night in town with Colleen." Ian finished the bottle of beer and rolled it between his hands.

"She's back?"

"She was, but we spent the night together at a hotel downtown and when I got up she was gone. She left a note saying she'd made a mistake and she was sorry," Ian said.

"She just left with no other explanation." It pissed James off to know that Colleen had done this to Ian once before, but to come back and do it again when he was finally starting to move on was just cruel.

"Apparently she ran into Jess at the flower shop and asked her to get me to call her because she had something important to tell me." Ian shook his head. "The only thing she told me was I looked hot and the next thing I knew we were naked in a hotel room."

"I guess Sandy found out?" James asked.

"No, she doesn't know, but I haven't talked to her." Ian turned and stared at James. "I know we aren't really dating, but I care about her and things were heading that way. We were supposed to go out on our first date the day I met with Colleen. I ended up standing her up, but I didn't mean to." Ian stood up and pressed his fists into his eyes. "I'm a fucking idiot."

"Don't be so hard on yourself. You and Colleen have history, but you really need to talk to Sandy." James cupped his brother's shoulder and it was filled with tension. "The first thing you have to do is apologize to her."

"She's still out of town, and Keith won't tell me how to get in touch with her," Ian grumbled.

"She'll be back. Just make sure you make things right."
James was about to turn and go into the house, when he caught
something move out of the corner of his eye. Ian must have noticed
it, too, because he took off in a sprint into the woods across the
street. James ran after him but he didn't know exactly what they'd
seen.

James scanned up and down the road while he waited for Ian
to come out of the woods. He started to walk into the woods where
Ian had disappeared. He was about two feet into the trees when he
heard Ian yelling.

"Get back here, you little fucker." He listened to see the
direction Ian's voice was coming from but with the trees it was hard
to tell.

"Ian?" James shouted but there was no answer. "Ian?" He
cupped his hands over his mouth and called out again. As he pulled
his phone out to try to call Ian's cell, his brother came through the
path a little out of breath.

"I lost whoever it was." Ian bent over to catch his breath.

"I know I saw something, but I'm not sure. Maybe it was a
moose." James scanned the tree line.

"That was no fucking moose but the bastard can run." Ian
stood up straight and took a deep breath

A chill ran down his spine. "Listen, don't say anything to Marina. I don't want to scare her because she'll think it's Marc." They walked out of the pathway and James glanced at the house.

"I won't, but if you want, I can crash on your couch tonight just in case," Ian suggested.

"No, I need to talk to Keith. You just don't want to go home in case Sandy comes back and she wants to beat you with a bat." James nudged him.

"She's gonna fucking hate me." Ian walked next to him back up the driveway.

"She'll be pissed yeah, but you should talk to her," James advised. Ian nodded as they walked into the front door.

"I should apologize to A.J., too." Ian groaned.

"Nah... he deserves a good choke hold every now and then." James chuckled.

"I heard that," Aaron yelled from the living room.

Marina was upstairs getting the boys in bed and setting up the movie. James pulled Keith and John aside to tell them what had happened. Keith immediately called one of his guys to keep an eye on the house for the night. James couldn't be sure it was Marc, but he wasn't taking any chances with Marina or Danny's safety. For all he knew, Mason could be in danger as well.

"It may not have been him at all," Ian said when Keith ended his call.

"I don't care. We're not taking chances here," John snapped. "I let Stephanie take chances and it nearly got us both killed." John was referring to when he and Stephanie first got together. A crazy woman got the notion that killing Stephanie would make her boyfriend propose to her. Probably because the guy was Stephanie's ex.

"John's right; we can't take any chances with Marina or Danny." He wasn't going to lose them. "I just got the gut feeling something is off about this guy besides the obvious."

"Why don't I get Sandy to see what she can find out about him? She just got back in town," Keith said. Sandy worked for him and was a computer genius. From what he knew, Sandy Churchill could find anything on the computer. Aaron had joked one time that she was the Penelope Garcia of Newfoundland and from what Kurt and Keith told him, she was.

"Why the hell do you have to get her involved in all this?" Ian snapped.

"For one she's the best at finding stuff people don't want found and two she needs something to do since you've been a stupid ass." Keith snapped back.

"Fuck you!" Ian growled and stomped out of the kitchen.

"Give him a break, Keith. His head is all fucked up." James warned but he wouldn't say any more than that. If Ian wanted the rest of his brothers to know what happened, then he would have to tell them.

"He's fucked up all right. Sandy's really hurt. She's head over heels for him," Keith snapped.

"Just let him figure it out." James' tone said it was the end of the conversation. Keith nodded and pulled his phone out. James and John sat at the table listening as he gave Sandy all the information they knew on Marc O'Reilly. With any luck she'd find out where the hell he was and James wouldn't be worried about him hurting Danny or Marina again.

Chapter 17

Marina stepped over the last couple of boxes laying in the hallway. It was the last of her things that had been brought from her house or Ian's house, now. Things between her and James were great and she was glad she'd let him get his brothers to help the previous night. She never realized how much stuff she had left in the house, since so much of it had been destroyed. There were still a lot of things that were stored in the attic and the basement that Marc hadn't touched. James was going to put it in his attic, but she said she wanted to go through it and figure out if any of it was worth keeping.

It was a hectic morning. Her first day back to work and James was also working the early shift. Thank god she didn't have to worry about dropping the boys off because one of Keith's guys would be driving them. It was a safety precaution and she was glad. This morning, Keith was doing it himself and the boys were extremely excited. They loved riding in Keith's old Army jeep. Marina didn't know how old it was, but it seemed ancient. Although, James told her it ran like a dream and it was a tank in the wintertime.

She didn't know what that meant but she assumed the boys would be safe.

She was still nervous about letting herself be too happy because she was still waiting for Marc to do something to destroy her happiness. It was what he seemed to thrive on.

Marina loved waking up every morning with James next to her and his arms wrapped tightly around her. If she was feeling anxious or upset, all she had to do was think about James and she smiled. Next to Danny, she couldn't love anyone more. She also realized she hadn't had any nightmares since the first night she stayed at James' house—or their house now. It showed just how being near him made her feel safe.

"Good morning, my beautiful lady." He walked into the kitchen and wrapped his arms around her while she was flipping pancakes. The smile appeared again and she turned her head so she could kiss his lips just as Danny and Mason ran into the kitchen. As had become the norm, they started to make retching noises.

"Mommy, that's so icky." Danny wrinkled his nose.

"Oh you think so, do you?" James picked him up and tossed him into the air making him squeal.

"Kissing girls is gross." Mason made a gagging sound. James grabbed him and tickled him until the squeals became hard on her ears. The scene made her heart so full that she thought it would burst, and she hadn't even realized she was smiling.

"And just what are you smiling at." He walked towards her, and she gazed up at the man who'd opened up her heart again.

"You." She laid her hands against his chest, and he kissed her lips softly.

"Ewwwww." The boys groaned as they climbed onto the chairs next to the table. Marina giggled when James shook his head. As long as the boys were in the room, they would have to keep the kissing to a minimum. He kissed her forehead and grabbed a cup from the counter. She'd poured his coffee already. It had become a habit since they'd been living together over the last few weeks.

Keith arrived just as Marina was about to tie the boys to chairs to calm them down. They were squealing and almost knocked Keith over running to meet him. As serious as he was, when he played with the boys, his face lit up. The only time she'd seen the man smile was when he was playing with the kids.

James came downstairs clipping his flak jacket, and all the air whooshed out of her. The sight of him in his uniform always made her want to tear it off and have her way with him. He was sexy as hell in full uniform. She was about to tell him just how hot he was but she stopped when Mason and Danny ran into the kitchen.

"Come on, boys, we don't want to be late." Keith had their jackets in his hands but they were standing next to each other and their faces were serious.

"James, Mason don't have a mommy anymore and my daddy is gone." Marina's heart jumped in her chest, and she glanced from James to Keith and back to Danny. "Well me and Mason was talkin, and you're a daddy, and Mommy's a mommy." Danny glanced at her and then at Mason. Mason nodded. "You think it would be okay if I call you Daddy and Mason called Mommy, Mommy?" Marina felt her jaw drop open and her eyes were becoming painful since she was sure they were the size of saucers by now. By the raised eyebrows and slack jaw, James was dumbfounded.

"I'll just leave the jackets here and go make sure the boys' seats are secure in the Jeep." Keith quickly left the kitchen. James seemed at a loss for words as he almost flopped on one of the kitchen chairs.

"Daddy, me and Danny would be like brothers. Just like you and your brothers. I don't have a brother." Mason climbed onto James' lap staring at him with the same hopeful expression her own son had. James glanced at her as if he was asking for help with a response, but all she could do was shrug. She was so glad they'd confronted James with this, because she didn't have a clue how to respond.

"How about you boys let Marina and I talk about this after work, and we'll let you both know."

The boys nodded.

"Now get your coats on so Uncle Keith can drop you off."

The boys struggled into their jackets, and Keith entered the kitchen again holding their back packs.

"You guys ready?" Keith asked but before he left, Danny ran to Marina and hugged her. He was almost out of the kitchen but he stopped and ran right to James for a hug. Mason followed suit and hugged both his father and Marina.

"See you two later." Keith chuckled as he followed the boys out of the house.

"Where the hell did that come from?" James shook his head.

"I have no idea." Marina walked by him to grab her purse from the table. He wrapped his arm around her waist and pulled her into his lap.

"I don't mind Danny calling me Dad. I love him, but how do you feel about it?" He stared into her eyes.

"You've been a dad to him, and I don't mind it at all. The question is how do you feel about Mason calling me Mom? I mean, how would it make Sarah feel?"

James stared at her for a moment almost as if he was trying to figure out the answer himself. "I know Sarah would want Mason to be happy and if Mason feels comfortable enough to call you Mom, then I think the question is, are you comfortable with it?"

Marina stared into his eyes. She'd fallen for the little boy a long time ago. Long before she realized she was in love with James.

"I don't mind at all." She cupped his cheek. "I love you both so much."

"We love you, too." James kissed her lips and she sighed. She was so happy at the moment, but there was a nagging voice in the back of her head telling her the happiness could be taken away in an instant. It was so hard to just enjoy her happiness because until Marc was found, that nagging voice wasn't going to go away.

"We better get going or we're going to be late for work." Marina pulled away from James and smiled.

"What's wrong?" James seemed to know her too well because he saw right through the forced smile.

"I'm just worried all this is going to be taken away." She closed her eyes.

"Marina, look at me."

She opened her eyes and gazed into the depths of his blue eyes. The eyes that always seemed to find a way to calm her frayed nerves and help her believe things were going to be fine.

"I've figured out pretty quickly that nothing in life is guaranteed, but living our lives worrying about what could happen is not a way to live. We need to stop wondering what if, and just deal with the hand we're dealt." He ran his finger down the side of her face. "You were dealt a crappy hand for a while but you came out a stronger person. Don't let your worries about Marc stop you from enjoying what we have together."

"I'm trying not to, but I'm so worried he's going to do something to take it all away." How James knew what had been going through her mind was a mystery, but it was also incredibly comforting that he could read her so well.

"I'm not going to lie; I'm worried about it, too, but for now we just need to keep our eyes open but not make our lives all about him." James kissed her cheek. "That gives him all the power."

He was right, of course, and she wasn't giving Marc the power over her again. She'd done that once, and it took her four years to let herself believe she was strong enough to get through his abuse.

The work day seemed to drag on forever, but she was glad to be back to work. She missed her coworkers, and her assistant was so excited to see her back. Her boss, David was equally glad to see her. It wasn't that he minded her working from home but he'd been worried she wasn't going to ever come back. She'd assured him she wasn't going anywhere and tried to keep her mind on her work for the rest of the day.

She was deep into a document David had sent her to check, when her cell phone vibrated in her pocket. She glanced at the screen and smiled as she tapped it.

"Hi, honey." She cringed because the words actually came out more of a sigh.

"Hi, sweetheart," James said.

"What's up?" She glanced the time on her computer and was surprised to see it was almost five.

"I wanted to let you know I had to pick Mason up early from daycare."

"Is he okay?" She shut down her computer and got ready to go.

"He had a fever, but Danny didn't want to leave with me because they were painting."

If Danny was painting, there was no way he was leaving. The kid loved it and for a four-year-old, he was pretty good.

"I'll pick him up. I'm just getting ready to leave now." She pulled on her jacket and grabbed her purse.

"Okay, drive safe," he said.

"Always,"

"Marina?"

"Yes?" Marina locked the door of her office and headed out of the building.

"I love you."

"I love you, too." She really did love him and just hearing him say it made her heart feel so full.

Walking through the parking garage, she kept her keys in one hand and her phone in the other. It was something Jess had told her to do whenever she was walking alone. She was almost to her car when a cold feeling ran down the back of her neck making the hair on her arms stand up. She turned quickly. There was nothing behind her or anywhere else in the parking area. She shook her head and continued to walk, but the eerie feeling of someone watching her wouldn't go away. She started to walk faster and as she got to her car, she yanked open the door. As soon as she was inside she locked all the doors and tried to calm her racing heart. It was the first panic attack she'd had in a while. What was wrong with her?

She started the car, but there was something told her she wasn't alone. She'd walked through the garage more times than she could count. It was the first time she'd ever gotten a feeling of dread coursing through her body. She probably should have gotten someone to walk out with her. She lay her head back against the headrest and took several deep breaths to calm her anxiety. Once she felt calmer, she pulled out of the garage and headed to pick up Danny.

She was still jumpy when she arrived at the daycare and managed to find a parking spot close to the entrance. The prickly feeling at the back of her neck made her snap her head around, but again she didn't see anyone except other parents coming to pick up their children. Was she imagining things? A young man held open the door to the daycare for her as she got to the entrance. She thanked him and quickly moved inside.

Danny was excitedly holding his masterpiece as they walked out of the building. Marina held onto his hand tightly mostly because she'd learned her lesson when he ran into the parking lot that day. It was then she had noticed a grey SUV in the parking lot with someone sitting in it. He was staring at her. She managed to get Danny buckled into his seat and jumped into the car. With shaky hands she pulled out her cell and tapped Keith's number. James had drilled it into her head that if she got into trouble, she was to call Keith. He had staff everywhere and could have someone with her in minutes probably even seconds.

"Marina, what's wrong?" Keith answered on the first ring.

"I'm outside Danny's daycare, and I'm probably just being paranoid, but there's a man in a grey SUV sitting there watching every move I make." Marina was talking quietly because she didn't want to frighten Danny.

"Grey SUV, bald guy, looks like a wrestler." Keith chuckled.

"Umm... yes."

"It's okay, Marina, that would be Bull. He's one of my guys, and I'm guessing James didn't tell you, but he's just there to keep an eye on Danny," Keith explained, and Marina didn't know to be relieved or pissed.

"Bull?" The name didn't escape her.

"Yeah, nickname, of course, but it's because he's six-foot-seven, and about two hundred and fifty pounds of solid muscle. The nick name is because when he hits someone, they say it's like being knocked down by a bull." Keith chuckled, and she was both surprised and amused because as long as she'd known the O'Connors, it was the most she'd ever heard Keith say at one time.

"Okay...I don't remember meeting him, but at least I know I'm not going crazy. I've got Danny now so you can tell Bull he can go home." Marina said.

"Hulk had a family emergency so Bull is filling in. I'll text him. Drive safe." The call ended and she glanced towards Bull. What a stupid name to call someone but when the man got out of the car her jaw dropped. He was huge. He nodded as he dropped a bag into his trunk and got back into his car.

"Bull...sheesh." Marina giggled and headed for home.

The eerie feeling of dread started again about halfway back to Hopedale. The long stretch of road was lined with trees on both sides and usually she enjoyed the beauty of it, but for some reason it seemed almost dangerous at the moment. She reached for her phone to call James. At least he could talk to her while she drove.

"Damn it," she groaned when she noticed her phone was dead. "One of these days I'm going to remember to keep that thing charged."

She glanced into her rearview mirror and noticed a car speeding up behind her. It started to pull around her, and she shook her head. She was driving the speed limit. This idiot seemed to be in an awful hurry. She'd reached to change the station on the radio when there was a loud bang and the car jolted to the side. Marina turned the wheel to keep from diving into the ditch at the side of the road.

Danny's scream muted the second bang, and her car lurched to the side again. She turned to see the car swerve at her a third time. She could see the driver was a man but she didn't recognize him. She saw the green car coming towards her again and smashing into her. Staying away from the embankment was getting harder and when she was hit again, she knew she couldn't avoid the ditch anymore. The car dropped off the side of the road and slid down until the side of the car crashed at the bottom of the embankment. The only thing she heard was Danny's screams and the screeching of tires as the mysterious car sped away.

"Mommy, Mommy help me," Danny screamed, but for a moment Marina was dazed. Danny's pleas brought her out of her stupor and she shook her head to clear her thoughts. Her car was on its side, and she turned to see her son still strapped into his seat. Her head throbbed, and something warm was running down the side of her face. She unbuckled her seatbelt and tried to open her door but it wouldn't open. The glass from her window was shattered but still there. The only thing she could think of was to use her elbow to knock the busted window out completely. She cleared most of the glass away while she explained to Danny what she was doing and tried to make sure her voice was soft and calm so he wouldn't know just how terrified she was. She leaned back and unbuckled Danny from his seat and he jumped into her arms making the car shake. Danny screamed again, and she pulled him tightly against her.

"Shhhh, we're okay. Now, Danny, I'm going to put you out through the window and I want you to stay right where I put you." Marina cupped his face so he was looking right into her eyes. "We need to be brave and get out of the car so we can get home."

"Okay, Mommy." Danny sobbed, and her heart broke as a tear ran down his cheek. Marina wiped it away and kissed his forehead.

"You're such a brave boy." Marina had to keep her tears back because the last thing Danny needed to see was her crying.

Marina eased him out through the car window and gave him a little push to sit on the embankment. The car shook again and Marina froze. She moved slowly to reach for her purse but it had fallen completely to the other side of the car. She didn't know how deep the ditch was and she wasn't taking any chances. She slowly eased herself through the window and kept her eyes locked on Danny as he watched her.

With both of them safely out of the car, she studied their situation. The ditch was deep and she knew she could climb up herself, she just wasn't sure Danny could. She peered into the car for her cell phone but she couldn't see it. It probably went flying across the car with her purse. She was about to climb back in to find it when she heard a voice above her.

"Are ya all right, my love?" A man's voice drifted down to her and when she glanced up, she could see an older man. His headlights were shining on back of him and all she could think was this man looked like an angel.

"Yes, I'm fine, I think. Someone ran me off the road. Can you help pull us up?" she called out.

"Send up the kid first." A younger man's voice sounded from behind the older man. Marina dug her feet into the side of the embankment and lifted Danny up until she felt someone pull him from her grasp. With a sigh of relief, she began her climb up and just as she was almost to the top, a hand reached down and grabbed hers. She glanced up into the face of the older man as he pulled her up the rest of the way. At the top she turned to see if Danny was okay, but she couldn't see him.

"Where's my son?" She scanned the road frantically.

"He's across the road with the young man over…" He pointed to an empty part of the road. "He was just there. He said he'd take him to the car out of the cold." Marina started to tremble and everything started to spin. Her legs buckled, but before she hit the ground the man caught her.

"Please, tell me you have a cell phone," she begged as he helped her to his car and seated her in the driver's seat. He nodded and reached into his coat pocket. He put the phone in her quivering hand and she frantically tapped in the number. It seemed to take forever for him to answer, but as soon as she heard James' voice she started to scream into the phone.

"Marina... calm down. What are you talking about?" Marina tried to explain, but she was sobbing so hard James couldn't understand her. The man took the phone and spoke to James as she sobbed.

"My name is Tom Roberts." The man wrapped his coat around her shoulders and rubbed her arms.

"Marina... Kelly." She had to clear her head because at the moment everything was spinning and her head was throbbing. The car that drove her off the road had a man in the front but she knew it wasn't Marc but deep down she knew her ex-husband was behind it.

"I wish we could have met under better circumstances, but your husband said he'll be here soon." She didn't even have the energy to correct him. She just needed James to get there fast.

"Marina, your head is bleeding. I've got a first-aid kit in my trunk. Let me clean that for you." The man reminded her of someone, but she couldn't quiet put her finger on it. He returned a few seconds later with a red bag in his hand and he crouched to clean up her wound.

"I need to find my son." Marina tried to stand up, but she fell back and Tom caught and eased her back into the seat.

"My dear, you just stay seated until the ambulance gets here." Tom held her hand.

The sound of sirens had her head popping up. Tom helped her stand and walk around the front of his car. The ambulance pulled in to the side of the road and two police cars stopped on the other side. Marina heard his voice before she saw him. James ran from behind Tom's car. She hadn't noticed his truck pull up behind but as soon as she saw him all she could do was cry. James enveloped her in his arms.

"I'm sorry, I didn't realize da young man would take da lad." She heard Tom say to James.

"It's not your fault, Mr. Roberts, but thank you for stopping to help," James said.

"If there's anything, and I mean anything, I can do ta help, don't hesitate ta ask." Tom touched Marina's arm.

"Well maybe you can give the officer getting out of that cruiser all the information you have."

Tom nodded and walked away from them. Marina never realized it was Aaron until James called out to him.

"Let's get you to the hospital." James guided her to the ambulance.

"No, I need to find Danny." She started to walk towards James' truck but everything started to spin.

"Sweetheart, you need to get checked. You aren't going to do anyone any good if you pass out." James held her shoulders and forced her to look at him.

"I'm fine," but as soon as the words were out of her mouth she knew it was a lie. She was seeing double and her head was pounding.

"No you're not." James wrapped his arm around her shoulders and turned her towards the ambulance. "Please, go to the hospital and get checked. I'll be there right behind you."

"Find him." Marina said as the paramedic helped her lay down on the stretcher.

Marina didn't want to go to the hospital. She wanted to find Danny, but James was right, she was dizzy and her head hurt. The last thing she saw before the doors closed was Tom talking to Aaron and the flashing lights of the police cruisers.

Chapter 18

James surveyed Marina's car and the first thing he saw was the smashed side. His whole body was convulsing with anger but he slowly lowered himself down into the ditch and examined inside. Marina's purse lay on the floor of the car in the front and Danny's backpack was on the floor in the back. Luckily the car was wedged securely against the bottom so he didn't have to be concerned with the car falling any further when he reached in to grab their things.

"James, be careful." He glanced up as he pulled his body out of the window. Greg Harris stood at the top of the embankment with a flashlight pointing at the car.

"I had to get their things." James threw Marina's purse and Danny's backpack around his neck as he climbed back up. When he was at the top, Greg grabbed his hand and to help him over.

"The tow truck is on the way. I would have gotten it," Greg said.

James didn't really want to talk at the moment—he just wanted to get to the hospital. He nodded at Greg as he stomped back to his truck and tossed the things to the passenger side. He sat in the truck for a moment and scanned the road. Aaron was talking with Tom as Greg and a couple of other of his coworkers were searching the side of the road. He didn't need them to find any evidence to know that Marc was responsible for all this.

"Fucking, fucking cock sucking bastard," James growled through his teeth as he punched the steering wheel. He had never wanted to kill someone in his life but the way he was feeling at the moment he could probably kill Marc with his bare hands. "Fuck." One more punch at the wheel and he pulled onto the road. Before speeding off he stopped next to Greg and asked him to call as soon as he knew something.

The whole drive to town he cursed the day Marc O'Reilly was born. He didn't need an investigation to know who drove Marina off the road and took Danny. His stomach threatened to revolt as he thought about the bastard having Marina's little boy. They didn't know if Danny was hurt from the accident and he was pretty sure Marc wouldn't care anyway.

At the hospital James checked his phone and noticed a text from Aaron telling him he'd called the family. John and Stephanie were on the way to tell her parents since Doug and Janet had gotten home from their vacation that morning. James breathed a sigh of relief because the last thing he wanted to do was tell Marina's mother and father their grandson was missing. Again. The text also said his brothers had jumped into action and were already searching for Danny.

He walked down the hall to the small examination room where Marina was being checked. The nurse leaving the room said she'd been given a sedative because she kept trying to get out of bed and leave. Otherwise, she was fine. James thanked her but knew Marina wasn't going to be completely fine until Danny was home.

A cold chill ran down his spine as he remembered the last time he'd been at the hospital. It was just after Sarah died, and they'd brought John into the emergency after he'd hit a moose on the highway. It was the same day he'd buried Sarah. He'd hated hospitals ever since.

Losing Sarah was incredibly painful and almost losing his twin brother had just about killed him. He walked into the exam room and the sight of Marina lying in the bed with her eyes closed and a white bandage on her head, hit him like a punch in the gut. His eyes filled with tears and he swallowed hard as he pulled a chair next to the bed. When he touched her hand, she didn't move and as hard as it was to see her so motionless, he knew she needed to rest. She was going to need her strength to get through this.

Stephanie and her parents arrived at the hospital and from the look on Doug Kelly's face he was ready to put a world of hurt on someone. James was sure if Janet wasn't linked into the man he would be punching someone.

"Now, Doug, hold your temper. I don't want you upsetting Marina," Janet whispered but James had no trouble hearing it.

"I just want to know what the hell happened." Doug's voice was not nearly as quiet as Janet's. James was glad Marina was still out.

"Doug, we're on it," John said from behind them.

"Then where the hell is my grandson?" Doug snapped at John.

"We'll find him, but you need to keep yourself calm for your daughter's sake." John whispered.

"Don't tell me what's good for my daughter. You may be married to one of them but they are my little girls and I know what's best for them." Doug turned to James and his face was inches away. "You promised to keep them safe."

"Doug that's enough." Janet pulled on Doug's arm and low and behold the man seemed to calm instantly but the truth was the man wasn't wrong. James did promise and it was killing him that he broke that promise.

He sat quietly holding Marina's hand while Stephanie and her parents talked in the corner of the room. John left to help search for Danny and made it clear James was to stay with Marina. Although her father didn't seem to agree from the constant daggers he was sending at James with his eyes.

Marina's eyes fluttered open and darted around the room. She locked eyes with James and he tried to make sure she stayed calm. That went out the window when Janet and Stephanie moved to the other side of the bed and Marina's tears started to fall.

"How do you feel, pumpkin?' Doug was surprisingly calm but the tears in the man's eyes as he gazed at his daughter almost made James lose it himself.

"I'm fine, but I'd feel much better if you said you have Danny." Her quiet sobs were breaking his heart and from the look on Stephanie and her mother's faces, he wasn't the only one.

"Rina, they'll find him." Stephanie sat on the bed and James prayed she was right, because he really didn't have a clue where Danny was and what Marc was going to do. Although, it hadn't been proven that Danny was with Marc, but he was sure Danny was with the asshole.

"I've got to get out of here." Marina threw the blankets back and tried to stand.

"Whoa, there." James caught her as she began to sway.

"I need to find Danny." She tried to push him away but with the sedative and the bump on the head she wasn't exactly steady on her feet.

"Marina, get back in the bed." Doug's voice was deep and had that fatherly tone that said don't disobey. "You're in no shape to go searching for anyone. The police and the O'Connors are out searching."

At first he didn't think Marina was going to pay any attention to her father's orders, but she sat back on the bed and sighed. James helped her settle in and covered her again but by the look on her face she was so pissed she could chew nails.

James backed away from the bed to give Marina's family more room. He glanced at Doug and his eyes almost begged James to do something. A soft knock on the door had everyone turning. James opened the door, and Tom Roberts walked in holding a large vase of flowers.

"I'm sorry to intrude, but I had to come check on the young lady."

"Come in, Mr. Roberts." James reached out to shake the man's hand, but when Marina saw him she held out her arms. Tom sat next to her on the bed and she wrapped her arms around him. Doug, Janet and Stephanie were staring, obviously completely confused as to why Marina was hugging a total stranger.

"Thanks for coming, Mr. Roberts." Marina released him from her embrace.

"Please call me Tom." He kissed Marina's cheek.

"Tom, these are Marina's parents Doug and Janet Kelly, and this is her sister, Stephanie O'Connor."

"I wish we were meeting under better circumstances." Tom shook Doug's hand and nodded to Stephanie and Janet. "I had to see if there was any news and remind you if you need anything, let me know." He pulled out a card from his pocket and handed it to James. "That is my personal phone number. Don't hesitate to use it." He squeezed Marina's hand and after a few goodbyes, he started to walk out of the room but motioned to James to follow him.

"I'll be right back," James told Marina and followed Tom out of the room.

"James, I have a lot of resources at my disposal, so please if you need anything call me." James couldn't understand why Tom seemed so set on helping, but he appreciated the man offering. He watched Tom as he disappeared into the elevator. The man was kind to help, but what could a gentleman of his age possibly do? What could anyone do? A nurse walked up next to James with wide eyes.

"Wow, you know Thomas Roberts." She seemed excited.

"We don't know him, really. He helped my girlfriend," James said.

"You have no idea who he is, do you?" She chuckled and James shook his head. He assumed Tom was just a kind man who wanted to help someone in trouble. "Thomas Roberts is one of the richest men in the country. He owns companies all over Canada and specializes in computer software for security companies and military." James couldn't help it but he laughed. There was no way she was talking about the man that just left Marina's room.

"You must be mistaken." James chuckled. The nurse shook her head and held up her finger. She hurried behind the nurse's station and returned with a magazine that she handed to James. On the front cover smiling back at him was Tom Roberts.

"If you read the article inside, it says that the man spent his whole life building up his companies. He jokes about being married to his company. He has no family but he says his employees are his family. He's one of the biggest contributors to the children's hospital and is one of the biggest philanthropists in the province."

James stared at the nurse. "How do you know all this?" James shook his head.

"My boyfriend works for TAR technologies. It's one of Mr. Roberts' companies." James knew of the company because he'd heard Keith mention it was the company that set up his computer systems. James thanked her and hurried back into Marina's room.

"Do you know who Tom is?" James held up the magazine.

"I thought he seemed familiar." Doug glanced at the cover.

"He's a very kind man to stop and help Marina." Janet squeezed Marina's hand.

"It's too bad he couldn't be useful in finding Danny." Stephanie sighed and tears started to run down Marina's cheek. What was he going to do? He should have put his foot down and made Danny go home when he picked up Mason, but he didn't want to upset him. Plus, Keith's guy was watching the daycare. Nobody suspected Marc was crazy enough to run them off the road. Then again they should have thought of every scenario. Now Marina's son was missing because they'd underestimated Marc. How stupid was that?

The doctors were keeping Marina overnight for observation even though she'd argued and told the doctor he was being an ass. Her father finally convinced her she had to stay because she wasn't going to be any help if she wasn't healthy.

She'd received four stiches in the small cut on her forehead and she had a couple of other bumps and bruises, but otherwise she was okay. James was concerned about how hurt Danny was in the accident. Marina said she hadn't seen any cuts on him, but it was dark and she had been so concerned with getting them out of the ditch.

His parents and cousins had shown up, and James was relieved to see them. Since his brothers were helping in the search, he'd asked his father to make sure that Marina's injuries were as mild as her doctor had told them. Not that he didn't trust the doctor but he trusted his father more. His dad assured them that Marina was only being kept for observation. He was a doctor and knew the doctor that admitted Marina.

John finally convinced Marina's parents to go home and rest, but not before Doug pulled James aside.

"Find. My. Grandson," Doug said through clenched teeth but James was sure it was because he was trying to keep the tears back.

"I won't rest until Danny's home, Doug," James assured him because he wouldn't sleep until Marina had her son back in her arms.

Greg and Aaron arrived together and right behind Keith. James knew someone was going to be coming because Marina needed to be questioned. They didn't get a chance right after the accident because she was ready to pass out. Both Aaron and Greg agreed it was better if Greg was the lead since there was no family connection. Before he entered the room, James pulled him aside.

"What do you know so far?" James asked.

"You know procedure says I can't tell you everything, but Mr. Roberts gave A.J. a description of the car and the suspect, but he didn't get a plate number. Mr. Roberts agreed to talk to the sketch artist." Greg shook his head. "Well, look at that. I can tell you everything we know."

"Thanks, pal. I appreciate it." James shook his friend's hand. "Greg, this woman means the world to me, and this is killing her." James swallowed hard and Greg squeezed his hand.

"You know we'll do everything to get her boy back." James nodded and Greg followed him into the room.

Marina answered the questions, but James could see her getting overwhelmed. When Greg asked again if she knew where

Marc would hide out, James shook his head, making it clear that Marina had enough. A nurse entered the room with a sedative for Marina just as Greg finished up. James was relieved because if she didn't have something to relax her, she wasn't going to get any rest. Stephanie stayed with Marina while James headed to the waiting room to put together some sort of game plan to find Danny.

He knew the department was doing everything they could, but Danny was like his own son and his brothers knew that. The only thing making it hard for James to concentrate on what everyone was saying, was thinking about how scared Danny must be. It was tearing him apart. Was he cold, hungry, was he crying? Did he know everyone would be searching for him? Marc didn't hurt him last time but who knew what the crazy bastard was up to.

"You'll drive yourself crazy if you keep it all inside." John sat next to him and leaned his elbows on his knees.

"Just hoping Danny's okay." James watched Keith pace back and forth in the waiting room with his phone to his ear talking in a low voice.

"That bastard better be taking care of him." John had his hands clasped together in front of him and it was obvious John was as restless as he was.

"Sandy, find out whatever you can about this son of a bitch. Check for bank cards, credit cards, anything you can find on him. He has to be somewhere. I want to know everything you can dig up on this guy. He's out there somewhere with Danny." Keith listened for a minute. "I don't know, but maybe Stephanie can give you something on him. Stephanie has her phone in the room." Keith listened again and then ended the call.

"Okay, Sandy is going to dig and find out what she can. How's Marina?" Keith crouched in front of John and James.

"Pissed and scared. If they hadn't given her a sedative, I think she'd be marching out of here looking for Danny," James said.

"We're going to find him, bro." Keith sounded so sure. James was trying hard to be positive, and Keith had resources that the police didn't. He also had all his available employees searching.

"I know, but how long is it going to take and is he taking care of Danny?" James just couldn't stop the sick feeling in the pit of his stomach. Marc didn't want Danny because he suddenly wanted to be a father, James was sure of that. Marc wanted something and he'd taken Danny for leverage. What the hell was it?

"How the hell is this bastard managing to be a step ahead of us every fucking time? I should have had Bull follow her home," Keith said.

"Hind sight is twenty-twenty, bro." John sighed.

Two fucking days and they were still no closer to finding Danny. James was wound so tight; he was ready to snap. The only reason he was at least attempting to keep himself under control was for Marina's sake. She'd gotten out of hospital the day after the accident and had been wound up tighter than a drum.

Greg dropped by earlier in the day to let them know Marc's car was abandoned about two kilometers outside St. John's, but nobody had seen him or Danny. Danny's picture was all over the news, as well as Marc's, and they'd received dozens of leads, but nothing had panned out. That wasn't unusual because for some reason there were people out there who just wanted to get involved whether they had information or not. It was a waste of the police resources but every call had to be checked out. The worse thing was the man that Tom described didn't match Marc's description. That only meant the bastard had someone helping him.

James begged his Uncle Kurt to let him help out with the investigation, but Kurt told him he was too close to the case. He'd even taken Aaron off the investigation, which didn't go over well with his little brother. Although Kurt did give Greg strict instructions to keep them in the loop. Since the car had been found, the search parties started around that area, but everyone knew Marc wouldn't be stupid enough to stay close to where he left the car. They'd also found another set of tire tracks telling them Marc had another car waiting for him. Which supported the theory he wasn't working alone.

James walked into the house, slammed the door, and punched it. He'd spent the day with one of the search parties and the only thing they found was an open area where people were dumping garbage.

"James?" Marina stood at the bottom of the stairs. "Why are you punching the door?"

He walked towards her, but she backed away. The fear in her eyes made him want to punch himself. "I'm sorry, I'm frustrated." He shoved his hands into his front pockets as the lump he'd been swallowing all day formed in his throat again. "Uncle Kurt won't let me help and I feel like all we did today was walk in circles. I feel useless."

"You're not useless. You're keeping me from falling apart." She cupped his face in her hands and stared into his eyes.

"I'm going to head home now." Jess walked out of the kitchen. "Nan left some food in the fridge and said to make sure you eat."

"I'll get something in a bit, Jess. Thanks for keeping Marina company." James smiled at his cousin.

"No problem, I just wish there was more I could do. Kristy is coming tomorrow and make sure you both eat. I'm not having Nan jump down my throat because you didn't." Jess pulled on her coat.

"I'll make sure we eat. You don't need the wrath of your grandmother on you." Marina smiled. Jess hugged her and kissed James' cheek before she headed out the front door.

"I'm going to get a quick shower and then we can eat." James kissed Marina's cheek before heading upstairs.

"Mason was waiting for you to come home." Marina called after him. "He fell asleep but maybe you should let him know you're home."

James opened Mason's bedroom door and stared at his son curled up on his bed holding something. When James walked closer his heart almost jumped out of his chest. It was the picture of Sarah that he'd put in his dresser with his wedding ring a few weeks back. He'd wondered how the picture was constantly showing up on his dresser after he'd put it in the drawer. James kissed Mason's head and turned to leave.

"Daddy?" He heard Mason's soft voice.

"Go back to sleep, buddy. It's late." James sat on the side of his bed and covered him up.

"Did you find Danny?" Mason sounded hopeful and James hated to dash his hopes.

"Not yet, buddy." James ran his hand over his son's unruly curls.

"I asked my angel mommy to help you find him. Nanny Betty said she works for God now." Mason held up the picture.

"Thank you, Mason. I hope she can help." James kissed his cheek. His son had his Sarah's heart.

"Daddy, she can't help but Nanny said she can watch Danny until you find him." Mason said.

"I hope you're right, pal. Now I think you need to get some sleep," James said.

"Okay, Daddy, but I gotta say my prayers." Mason sat up in the bed.

"Okay." Mason put Sarah's picture on the bedside table and knelt on the bed. He clasped his hands together.

"Thank you for my family and my friends. Please watch over them." Mason stopped and then closed his eyes. "God, can you please help Daddy find Danny because I really miss him. Amen." The tears burned his eyes and he closed them to hold them back. Mason blessed himself and crawled under the blankets. "Goodnight, Daddy."

"Goodnight, Mason." James kissed his son's forehead and covered him up. Before he left the room he turned and noticed the picture on Mason's bedside table.

"Sarah, help us find Marina's little boy," James whispered and left the room. Mason truly believed Sarah was watching over Danny, so who was he to doubt him. They had to find him soon.

Chapter 19

Three days they'd been searching for Danny and Marc but they seemed to have disappeared off the face of the earth. She and Stephanie spent the day walking around the streets with pictures of Danny and Marc showing everyone she walked by. They would all look at the flyer but nobody saw them.

As they drove back to Hopedale they passed the area where she'd gone into the ditch. The only thing there was the skid marks where she tried to stop the car. Other than that it was as if nothing changed. Except something did. Her son was with someone he didn't know and she knew in her heart he was scared to death.

James' parents' house had become the command center for the search parties. They'd all end up there after they'd spent the day searching and see if there was any news. She walked in and was greeted by Nanny Betty and Cora. The first thing she was made to do was eat and she did. James' grandmother wouldn't give up until she ate something.

"Jimmy's at de station. He should be back in a bit." Nanny Betty told her as she poured up a hot cup of tea.

"Thanks, I don't know what I would do without all of you." Marina hadn't taken the time to thank any of them because she was so focused on getting Danny home.

"No need for thanks. Dat's wat family is for." Nanny Betty gave her a hug and moved on to making sure Stephanie was eating.

James walked into the house with his father. He walked right to her, crouched and took her hand. For a few minutes they just stayed there watching the dozens of people coming and going. A lot of the people she didn't know but had been told they were off duty police who'd brought their families to help. Keith's guys were there as well being bossed around by Nanny Betty because they weren't eating enough. Any other time she'd find that funny.

"I think it's time we head home and try to get some rest," James said.

"Yeah, I think Mason is ready for bed." Marina saw the little boy sitting on Kristy's lap with his head resting on her shoulder.

"Let's go."

A couple of cars drove up and down the street the same as they always did. It was like nothing in the world changed, but something did change. Her world was turned upside down. How could all these people driving around not know the pain she was going through? What a stupid thought. None of these people driving to their destinations knew Danny, and they didn't know what an amazing little boy he was. None of them knew his smile could light up a room and none of them knew how her chest hurt without him.

The first flurries of the year were starting to fall. Any other time she would consider it beautiful, but at the moment all she could think about was if Marc was keeping Danny warm enough. Danny had his heavy jacket on when Marc took him, but she wondered if he was inside or were they out in the cold?

She glanced at the clock on the wall and swallowed the lump in her throat that had become permanent since Danny disappeared. It was his bedtime, and he was used to her tucking him in every night. He'd even gotten used to James singing the 'tough boy song' every night. Would Marc make sure he went to bed on time? The lump threatened to choke her and her eyes burned with tears yet again. She didn't want to cry anymore because she was sick of feeling weak. It was more than seventy-eight hours since she'd seen her son, and her heart was hurting.

She turned when she felt something touch her hand and saw Mason staring up at her. His big blue eyes stared up at her and she realized he was just as lost as she was.

"Auntie Marina?"

"Yes, sweetie?" She tried to control the tremble in her voice.

"Do you need a hug?"

Marina nodded and knelt on the floor in front of him as his small arms wrapped around her neck. She closed her eyes and tried to hold back the tears. She didn't want him to see her cry. He was trying to make her feel better, and if she was crying it would upset him.

"That's from me and Danny," he whispered against her cheek, and she couldn't stop the tears anymore. They rolled down her cheeks as she hugged Mason tightly against her, and he didn't flinch. It was as if he had some sort of instinct that Marina needed to just hold him for a while.

"Thank you, Mason." She kissed the top of his head and he put his head on her shoulder. When she opened her eyes, James was standing in the kitchen with his hands in his pockets. The glistening in his eyes said he was moved by his son's concern. She'd grown to love this child as much as her own.

"Mason." James' voice cracked as Mason turned around. "It's time for bed, buddy. You go get ready, and I'll be up to tuck you in." Mason gave her another hug and she couldn't hold the tears back anymore.

"Don't cry, Auntie Marina. Danny'll be home soon. I know he will." He seemed so sure and she wished she had his confidence.

"I hope you're right, sweetie." Marina kissed the top of his head and he ran out of the kitchen. She stood and turned back to the window. James walked up behind her and wrapped his strong arms around her. She knew he was missing Danny, too because she'd saw him staring at the flyers his family made. It was as if he was willing the picture to tell him something. Marina turned into his arms and pressed her cheek against his chest. His hands stroked her back and she closed her eyes.

A few minutes went by, and she heard Mason call out from upstairs. James kissed the top of her head and she felt the loss immediately. The cold thoughts entered her head again. She couldn't think the worst, but sometimes her mind just went there. Would she ever see her son's smiling face again?

Her phone vibrated in her pocket and she frantically fished it out. She glanced at the screen and although she loved her parents, she was disappointed that it wasn't someone telling her they'd found Danny.

"Hi, Mom." Marina held the phone to her ear.

"Is there any news on your end?" her mother asked.

"Not yet." Marina sighed as she stared out of the window.

"He'll be home soon, honey." As positive as her mother was trying to sound, Marina could hear the doubt.

"What if Marc's not taking care of him?" Marina didn't know where the tears were coming from but they'd started again.

"I can't believe he'd do anything to hurt his own son. He's just trying to hurt you, honey." That wasn't all he wanted and she knew it. Marc wanted something but she had no idea what it was.

"I hope you're right, Mom." Marina wiped the tears from her cheeks.

"If you need anything let us know." Janet said. "Your father is out with Sean and Kurt searching the woods."

Marina hadn't even realized they were still searching since it was snowing and dark. "I hope they're not too deep in the woods because the snow is starting to get heavy out here." Marina said.

"I'm sure they'll be smart enough to get in out of the weather." Janet said and Marina shivered. The thought of Danny being out in bad weather with someone he didn't know was making her want to throw up. She tried hard to keep the contents of her stomach down and talked to her mother for a few more minutes. Her mother ended the call just after her father had arrived home. Janet wanted to find out if Doug had found out anything. Marina wanted to know, too, but when she was about to ask her mother to talk to him, she heard James yelling.

Chapter 20

James sat on Mason's bed reading but he noticed his son kept glancing at Danny's bed. Mason had to be missing Danny so much. The boys were like two peas in a pod. They did everything together, especially since Marina moved in but over the course of the last day or so, Mason had become really quiet.

James was almost finished the book when Mason took it from his hand and crawled onto his lap.

"Daddy, if someone told you to keep a secret but the secret was something that could make everyone happy again, would you tell?" The expression on Mason's face had James hair standing on end.

"What are you talking about, buddy?"

Mason seemed to be struggling with his thoughts as he stared at Danny's bed.

"Mason, is there something you need to tell me?" Mason jumped down from his lap and walked to Danny's bed. He glanced at James for a moment and then got onto his hands and knees and pulled something from under Danny's bed. When Mason stood up, he was holding a small box about the size of a ring box. He held it in his hands as he stood in front of James.

"You can tell me anything, Mason, you know that?"

He put it in James' hand and put his hands behind his back. James opened the box and inside it contained a piece of paper with a key. James opened the paper and on it was instructions to opening something with the key and a phone number.

"What's this, Mason?"

Mason crawled onto the bed, but he kept his head down. He still seemed to not want to break Danny's trust.

"Mason, if you know what this is, you need to tell me," James said firmly and when Mason glanced up at him, and James felt terrible for raising his voice. Mason's lower lip stuck out like it always did when he was about to cry.

"I'm sorry, buddy, I didn't mean to raise my voice. It's just this could be really important and I know you promised to keep a secret, but this could help us bring Danny home."

"Daddy, 'member when the man took Danny at the park?"

James nodded.

"He gived Danny that box and told him that he needed to find a box with a lock on it that Auntie Marina had and it belonged to the man. He said Danny had to open the box with that key and when he got all the stuff in the box he had to phone him on that number." James' mouth hung open as he listened to what his son was telling him.

"Did Danny give him the things in the box?" James was trying to stay calm but the phone number could lead them to Marc and Danny.

"No, 'cause we couldn't find it. I even helped him but we couldn't find any box with a lock, and Danny was 'fraid to ask his mommy because the man said she'd be real mad." Mason huffed out a long breath. "Daddy, did I help?"

James smiled at Mason and kissed the top of his head. "I hope so, buddy. Thanks for telling me, but you need to get some sleep."

Mason snuggled down in the bed and yawned. He seemed relieved to have it off his chest.

"Goodnight, buddy."

"You don't have to sing the tough boy song tonight, Daddy. I'll wait until Danny's home." Mason closed his eyes, and James hurried from the room.

James wasn't sure if the key and number was going to help find Danny, but at least they had an idea of what Marc wanted. James just wanted to know what was in the box. He bounded down the stairs two at a time, calling out to Marina.

"What's wrong?" She was still in the kitchen in front of the window.

"I need you to think really hard about this. Do you still have anything belong to Marc? Like a box that this key would unlock?" James held up the key, and Marina stared at it.

"I don't have anything that belongs to him. When he left I packed everything and he had one of his friends pick it up. Anything that was left, Dad stored for me." Marina took the key and studied it. "But this key looks familiar. Where did you get it?" James led her to the living room and told her what Mason had said.

"Mason said he and Danny looked for the box but couldn't find it," James finished.

"I've got no idea what box he's talking about," Marina said.

"I've got to call Keith and see if he can find out anything from this phone number." James pulled his phone out of his pocket.

"Maybe you could call Greg and your uncle first and let them know about it." She stared at the key in her hand as if willing it to tell her something.

Keith arrived not a minute before Kurt and Greg walked into the house. John, Aaron, Nick, Ian, and Mike arrived a few minutes later. Stephanie, Kristy, and Isabelle showed up together and kept Marina company while Keith was on the phone with Sandy, seeing what she could get from the phone number.

James paced the floor and Marina's phone rang almost every ten minutes because her parents wanted an update. James had stopped answering his phone since Nick started to keep their parents and Nanny Betty up to date. Not that there was much to find out. The phone number they found belonged to a Martin Tapper, but Sandy believed it was an alias Marc was using because the photo ID came up with Marc's picture. Keith asked her to keep searching for anything and ended the call.

"So the phone number is no help," Keith said.

"It's a burner I'm guessing," John said.

"I'm not sure, but Sandy's going to do a search on this Martin Tapper alias Marc is using," Keith said. "She wants me to find out how much Marina knows about Marc's past. Some of what she can tell us might make the search faster."

"Is that really necessary?" James knew the answer before he asked the question.

"I'll try not to upset her," Keith promised.

James followed Keith out of the kitchen and into the living room where the women were sitting. James didn't need to look to know that the rest of the men were following as well. Marina met his gaze and he nodded as Keith sat on the coffee table in front of her.

"Marina, I know this is probably going to be hard, but I need to know everything you can tell me about Marc," Keith said.

"Like what?" Stephanie answered for her.

"Everything you can remember he ever told you about his past." Keith said. James sat next to her and she immediately leaned into him.

"He didn't talk much about his past. The only thing I know is his biological parents were killed in a car accident when he was three and he was placed in an orphanage. The O'Reilly's adopted him when he was four. Mr. O'Reilly was killed in an industrial accident when Marc was eighteen, I think, and Mrs. O'Reilly was so devastated she killed herself just over a year after that. Everything was left to Marc because he was their only child, but they didn't really have much. He used the money that he got from the sale of their house to put him through chef school. I met him just after that."

"Do you know the names of his biological parents?" Kurt asked.

"He never told me and I never asked because it was hard for him to talk about." As hard as Marc had it, James didn't feel any sympathy for the man because of what he was putting Marina through. A difficult childhood was no excuse to put someone through this turmoil.

"You don't have any idea what box he's talking about?" Greg asked.

"I told James, I've never seen any box." Marina sighed.

While they were talking to Marina, the front door burst open and Sandy ran in struggling to catch her breath. James didn't miss the glare she gave Ian, but she hurried by him and right to Keith.

"Why don't you answer the damn phone?" she snapped at Keith and James couldn't help but smile.

"It didn't ring." Keith stood up and she didn't back away. She put her hands on her hips and glared up at him.

"I called ten times." Keith reached in his pocket to pull out his phone but didn't find it. He hurried into the kitchen and came back with it in his hand.

"Sorry, I left it on the kitchen table. What's up?" Keith shoved the phone into his pocket and James chuckled when Sandy mumbled something under her breath about brothers being alike.

"Well, if you had not left your phone on the table, I could have told you that I pinged the phone and have a location where to find it." She held out a tablet in her hand.

"This is in town," Keith scanned the tablet.

"Not exactly. Shea Heights is kind of in town and out of town but it's way up in Maddox Cove Road," Sandy said pointing to something. "It's like it's back in the woods."

"Wait, Marc's family used to go up there camping when he was a little boy. They even towed an old trailer up there." Marina stood and looked over Sandy's shoulder. "I went up there with him once. It was way back in the woods, but you couldn't drive in there.

We had to take a four-wheeler but we only went there once because it was in pretty rough shape."

"Would you remember exactly where it was?" Keith asked.

"I don't know. That was when we first started dating." Marina shook her head. "I do remember there was a big yellow sign at the entrance of the path that said 'O'Reilly's get away,'"

While Marina tried to give them directions on how to get to the camping spot, Kurt called the station to set up a team to go. James, John and Aaron were only permitted to go if they stayed back and let the others go in first. Keith never agreed and made it clear to their uncle he wasn't his boss.

"I'm going with you." Marina was heading out of the living room behind Kurt.

"I'm sorry, Marina. I can't let you go. I'm already bending the rules by letting James, John and A.J. go." Kurt was pulling on his jacket.

"He's my son." Marina stepped right in front of Kurt with her hands on her hips and her face inches from his uncle.

"That's why you can't be there." Kurt was calm. Probably because Marina was doing a good impression of Nanny Betty at the moment, and Kurt had dealt with his mother's wrath a time or two.

"Why, because I'm not some big bad cop?" Marina was poking Kurt in the chest with her index finger. "I'll have you know your daughter has been teaching me a thing or two about self-defence and the way I'm feeling right now I could probably kick your butt." Kurt's lips twitched as if he was trying to hold back a grin. James couldn't hold it back and as he glanced around nobody else was either.

Kurt wasn't worried about Marina kicking his ass in the least. For one the man was a fourth-degree black belt and taught him and his brothers as well as his own daughters. Jess, Ian, and Keith stuck with the sport over the years. The rest of the brothers and cousins got as far as brown belts.

"Marina, it's better if you stay here. It would be safer for Danny because if Marc sees you he may do something." Stephanie had pulled Marina back from Kurt but there was still rage in her eyes. She seemed to be like a caged animal as they all got ready to leave. He had to admit he was pretty proud of her standing up to his uncle the way she did. Kurt was a big man, but his mother always said a mother bear will do anything for her baby. Even if it endangered her own life.

"Marina, I'll call you as soon as we know something, I promise." James pulled her aside and held her in his arms.

"Please be careful and find him." Marina clung to him.

"I'll do everything I can to bring him home." James lifted her chin so he could see her eyes. "I love you."

"I love you, too." Marina stood on her toes and kissed his lips softly. James hugged her and followed the team of men out of the house.

Chapter 21

He looked around the cold, dark room when the man closed the door. He slowly moved towards the old bed and climbed onto it. It made a scary, creaking sound and he didn't like it. He was really scared and he wanted to go home to Mommy, Uncle James and Mason. He wrapped his arms around himself and rocked. Mommy always made him feel better when she rocked him. What if he never saw Mommy any more? He couldn't run away because he didn't know where he was and the man was so big.

Besides, Mommy said he should never run away because he wasn't happy. The man said he was his daddy, but how could that be? He was mean and he yelled. Uncle James didn't yell at Mason. He missed Uncle James and he wanted him to be his daddy, not this mean man. He curled up on the bed and cried until he fell asleep.

He woke up a while later shivering. He was so cold, and it was dark in the room. He jumped down off the bed and ran to the door to open it, but it wouldn't open. He banged on it and screamed as loud as he could. He didn't like being locked in the room. He screamed so loud his throat hurt. He was kicking the door when it swung open and knocked him to the floor.

"I want Mommy," he screamed at the man.

"I don't want you here anymore than you want to be here, but you need to shut the hell up so I can get your mother on the phone. Now get in that bed and go to sleep before I give you something to scream about." The man towered over him, and he didn't like the way he looked at him. He was like a monster.

"I'm cold and thirsty." He sobbed and hiccupped.

"Come out here, you pain in the ass." The man grabbed his arm and it hurt. He sat him at the table and put a can of root beer in front of him. "Drink that and here's a blanket." He tossed the blanket on the floor and sat on the couch.

"I need to pee." He pulled back when the man jumped up and lunged at him.

"Jesus Christ, kids are a fucking pain." He opened up another door and pointed. He really had to pee badly but he was afraid the man would lock him in the bathroom. He slid off the chair and walked slowly to the open door. At least there was a light.

"Hurry the fuck up, kid."

After he used the dirty toilet he walked out of the bathroom. The man was standing with the blanket in his hand and pointing to the dark room. He really hated the dark, but he knew the man would get mad if he asked to leave the door open.

"Get in there and go to sleep." He pushed him into the room and threw the blanket at him then closed the door, leaving him in the dark again. He climbed up on the noisy bed and curled up under the blanket. It smelled funny but he was warm. He started to cry until he was too tired to stay awake.

****

The sign Marina told them about was still there but faded. James thanked their lucky stars, because without the sign, they'd never find the entrance. Like he promised, James stayed back and let the others go ahead of them. The pathway was rough and full of debris, almost as if nobody had been through there in a long time. It made his heart sink.

"I don't know how anyone would get through here with a kid in tow," Aaron said as if he was reading James' mind.

"I don't think any vehicles have been up this way, but maybe there's another way to get there that we don't know about," John said.

"This snow is not making it any easier to find the fucking thing either," Aaron complained. James knew his brother was getting frustrated because he'd been cursing Marc the whole way into town. Aaron didn't get angry often but it seemed Marc was bringing the worst out in all of them.

The snow had slowed a bit but it was still making it difficult to find the trailer Marina had described. Kurt had turned around several times and the look on his face said Kurt was thinking the same as everyone else. They probably wouldn't find their way to the place in the dark with it snowing, even with the flood lights.

James was ready to give Kurt the word to stop the search, when he heard Greg's voice up ahead.

"Newfoundland Police Department, open the door." Greg's voice boomed through the woods and by the time James got through the opening, one of the other officers had pulled open the door. The trailer had broken windows and it was rusted badly. His heart sank at the sight. There was no way they'd find Danny and Marc in there. Greg and Cory came out through the door of the trailer. Their faces showed nothing as they walked up to Kurt and Keith. James wasn't staying back any longer and jogged up to the group.

"Nobody's been in that trailer in a long time," Greg said.

"I'll call the coroner." Kurt turned from the group and put the phone to his ear.

"Wait? Coroner?" James legs almost gave out.

"James, it's not Danny," Cory grabbed James before he went to his knees.

"Then why are you calling the coroner?" John had joined the group.

"We found human remains inside but they've been there for a while." Greg said. "The remains are chained to a chair." All the air whooshed out of him and he went to his knees. Aaron and John knelt next to him and listened as Greg explained what they found inside. "It looks like whoever it is was kept there against their will. I think it's a male, but the remains are badly decomposed."

"So Marc and Danny haven't been here?" Aaron sighed.

"I'm not going to say no, but I really don't think so," Greg said.

"So now what do we do? Sandy said the phone signal came from up this way," Keith said.

"We have to wait for forensics to go through there, but if the phone is here at least we know Marc has been here." Kurt had rejoined them.

James stood up again and glanced around the clearing. He just wanted to scream and run at the same time. He'd have to go home and tell Marina they didn't find Danny and she was going to be devastated. He turned and headed back to the main road because he just wanted to get away from everyone so he could catch his breath.

"We'll find him, bro." Keith was behind him, and James nodded but didn't speak. He wouldn't be able to control his emotions if he spoke at that moment.

He managed to find his way back to the main road alone, but the road was pitch black. Not unusual around the area because there were very few street lights. Not many people lived out that far. James just wanted to get back to Hopedale and see Marina. He pulled out his phone and sent a text to John and Keith telling them he was heading home. There were enough vehicles so he didn't worry about anybody not having a way home, and besides, he just wanted some solitary time to figure out what he was going to say to Marina.

By the time he got into Hopedale, the snow had almost stopped but the roads were completely covered and he had to take his time once he turned onto his road. He managed to get his truck into the driveway without much trouble, but getting out of the truck seemed to take everything he had. Going into the house and telling the woman he loved that he didn't find her son was tearing him apart. As much as he had promised himself he wouldn't get his hopes up, he had and the disappointment was gut wrenching.

The front door opened before he made it up the steps, and Isabelle stood there with a sombre look on her face. For a moment she just stared at him but then she walked out and closed the door behind her. She wrapped her arms around him and hugged him tightly.

"John called and told us what happened," she said when she stepped back. "Uncle Sean came by and gave Marina a sedative. Mostly because she kept saying she can feel how afraid he is. I don't know how true that is but Nan seemed to believe her."

"Fuck, fuck, fuck." James hissed through his teeth.

"Nan managed to get her to go to bed and told her we would send you up as soon as you got back."

James wrapped his arm around Isabelle's shoulder and kissed the top of her head. "Thanks, cuz. I don't know what I'd do without all of you." He opened the door and was greeted by Nanny Betty.

"I jus' made some tea and coffee, if ya want some, but ya get upstairs and see da lass. She's fightin' the medication Sean gave her because she's waitin' for ya." Nanny Betty reached up and cupped his face in her small hands. "Doncha worry, Jimmy, we'll get little Danny back."

"I hope you're right, Nan." James tried hard to keep the tears from spilling out of his eyes, but since Nanny Betty pulled a couple of tissues from her pocket and handed them to him, he was pretty sure he didn't succeed.

He heard her soft sobs just as he got to the bedroom door. He swallowed hard and opened it. She was curled on her side facing the window and didn't seem to hear him coming into the room.

"Marina?" James voice cracked as he said her name.

"He's scared, James. I can feel it." Marina sobbed.

"Baby, we'll find him, and I'm sure Marc will get in touch with us soon." James lay next to her on the bed and pulled her into his arms.

"I don't want to cry, but I can't stop and it makes me feel weak." Marina turned into his embrace.

"Marina, you're not weak. You're a mother missing her child and you can cry all you want. I'll be here to hold you as long as you need me to, but don't ever think for one second that makes you a weak person." James pressed his lips against the top of her head and held her until her sobs stopped and her breathing became deep and even. She'd fallen asleep and hopefully the sedative would help her get a good night's sleep.

Once he untangled himself from Marina and covered her, he made his way downstairs. He knew everyone was back from town and they'd all congregated in the kitchen. James walked in and the conversation stopped. That wasn't good at all.

"What's going on?" James didn't like the look on Kurt's and Keith's faces, and John was averting his eyes.

"We found the phone," Kurt said. "It was about a hundred feet from the trailer."

"Why do I get the feeling that's not good news?" James leaned against the counter next to John.

"The phone case was inside a plastic bag with this." Keith handed him his phone and James glanced at it. A picture of Danny was on the screen. He was stood in front of the trailer and from the red rims around his eyes, he'd been crying.

"So he was at the trailer." James tossed the phone back to Keith.

"I had a feeling he knew we were going up there, so I brought the box the key was in to one of our techs," Kurt said.

"There was a listening device embedded into the bottom of the box under the insert."

"So he heard everything we said and where we were going." James sighed.

"I think he has to be close by that trailer, so in the morning we're expanding our search area and pulling in more people to help," Kurt informed him. "I'm going back to the station and making the calls. Keith is calling in all his available men and women."

"Kurt you can drop me off home so I can start getting some food ready for all those people tomorrow." James turned to see Nanny Betty pulling on her coat.

"Mudder, we won't need any food," Kurt said.

"Doncha be so foolish. Ya can't have all dem wonderful people tramping through de woods and snow and not feed 'em."

"Mudder, it's their jobs and they don't expect to be fed for doing their job." Kurt sighed.

"Jobs or not they're helping our Jimmy and Marina find dere son. Now are ya gonna drive me home or will I walk." Nanny Betty pulled her wool hat over her head.

"I'll drop you off, Mudder." Kurt shook his head as he left the kitchen. James knew, like everyone else in the family, there was no arguing with his grandmother and just because it was after ten at night didn't mean she wasn't going to go home and pull in Kathleen,

Cora, and Alice to get lots of food together so everyone would be fed.

"We'll make sure ta have a big scoff ready when everyone gets back with our boy." Nanny Betty followed Kurt out of the house. A scoff was what Newfoundlanders called a huge home cooked meal and nobody did it like Nanny Betty and his mother.

"Nan does realize that the search is not in Hopedale, right?" Aaron said.

"Shut up, A.J. She might pack up her car and follow the search party out there." John chuckled.

It was well after midnight and everyone had left except for John, Stephanie and Nick. They'd decided to stay for the night. Aaron and Mike had gone to stay with Ian at his house. Keith had gone to his own house. James stood on the back deck staring out at the ocean. He never got headaches, but his head felt like it was going to split in two. The last time he could remember having a headache was when Sarah got sick. Stress did funny things to a person. A hand clamped down on his shoulder, and he jumped with his fist ready to strike.

"Jesus, John, give me a stroke next time."

"Sorry, I thought you heard me come out." John sat next to him and handed him a shot glass. "Thought you may need this. You know the family motto."

"A shot of screech calms your nerves." James chuckled and quickly downed the dark liquid. He didn't drink it often and the burn that was currently in his throat reminded him why. He was glad it was John who followed him outside. John knew him well and knew if he wanted to talk or just be quiet. "Thanks, bro."

"For what?"

"Just for being here."

"Since conception, bro," John said.

"I don't know how much more she can take." James swallowed hard.

"I don't think you've got to worry about Marina. She's a tough cookie. First she got herself out of a bad marriage. She's been raising Danny by herself and working full time and did you see her with Uncle Kurt? I thought she was going to throat punch him." John chuckled and then put his hand on James' shoulder. "I'm worried about you, though. I know how you feel about Marina and Danny."

"He's like my own son."

"I know." James tipped his head back, closed his eyes and silently prayed for some help. He couldn't watch the woman he loved go through this turmoil anymore, and he didn't know if he could take much more himself.

Chapter 22

The room was so cold and the blanket wasn't keeping him warm anymore. He slid off the bed but kept the blanket wrapped around him. He walked to the door and turned the knob and it opened. A man was laying on the couch and his eyes were open wide but it wasn't the man who said he was his daddy. This man was dirty and smelled really bad.

"I need to use the bathroom," he said but the man didn't even look at him. The door to outside was open and there was snow all over the floor. He slowly walked towards the man and saw white stuff coming out of his mouth. It looked like soap but why would the man eat soap? He touched the man's hand. It was really cold but the man still didn't move. He was just staring at the wall. "I'm going to pee."

After he used the bathroom, he walked back to where the man was still on the couch. He must be really tired, because the man didn't even move when he walked to the front door. He peeked out and saw all the trees around the house and stepped outside. He glanced back, but the man still lay there. He walked back inside and saw his coat and boots next to the door and he pulled them on. He wasn't staying here anymore. He was going home.

"I'm going home to Mommy and you tell my daddy I don't want to come with him no more. I want Uncle James to be my daddy." The man didn't say anything so he rolled up the blanket under his arm and walked out of the house. He was suddenly really scared since he wasn't sure if he remembered how they got there. He remembered his poppy Kelly telling him once when they played hide and seek that he found him because he saw his footprints in the snow. He saw small round holes in the snow towards an opening in the trees. He crouched to look at them. He stood up and looked where they disappeared down the pathway.

"I'm goin' home," he whispered and followed the holes away from the house. He turned several times to see if the man was following but he was by himself. It was scary walking in the woods alone but he wanted to see Mommy, Uncle James and Mason.

He'd been walking a long time and he was getting really tired. He saw a stump on the side of the path and sat down. He looked back at the house and thought he should go back. Mommy told him he should never run away just because he wasn't happy. He stood up and turned towards the house, but something moved behind him and he turned around. A big white dog was standing in the pathway and it was staring straight at him. Mommy said not to go near strange dogs, but this dog didn't seem mean.

"Hi, doggie, are you lost too?" He said and walked slowly to the dog with his hand out. Uncle John said dogs needed to sniff people to make sure they were nice people. The dog sat down and wagged his tail. "I'm lost, too," he said as he put his hand in front of the dog's nose. The dog licked his hand and it tickled. He rubbed the dog's head and looked around. He really was lost.

The dog barked and he watched it walk down the path. "Do you know how to get home, doggie?" The dog barked again and backed up. "Do you want me to go with you?" The dog jumped up, barked and started to walk down the path. Maybe he knew how to find someone who could call Mommy, Uncle James or Uncle John. Maybe the dog could take him home. "Wait up, doggie." He ran up next to the dog and grabbed onto the collar. "I'm gonna call you Buddy 'cause that's what Uncle James calls me." The dog barked again. "You like that, Buddy? Good." He walked, holding the dog with one hand and the blanket rolled up under the other arm. He was going home to Mommy.

****

Marina woke up calling out to Danny, but he didn't answer. Of course he didn't answer because his crazy father had taken him. It had been four days now and still no word from Marc or any sign of where they were. She knew Danny was scared because she could feel it, but she didn't know how to explain the feeling. James' grandmother said she completely understood.

"One summer when my Sean was eight years old, he got lost in da woods and I could feel it in da pit of me stomach how scared he was. It's a connection mothers have wit their children, and it never goes away. Kathleen can feel how scared James is with Danny missing." Nanny Betty told her as they sat in the kitchen drinking a cup of tea later that morning.

"It's different today, though. I feel his fear but there's something else. Almost like he's hopeful?" Marina didn't know what it meant.

"It might be a sign dat we're going to find da lad soon." Nanny Betty reached across the table and clasped her hand. "We've all been prayin' ta bring him home." Marina wasn't a really religious person. The first time in years she'd been in a church was when Danny was baptized, and then Stephanie's wedding, but over the last few days she'd prayed more times than she could count. It felt hypocritical since the only time she prayed was when she needed something, but praying seemed so natural when she was struggling with something.

"I hope you're right, Mrs. O'Connor." Marina held Nanny Betty's hand tightly and it gave her a sense of calmness.

"Mrs. O'Connor was my mother-in-law and she was da devil incarnate. Ya call me Nan like all me udder grandchildren." Nanny Betty squeezed her hand and stood to put her cup in the sink. There was a firm knock on the front door and Marina jumped up to go answer it. Since everyone was out searching, Nanny Betty had drawn the short straw to stay with her. James still insisted that she stay home in case Marc called. She opened the door and gasped.

"Mr. Roberts? What are you doing here?" Marina stared at the man standing on the step.

"I know you still haven't found the little fella, and I wanted to help with anything I can." He said as she motioned him inside.

"I don't know what you could do, but the thought is wonderful. Why don't you come in and have a cup of tea?" Marina took his coat and hat. He reminded her of Dick Van Dyke with his white hair and blue eyes. He had a friendly face and from what she knew about him he was in his early seventies.

Marina hung up his coat and hat and he followed her into the kitchen where Nanny Betty was busy washing dishes in the sink again. She refused to use the dishwasher and told James several times it was the lazy man's way.

"Nan, this is the man who helped me the other night." Marina said but when Nanny Betty turned around her face lost all it's color and her hand flew to her chest.

"Elizabeth Power, well as I live and breathe," Thomas said.

"Tommy Roberts. Dear God it is you." Nanny Betty seemed as if she was about to pass out.

"Yes, it's me." Tom's smile made him appear years younger, but the expression on Nanny Betty's face gave new meaning to the words 'if looks could kill.'

"I didn't think you were ever coming back to Newfoundland for love nor money." Nanny Betty crossed her arms over her chest but Marina heard the slight tremor in the woman's voice. Not typical for Nanny Betty to be nervous around anyone.

"I've been back in Newfoundland for about three years, Elizabeth." The way Tom said the name made it sound almost intimate.

"It's Betty. Nobody calls me Elizabeth since me fadder died." Nanny Betty snapped and turned back to the sink.

"You'll always be Elizabeth to me." Tom said. Either Nanny Betty didn't hear him, or she'd chosen to ignore him. "I didn't realize you were related to her." Tom had turned to Marina and smiled.

"She's James' grandmother." Marina corrected him. It was like a light went on in his eyes and he chuckled.

"Ah… So Jack won the prize did he." Tom said. "Where is the son of a gun?" Marina saw Nanny Betty's back stiffen and she turned around slowly. Her face was so red it almost looked purple.

"For your information, Mr. Roberts. I won the prize when I married Jack and if you must know we lost the love of my life six years ago." Marina was getting concerned with Nanny Betty's reaction. The woman was never out of control but she seemed ready to snap at any time.

"Love of your life, huh? I remember he wasn't always," Tom said.

"He always was but I was too blind ta see it at first, but thank da lord my mistake left da province for bigger and better things." With that statement Nanny Betty turned on her heels and stomped out of the room.

"Over fifty years since I've see her and she's still as high spirited as ever." Tom chuckled.

"I'm guessing there's a story there?" Marina asked as she pointed to the kitchen chair.

"Yes, but I don't have the right to share that story." Tom sighed. "So, what can I do to help?"

Marina flopped into the chair across the table from him. "I'm not sure, but I'll have James call you if he can think of something," Marina said.

"Marina, I've never been married or had children and I can't imagine what you're going through, but whether it's monetary or otherwise. I want to help."

"That's so nice of you. I promise, I'll let you know or have James call you." Marina smiled at him.

"Yar still here." Nanny Betty grumbled as she stomped into the kitchen.

"I was just leaving, but you have my number, Marina, if you need anything." Tom took her hand and squeezed it gently. "Elizabeth, I hope to see you again." Tom turned and walked out of the kitchen. Marina heard the front door close and turned to Nanny Betty.

"How do you know Tom?" Marina had to hold back a giggle when Nanny Betty called Tom everything under the sun and some names Marina was sure Nanny Betty had made up.

"Tommy Roberts is not worth talkin' about my dear." Nanny Betty said nonchalantly as if he were no better than a piece of dirt on her shoe. "I'd just like ta know wat he thought he could do dat my boys couldn't." There was the hostility that Nanny Betty had showed earlier for Tom.

"He was offering to help find Danny," Marina explained.

"Well, din. Dat was nice of him, but I don't know wat he thinks he could do." Nanny Betty stood in front of the kitchen window staring out into the darkness.

"I don't either." Marina admitted.

James had gotten home a few minutes later and Nanny Betty quickly made her exit with nothing more than a quick see ya later. She was really out of sorts since she'd seen Tom and Marina was really curious as to what the story was.

After a shower James came back into the living room where she was talking to John and Stephanie. She'd told them about Nanny Betty's reaction to Tom and how Tom had reacted to her.

"Do you suppose they dated before she met your grandfather?" Stephanie asked John.

"I think Tom knew him because he said something about Jack winning the prize." Marina remembered the comment and thought it was a weird thing to say.

"As far as I knew Grandda and Nan have been together since they were teenagers," John said.

"I don't know. All I know if Tom can be of any help, I've got no issue with asking him, if it helps us find Danny." James sat next to Marina and kissed her temple.

"Mason was excited to go stay with your parents tonight." Marina said.

"I know, I stopped there on my way home. He wanted to know when Danny was going to be home." James sighed. "What am I supposed to tell him?"

Marina didn't know either, but over the course of the evening the feeling of dread she'd had over the past few days seemed to change to something else. She didn't feel the same fear she'd been feeling for the last few days, and it worried her because she didn't know what it meant. Actually, she was afraid of what it meant.

For the second night in a row John and Stephanie spent the night with her and James. Ian was now hosting three of the other four brothers. They all seemed intent on staying in Hopedale until Danny was found. Marina was getting ready for bed when she heard her cell phone ringing and ran to grab it. She glanced at the screen but it was a blocked number. It made her heart pound in her chest.

"Hel…hello," she stammered.

"I'm looking for Marina Kelly," the soft female voice asked.

"I'm Marina Kelly."

"Ms. Kelly, do you have a son Danny?"

Marina started to shake and her legs were about to give out. She went down on her knees before she answered.

"Yes, I do. He's been missing for the past four days." Marina tried to keep her voice calm, but she hiccupped halfway through her response and the tears started. James walked into the room as she went to her knees. He was at her side in seconds, and Marina hit speaker on her phone so he could hear.

"My name is Barb Druken and I live on Shea Heights. I train K9 dogs for the R.C.M.P and the N.P.D. One of my dogs escaped the kennel earlier today and when he came back he had a boy with him. The boy said he's name is Danny Kelly and gave me your number." Marina gasped and covered her mouth with her hand as the tears flowed.

"He's okay?" Marina sobbed.

"He's a little cold, but I've got him wrapped in blankets by the fireplace," Barb told her. "Would you like to speak with him?"

"Oh my God, yes." Marina almost screamed and James ran out of the room, returning seconds later with John and Stephanie.

"Mommy?" Danny's voice echoed through the phone and her tears flowed down her cheeks.

"I'm here, baby. Are you okay?" Marina sobbed.

"I wanna come home." His pleading voice made her want to run right to him.

"We're coming to get you, baby. Don't worry. Can you put the lady back on the phone?" Marina was on her feet and heading out of the bedroom.

"I'm here Ms. Kelly," Barb said.

"I need your address," Marina said but before Barb could answer John interrupted.

"I know where she lives," John said. "I was with Cory when he picked up a couple of the dogs last year."

Marina thanked her and she didn't remember getting into the truck but the next thing she knew they were driving on the highway towards St. John's. John had made the calls to the family on the drive and Kurt had warned them not to ask Danny anything. He needed to be interviewed by someone outside the family. Marina didn't care who questioned him. All she cared about was having Danny out of Marc's clutches and having him in her arms.

The drive to town never seemed so long before, but when she thought they were never going to get there, John told James to turn into a driveway off Blackhead Road. Marina was out of the truck before James had a chance to put the truck in park. She ran to the small bungalow at full speed and almost tripped as she ran up the steps to the door.

The front door opened and an older woman smiled at her. She motioned for Marina to enter and held the door open as the rest of them made their way to the house. Marina looked at the couch next to the fireplace. Danny was sound asleep curled up next to a huge white husky. The dog raised its head as Marina approached and at first she didn't think the dog would let her near Danny.

"His name is Cloud." Marina heard Barb behind her. "He's the one that brought Danny here, but Danny seems to insist on calling him Buddy." Barb chuckled.

"Well, Cloud, thank you for finding Danny." Marina crouched and carefully petted the dog's head. "You are a handsome boy, aren't you?" Marina smiled when the dog sat up and licked her face.

"Mommy?" Danny's eyes were open and she couldn't stop herself from pulling him into her arms. At that point she didn't care if the dog tore her arm off.

"Danny, are you okay?" Marina held his face between her hands and examined him.

"I'm okay, but I don't wanna go back to that house anymore. It smells bad and the one man wouldn't talk to me and the other man said he was my daddy, but he left." Danny had tears in his eyes.

"You aren't going back there. You're coming home with me and James." Marina pulled him into her arms and hugged him to her. Cloud seemed to want to get in on the action because he began to lick Danny's face, making him giggle.

"Barb, I don't know how to thank you," James said from behind her.

"It wasn't me. I don't think Cloud is going to make a good K9, but he seemed to know that Danny was in trouble and escaped the kennel to find him," Barb said.

"What are you doing with him?" Marina asked.

"I've been searching for a family for him, but until then he'll stay with me." Barb bent down to ruffle the dog's head.

"We'll take him." Marina and James said together. They looked at each other and laughed.

"How could we not take him after what he did?" James smiled at the dog.

"What do you think, Cloud? Would you like to go live with Danny and his family?" The deep bark from the dog and the excited jumping had Marina believing the dog knew exactly what they were saying.

"When can we take him?" Marina asked. Barb explained that he'd already been released as a potential K9, but she'd still have to do some background checks.

"No offense but I need to make sure he's going to be cared for and you have the space for him," Barb explained.

"We understand." Marina glanced at Danny. "Do you want Cloud to come and live with us?" Danny nodded and giggled when the dog began to lick his face again.

"I need your address so I can do a home visit and once the checks come back, I can release Cloud to you." Barb shook James' hand and nodded to Stephanie and John.

"Let's go home, Bud." James ruffled Danny's hair. "I know someone else who's been really missing you." Marina knew he was referring to Mason.

As much as Marina didn't want to let Danny out of her arms, she knew she had to put him in his car seat. She sat in the back seat of the truck with Stephanie and held Danny's hand the whole way home. She gotten a rancid smell from him when she hugged him first but she really didn't care at that point, but in the confines of the truck the smell was pungent. Danny had fallen asleep and she turned his hand over to see the dirt caked into his palms.

"What are you looking at?" Stephanie whispered so she wouldn't wake Danny.

"His hands are filthy," Marina whispered. "And he smells really bad."

"I noticed," Stephanie said.

"I'll give him a bath when we get home," Marina whispered as she pushed back his hair from his forehead.

She sighed when they pulled into the driveway and saw the front door open. Her father and mother were on the step next to James' parents. Kathleen was holding a wiggling Mason in her arms, and Nanny Betty was in the doorway with her hands clasped in front of her chest and tears in her eyes.

"Danny, we're home, baby. You've got to wake up now." Marina spoke softly as to not startle him. His eyes fluttered open and he stared at her.

"I'm really home," he said sleepily.

"Yeah, pal, you're home." James stood outside the truck holding open the door. Marina released the car seat harness and Danny jumped into James' arms.

"Can I call you daddy now?" James looked at Marina, and she nodded.

"You can call me anything you want, buddy." James hugged him and Danny wrapped his arms around James' neck. With all the happiness of having Danny home, Marina still knew Marc wasn't finished with her, but she put that in the back of her mind and just let herself enjoy the moment of happiness. Waiting for the other shoe to drop would only drive her crazy and take away the joy of finding her son.

Danny wasn't happy about taking the time to get a bath, but with James and his negotiation skills, Marina managed to get him to take a short one. James also managed to put off the questioning until morning by promising Kurt and Greg nobody would ask Danny anything about what happened.

It was after three in the morning and way past the boy's bedtime, but considering what they'd been through the last few days, it didn't seem important and with the family filling the house, there was no way Danny and Mason would make it easy to get them to bed.

"I love seeing that smile." James stood behind her as she watched Danny play a video game with Aaron and Mason.

"He seems okay. I don't think he's been too traumatized by Marc." Marina leaned back against James, and he wrapped his arms around her.

"Dad checked him out and physically he's fine, but it will probably take a few days to know if there's any psychological trauma," James said.

"I know."

The sun was coming up when Mason and Danny passed out on the couch. Everyone except for Keith and Bull had gone home. Bull was now permanently assigned to Danny until Marc was found. James brought both boys up to bed and tucked them in while she had a minute to herself. She hadn't taken her eyes off Danny since the minute they picked him up. Even after a long hot bath she stood in the doorway to the boy's bedroom and just watched him sleep.

"I think you need to get some sleep, Ms. Kelly." Marina turned to see Bull sitting at the end of the hallway reading.

"Aren't you going to sleep?" The man had to be a robot.

"I'll get a few hours when Keith takes over at eight," he said.

"Do you want a cup of coffee or something?" Marina felt the need to make sure he wasn't going to fall asleep on the job and get in trouble.

"James has a pot of coffee already made for me when I need it. He's just locking up downstairs." He told her.

"He's finished locking up and agreeing with Bull that a certain Ms. Kelly needs to go to bed." Marina glanced towards the top of the stairs to see James leaning against the rail.

"Wow! Men really do think alike." Marina smiled.

"Come on, sweetheart, I think we both can use some sleep." James led her to the bedroom. "Bull, coffee is ready whenever you want it and if you want a bite to eat, Nan left a ton of leftovers in the fridge." Bull nodded and made his way downstairs.

"You know there may not be enough food in the fridge to feed him." Marina giggled.

"I'm sure it's enough for a few hours." James closed the bedroom door and pulled Marina into his arms. "Right now I don't care if he eats everything in the house. I just want to crawl into bed and hold you all night long."

"That sounds like heaven." Marina leaned her head against his chest and sighed.

She never realized how exhausted she really was until she curled up in James' arms and closed her eyes. Between the relief of having Danny home safe and sound, and the warmth of James holding her, sleep was coming fast.

"I love you, James," she murmured before she started to drift off

"I love you, too, sweetheart," was the last thing she heard before she fell into a deep, content sleep.

Chapter 23

The fucking idiot had to overdose and the stupid kid didn't even find what he wanted him to find. So now he had no kid, no key for the box, no box and no way to get the money that was due to him.

"Now what the fuck do I do?" He flopped down on the end of the couch next to the dead druggie. He knew he shouldn't have left so much meth for Tucker. The guy would keep shooting up until he had none left, and the stuff he gave the dummy was high quality. It was way too easy to overdose.

He glanced around the cabin and wondered if his parents had spent time with him here. He remembered nothing about them and finding his brother had been no help at all. It pissed him off that his own flesh and blood refused to help him when he asked. Goes to show that blood is not thicker than water. Then he was saddled with that whiney bitch for far too long and it was like a halleluiah moment when she kicked him out. If she knew everything, she'd be devastated.

The only thing was, he couldn't cut ties completely until he had the papers in that fucking box. They were what he needed to get the money that was due to him, and with his brother no longer in the picture, and nobody really knowing about him, all that money was his. He just couldn't figure out how to get the box and the key back.

First, he had to get rid of the body before it started stinking up the place. He could dump it next to that old trailer, but when he'd gone by there earlier, the place was crawling with cops. They probably found what he'd left inside by now, so he knew it was only a matter of time before they figured things out. He jumped up, grabbed the old blanket off the back of the couch and spread it on the floor in front of the couch. He rolled Tucker onto the blanket and wrapped him as best he could by himself. The guy was not big, but the dead weight was heavier than he expected. He grabbed Tucker's feet and dragged him out through the door of the cabin. He didn't want to alert the cops by driving by them with his truck, so he dragged the body into the dense trees as far away from the cabin as he could get it. He also wanted to keep it far away from the old trailer so the cops wouldn't notice it. He hurried back to the cabin and grabbed a shovel out of his truck, and then he made his way back to the body. He covered it with snow and hoped it was good enough to keep anyone from finding it. He felt a little guilty for tossing his friend aside like garbage, but he really didn't have time to feel guilty. Maybe when he got his money he'd come back and give Tucker a proper burial.

Back at the cabin he grabbed a beer out of the fridge and chugged half of the bottle before he took it from his lips. Now he needed another way to get the box from that bitch. She was ruining his life even when she wasn't in it anymore. How anyone could love her was beyond him. Getting close to her was going to be impossible because her overgrown father, that do good boyfriend of hers, and his brothers were watching her twenty-four hours a day. Plus, there was that big guy who looked as if he could bench press a truck. There had to be a way. He wasn't taking the kid again. Not only would they have him in lockdown, he couldn't stand the constant whining and crying again. Being a father was not for him, and the kid was never going to get to know his real father.

He lay back on the couch and closed his eyes until he remembered not an hour ago Tucker lay dead on the same couch. He jumped up and plopped down in the armchair across from the couch. He'd be tossing that in the back of the truck and dropping it at the dump.

With his eyes closed, he searched his thoughts for an idea to get what was due him. Then it hit him and a grin formed on his face because nobody would ever suspect him to be so bold. He was going to get what belonged to him no matter what.

****

James tossed his phone on the desk after ending yet another call to the lab to see if they'd made any headway on the identity of the remains found in the trailer. Three days later and they were still working on it. Plus, forensics was still sifting through all the garbage they'd found inside and outside the trailer. He knew all of it had something to do with Marc, and he didn't need to be told Marc was the reason the John Doe in the trailer was dead. The thought of that man married to Marina sent a chill up his spine.

He hadn't really wanted to return to work, but Marina had insisted plus Keith and Bull wouldn't let anyone near her or Danny. However, he wasn't so relaxed about the staff meeting she'd be attending that afternoon. It was really the first time he'd argued with Marina since they'd been together and it wasn't pretty. He smiled as he remembered.

"Tell your boss you're not going because there is no way in hell I'm letting you leave this house." James rested his hands on the desk and stared down at her.

Marina slowly pushed herself away from the desk and stood up. James stood up to his full height and crossed his arms over his chest. "You're not letting me leave the house?" she said slowly as if she wanted to make sure she pronounced every word correctly. Then as if she was making sure she knew what the words meant, she repeated it. "You. Are. Not. Letting. Me." She pronounced each word.

"No. You're staying here until we find Marc." When she narrowed her eyes and slowly walked around the desk, James backed up to keep her at arms' length because the look in her eyes was kind of scary.

"James, thank you for caring but I'm going to say this once, and once only. Nobody is ever going to tell me what I can or can't do ever again. This is my job and I've got to go to this meeting. You aren't going to stop me from going, Keith is not going to stop me from going and even that overgrown ape, Bull isn't going to stop me. I'm not going to be bossed around by anyone. Ever. Again. You got that?"

He stood with his back against the wall while she poked him in the chest the same way she'd poked Kurt a few nights before. He decided at that moment to keep his mouth shut. She reminded him of his grandmother when she went on a rant. It was funny, yet it made him proud that she had the strength to stand up for what she wanted.

"Keith is sending Bull with Marina to her staff meeting. Trunk is at the house with Danny and Mason." James shook himself out of his thoughts and looked up to see Nick leaning his hip against the desk.

"Yeah, I know. Mason was so excited because he had no school today and was going to get to spend the day with Superman." James chuckled. "What are you doing here at the station?"

"After everything that's been going on over the past few years, first with Stephanie and now with Marina, I've decided being a lawyer for scumbags is just not what I should be doing with my life."

"Honestly, I could never get my head around you as a lawyer." James always saw Nick as a doctor, fireman or even a police officer. Nick never seemed the suit and tie kind of guy.

"Yeah, well it took working with corporate assholes to make me realize the same thing. So I just spoke to Uncle Kurt and filled out the application for the academy." Nick grinned.

"Holy fuck, another O'Connor on the force. We're being invaded." The voice of Rick Avery came from the other side of the office.

"Well I think I'll be the last of them for a while." Nick chuckled. "Well until Mason is older anyway."

"If you're half the cop your brothers and uncle are, we're lucky to have you." Rick slapped Nick on the back as he walked up to the desk.

"Just stay away from my little sister." Rick narrowed his eyes and grinned.

"Is she cute?" Nick wiggled his eyebrows.

"Don't even think about it, Casanova. I know all about you younger O'Connors, and neither of you are getting within a hundred feet of her. She's already been warned about A.J., and I will be giving her a head up on you too." Rick chuckled.

"Smart move." James laughed.

"Well, I'm hurt that you would think that of me, bro." Nick held his hand to his chest and stuck out his bottom lip.

"I don't think that of you, little brother. I know that of you." James stood and stretched his arms over his head.

"How's the boy doing, by the way?" Rick was one of the officers who volunteered his off duty time to help find Danny.

"He's doing pretty well, actually. He's had a couple of nightmares but Marina's been looking into getting him a therapist to talk things through. We picked up the dog yesterday and he hasn't left Danny's side. We had to explain to Mason that the dog helped find Danny and that now the dog was just making sure Danny was okay. Mason seems taken with the dog too so we put a dog bed in the room between their beds." James didn't tell them that Cloud seemed to know when Danny was feeling stressed and would lay next to him. He'd heard of therapy dogs and although Cloud wasn't trained as one, he certainly seemed to be a natural at it.

"I'm heading back to Ian's place. Are you off now?" Nick zipped up his coat.

"No, I've got another couple of hours," James said.

"I'll walk out with you. I'm done for the day," Rick said as he waved to James.

"Good. Then you can tell me more about that sister of yours." Nick laughed when Rick shoved him playfully.

"Not a chance, slick." James heard Rick say as they disappeared through the door.

Marina called him when she arrived at the office like he'd asked, but she hadn't been happy about it. He was pretty sure that, like his grandmother, it would take a lot of groveling for her to forgive his slipup.

"The meeting is going to take a couple of hours. I'll call you when I'm on the way home." She still sounded pissed.

"Are you still mad at me?" James asked and heard her sigh.

"Yes," she said softly.

"I don't like you being mad at me."

"I understand why you didn't want me to go to work but you can't order me around and tell me you're not letting me do something. It feels like you're trying to control me. Danny is safe and I'm not here alone."

"I'm sorry, sweetheart. I just don't want anything to happen to you. I love you so much." James leaned back in the chair and closed his eyes.

"How am I supposed to stay mad when you say those things?" She groaned.

"I do love you." James smiled.

"Argh, that's not fair, but I love you, too. You big ape." Marina let out a sigh. "The meeting is about to start. I'll see you tonight." The last thing he heard was her telling someone she was coming.

He'd been home for almost two hours and was pacing the floor. Marina said the meeting was going to be a couple of hours and when she was done she'd call him. That had been almost three hours ago and still no call. He'd called Bull and the man assured him that Marina was still inside the building.

So here he was waiting at home reading the unanswered texts he'd sent Marina over the last half hour. Keith was on the phone with Bull ordering him to go into the building to make sure Marina was still in the meeting. His stomach was in knots and his heart was thudding in his chest. Something was wrong and he could feel it.

"Daddy, what's wrong?" Mason walked into the kitchen.

"Nothing, buddy, I'm just waiting for a phone call." He didn't want to worry his son and he certainly didn't want to upset Danny.

"Where's Mommy?" Danny asked.

"Her meeting ran late. She'll be home later." James hated lying to the boys, but at this point he really didn't know if anything was wrong. "Both of you go upstairs and get ready for bed. I'll come tuck you in and when Mommy comes home, I'll send her up to say goodnight." Mason left the kitchen, but Danny didn't move. He was staring at James as if he knew James wasn't being honest.

"Is Mommy in trouble?" Danny asked with a small quiver in his voice.

"No, buddy. Why would you think that?" James crouched in front of him and held him by the shoulders.

"I got a funny feeling in my belly." Danny's eyes filled with tears.

"Mommy's fine, pal. Why don't you go snuggle in your bed with Cloud? He always makes you feel better." The dog had been a godsend for Danny. Before he had a chance to turn around, the dog was next to him and gave a little whine. It amazed James how the dog knew when Danny was distressed.

"Okay, Daddy." Danny held onto Cloud's collar and started out of the kitchen but before he left he turned around. "I like calling you Daddy." He smiled, and James' heart melted.

"I like hearing it, buddy." James swallowed the lump in his throat as Danny left the kitchen. He really did love hearing Danny call him daddy.

Keith had been sitting at the kitchen table with the phone to his ear waiting for Bull to find out why Marina wasn't answering James' texts. His low rumble and string of curses made James stomach tighten.

"What do you mean James called the secretary?" Keith snapped. "Why the hell would he pick her up when we had you there?" Keith's face was red with anger. "Don't let anyone leave that fucking building until I get there." He listened for another minute. "Find out where all the exits are, and if they have any video surveillance and if they do, call Sandy to go over it."

"What's going on?" James didn't really need to ask because the clenched jaw and grinding teeth told him exactly what he didn't want to hear.

"The meeting was over an hour ago and apparently you called and told Marina to meet you on the back of the building," Keith snarled.

"Marina... she's... missing?" James stumbled over the words.

"I'm afraid so, but I'm heading to town now and I just texted Uncle Kurt to meet me there."

"I'm going," James snapped.

"No... you..." James cut him off before he even finished speaking.

"Don't even try to stop me because I'm going," James said. "I just need to tuck in the boys and I'll be behind you. I'll get Mom to come here with the boys." Before Keith could say another word, James called his mother and was headed upstairs to make sure the boys were in bed.

"Okay, boys. I've got to run into work for a bit. Nanny Kathleen will be here, but I want both of you to go to sleep. Cloud is there to make sure everything is all right but please be good. This is really important, okay?" James spoke softly and tried to make it sound casual without worrying Danny.

"Is Mommy still at her meeting?" Danny asked.

"Yes, and she's trying to hurry up so she can say goodnight, but you go to sleep and she'll be here when you wake up." James hoped to God he was right.

When he got back downstairs, his mother and grandmother were sitting at the kitchen table trying to comfort Stephanie and Janet. It still amazed him how everyone got to his house so fast, but he was grateful for all of them. He pulled on his jacket and turned to leave the kitchen when he ran into the brick wall that was Marina and Stephanie's father.

"I don't want any arguments. I'm going with you or I'll follow you in my car." Doug's voice boomed, and James knew he didn't have a choice.

"We'll take my truck," James said as they left the house.

The drive to town was quiet with the exception of the radio playing softly. Well at least until Doug turned it off. James glanced at him and could see his jaw clenched. The man looked as if he was about to punch someone, and James prayed it wasn't him. If Doug believed this was James' fault, he wouldn't blame the man because he really should have put his foot down when she said she was going to the meeting. Then again, she didn't really give him a choice.

"This isn't your fault, James." Doug seemed to be reading his thoughts.

"I shouldn't have let her go knowing that asshole was still out there." James gripped the wheel tighter.

"Believe me, son, I know my little girl and if you'd fought her on this, she would've showed you how much she resembles her mother." Doug chuckled. "I see that spirit in her again. She lost it the last few months she was with that fucker."

James was somewhat taken back when Doug cursed. Marina told him once that she'd never heard either of her parents use foul language.

"But I know if you'd fought her on this, she'd have put your balls in a vice."

James smiled because he had no doubt Doug was right. He'd seen that earlier that morning when she'd backed him into the corner.

"I won't rest until I find her, Doug," James promised.

"I know you O'Connor boys keep your word." Doug reached over and clasped his shoulder. "I'm glad you came into her life."

"She gave me back mine." James choked out and held back the tears that were blurring his vision.

There were flashing lights in front of the building where Marina worked, and he pulled his truck in behind one of the cruisers.

Doug jumped out of the truck, and James was right behind him. It didn't take long for James to spot Kurt and Bull. They were surrounded by his brothers and Sandy. It was strange for her to be out in the field because she usually worked behind the computers getting the information they needed.

"There has to be a traffic camera showing what way they went," John snapped and James could see he was losing his patience.

"Stop shouting at her, John. She's doing everything she can." That would be Ian coming to Sandy's rescue, again. Although it didn't seem to cure the cold shoulder she was still giving him.

"I've contacted city hall, but there are no traffic cameras around this area." Sandy had her laptop on the bonnet of the car and her fingers were flying over the keys.

"You want to fill me in?" James stood next to Keith.

"The secretary told Kurt that she got a call from you saying you were trying to get Marina on her cell but it was dead. The guy told her that there was a problem with Danny and you and Bull were waiting at the back exit for her. The video feed confirmed Marc has her," Keith said. "You can't see it in the video, but it looked like he was holding something against her side. We found her phone next to the back door where she exited." Keith sounded so professional it was almost as if he had no emotions, but knowing his brother the way he did; James knew Keith's emotions were high.

"So you're telling us that bastard has my daughter." Doug growled and his large hands formed into fists at his sides.

"We'll find her, Doug, don't worry." John seemed as shocked with Doug's language as everyone else, but nobody was going to say anything to the bear of a man.

Kurt stood at the front entrance of the office building, and James heard there were officers at every entrance. Not that it made a difference, since the video already showed Marina leaving the building, but they had to make sure nobody was helping him. James scanned the crowd and saw Bull standing next to the building with his head leaned against the wall. Keith was in front of him and from the hand gestures, James could tell Keith was reprimanding him. James quickly headed in the direction. This wasn't the man's fault.

"Furthermore, you should have been inside the building and made sure Marina checked with you before she left the building." Keith wasn't yelling, but his tone was harsh.

"Keith, for the hundredth time she didn't want me inside the building. I tried to tell her I had to stay close and she about ripped my head off. She said she'd break her laptop over my bald head if I tried to go into the building. She said she would text me as soon as the meeting was over." Bull's voice was low and calm.

"Keith, this isn't his fault," James snapped.

"Don't interfere, James. It was his job to keep her safe." Keith put the phone to his ear. "Go home, Bull. You're under suspension until further notice."

"Now wait a God damn minute, Keith. I know he works for you, but he volunteered to do this. You can't suspend him for helping." James wasn't going to let Bull lose his job for trying to help him out.

"James, I said stay out of this." Keith growled.

"Fine, Bull, you can work for me. I won't be able to pay you as well as Mr. Perfect here but I do have funds to hire you as security for my sons until Marc is caught." James stared down Keith. He didn't have a lot of money but he did have life insurance money that he'd received from Sarah. He hadn't touched it because he was keeping it for Mason's education, but if he had to use it as payroll for a man that was only trying to help, he would no matter if it did piss off his brother.

"Oh for fuck sake. Fine, Bull, you aren't suspended. Jesus Christ, James." Keith then held up his hand as he spoke into the phone.

"Thanks, James. You didn't have to do that." Bull shook his hand.

"I know what happened wasn't your fault. I got a taste of how stubborn Marina is earlier today. We really should have made sure Marina was more careful about her calls and messages, and she's always forgetting to charge that damn phone." James never thought Marc would have the guts to call her office. Then again in hindsight, they should have thought of every scenario.

It seemed like days they'd been waiting for word on Marina, but in reality it had only been a few hours. Sandy called and said she had some news and needed everyone together. Keith said it sounded important. So here he paced waiting for her to show up.

"Wait until you see what I found out." Sandy struggled in through the front door carrying her laptop and a bunch of papers. Ian of course was the first to help her out. She thanked him but that was the extent of her conversation with him.

His kitchen looked like a command center with all the police and equipment around the room. Sandy was busy opening laptops and Keith was spreading out papers on the counter. Everyone else including the rest of his brothers, his father, uncles, aunts, cousins and Marina's parents were crowded into the kitchen.

"So, where do I start?" Sandy stood back as everyone's attention was on her. "Okay, when I found that alias Marc used I decided to do a nationwide check on that name, and boy what I found out was insane. Not only did Marc live in Edmonton, he also lived in Toronto and has a warrant for his arrest on a drug charge five years ago." Sandy handed a paper to Keith.

"Wait a minute, that's impossible," Stephanie said.

"I'm afraid not. That paper is the warrant and the file on Martin Tapper," Sandy said as she shuffled through more papers.

"Marina met Marc six years ago. They would have been married five years last month," Stephanie said. The room went completely quiet, but Sandy didn't seem the least bit shocked by the statement.

"That's because Martin Tapper and Marc O'Reilly are not the same person. They are however, wait for it, identical twin brothers." Sandy held up a picture with identical boys. "You see, I did some digging into Marc's time in the orphanage. The place was shut down a few years after Marc was adopted because they were not being completely honest with the adoptive parents. From what I can gather, Marc's adopted parents didn't know he was a twin, and only adopted Marc. Martin ended up in the foster care system, and was eventually adopted by a family in Edmonton when he was ten."

James' head was spinning with all the information he was getting from Sandy, but he didn't know what this had to do with Marina.

"He was removed from that household when he was fifteen because of physical abuse and remained in the foster care system in Alberta until he turned eighteen. He was in and out of jail for minor offenses. Then he moved to Toronto, where he got heavy into drugs and ran when he was going to end up doing hard time." Sandy took a deep breath and held up a finger.

"Here's where it gets interesting. I was talking to the sketch artist with the NPD and she put together this sketch of the skull they found at the trailer." She held up the sketch. and James' jaw dropped open.

"That's Marc." Janet gasped.

"I searched for dental records for Marc and discovered the last time he was at the dentist was eight years ago. I know, gross. Anyway they had x-rays of his teeth and compared them to the remains. It's definitely Marc and they're estimating his time of death as at least five years. Which means Marc isn't the one that has Marina."

"Dear God. No wonder there was such a drastic change in his personality. It wasn't the same guy. He killed Marc and took his place." Janet sobbed.

"So how the hell does this help us find Marina?" James snapped. He just couldn't wrap his head around what Sandy had told them.

"I did a search on property owned by both Marc and Martin and found a lot of land close to where the trailer is. There's a cabin built on the land and it was bought by Marc just before he and Marina got married. I'm assuming that it was going to be a gift, but he never got to show it to her. There's something else and I think it's what Martin is looking for. Their biological parents were well off and had a will that stated their estate was to be divided up between the brothers when they turned thirty. I contacted the lawyer that showed on the estate, and he said that he'd sent all the information to Marc. The lawyer said Marc was in shock because he didn't know he had a brother. He told the lawyer to hold off until he found his brother."

"Sandy, can you just forget all this and tell us where the damn cabin is?" Kurt seemed aggravated.

"Sorry, I just find all this amazing. She turned her laptop around and showed them where the cabin was located. James could see it was close to the trailer, but it had been far enough away that they'd never have thought to look there when Danny was missing.

"Son of a bitch." John growled. "We were right next to that when Danny went missing."

James had barely heard the rest of the conversation since he was pulling on his jacket and grabbing his keys. He was going to get Marina and nobody was stopping him, or at least that was his plan until Kurt grabbed him by the collar.

"Don't even think about it," Kurt warned. "You can't go in there half-cocked. He could have a gun or worse."

"You're not keeping me out of this, Uncle Kurt." James pulled away from him.

"If you go in there all Rambo like, you know it could screw up any case we have against him." Kurt was right but at this point

James didn't give a damn. This guy had already beaten Marina before and he wasn't letting her get hurt again by this man.

"I don't give a fuck about the case. He's not going to hurt her again." James suddenly found himself slammed against the wall.

"I said calm the fuck down so we can make a plan to get the bastard and get Marina out safely." He should have known better than to disobey Kurt. He could kill a man with his bare hands.

"Now, Kurt, ya calm down before I bust yar arse. Jimmy has every right ta be worried. Now get yar hands off yar nephew and help him get de woman he loves home safe and sound." Nanny Betty stepped in between him and Kurt. She was probably the only one of the family who didn't care what kind of skills Kurt had. To her he was still her little boy and she had no problem making him feel that way.

"Jesus Christ, Mudder, I'm not a kid anymore." Kurt groaned.

"Watch yar language." Nanny Betty slapped Kurt on the back of the head. "Dat goes fer all a ye. Ya can do all dis without using da Lord's name in vain and using bad language. Dere are two lads upstairs sleeping and they don't need ta hear any a dat. Now get ta work and get our girl home." James met Kurt's eyes and he couldn't help it, his lips twitched when he saw Kurt roll his eyes. Nanny Betty was the one in charge, just like any other time she was in a room.

"Well, I guess we better get to work." Keith tried to hide the smirk.

James paced the floor while Keith, John, Kurt, Aaron, Greg and Rick made a plan to infiltrate the cabin, but they really weren't sure if he was even there. It was possible he'd taken her somewhere else. They really couldn't have a perfect plan until they could see the cabin and know for sure that Marc was still there. No, it wasn't Marc. It was Martin. James still couldn't get his head around that bit of information.

He couldn't sit still in the rear of the truck because his whole body was on high alert. Kurt had sent in a team from the St. John's department to get a better look at the cabin and give him the information. They were warned not to go in unless they suspected Marina was being hurt. So far they were still just watching. The last report was that the suspect was outside the cabin pacing the front deck and talking to himself. The curtains of the windows were all closed and nobody could see inside to check if Marina was okay. That was the worst feeling in the world not knowing if she was safe.

They were all dressed in tactical gear with earpieces so they could keep in contact as they moved through the woods towards the cabin. Nobody wanted to do anything to let Martin know they were coming. He wondered if the asshole had told Marina that he wasn't Marc and that he'd been the one to kill her husband and take over his life. It was still surreal to him that someone would do that to his own brother.

"Sir, we just found a body out here." James heard the voice of one of the tactical team through his ear. He froze.

"Male or female?" Kurt asked and James held his breath waiting for an answer.

"Male, sir, and it looks like he's been dead for a while," the guy said.

James almost fell to his knees.

"Stay there and give the coordinates to the coroner." Kurt said. James felt a hand on his shoulder and he turned around. John stood behind him.

"Let's get her out of there," John whispered.

"Thanks, bro." James continued towards the cabin.

"Suspect is entering the cabin again. Will we move in, sir?" James knew the voice. He'd worked with Greg for years and had been in this situation many times with him, but this was the first time James was terrified of what would happen.

"Is everyone in place?" Kurt asked and everyone except James answered, but John replied for him.

"Move in slowly and see if you can get eyes on Marina before you go inside," Kurt ordered.

James had a full view of the front of the cabin. It was a quaint little house that would be great for spending a weekend away from everything, but now it looked ominous. He was ordered by

Kurt not to interfere with the team and he wasn't permitted to enter until they had Martin secured. It was the hardest thing in the world for him to do knowing Marina could be hurt or worse.

Chapter 24

"For the hundredth time. I don't have anything that belongs to you. I don't know what box you're talking about," Marina said.

"I know you've got it somewhere because he told me it was in the attic." Marc growled and Marina was starting to wonder if the man had completely lost his mind. He kept referring to himself in third person and he wanted a box that was in the attic. Even when they lived together, there was no attic because they lived in an apartment.

"Marc, please listen to me. I don't know what you're talking about. You never showed me any box." Marina tried to keep her voice soft and calm.

"Stop fucking around and don't call me by his name again," he yelled, and her first thought was he really had lost his mind. She didn't know what he wanted her to call him.

"Wh… What am I supposed to call you?" She needed to know how far gone he was, and how much danger she was dealing with.

"I can't fucking believe you're that stupid that you couldn't tell the difference." He laughed and it sounded more like a cackle than a laugh.

"The difference between…" His hand hit her cheek hard enough that her head snapped to the side and her ears rang.

"I don't want to hear another fucking word out of your mouth except to tell me where I can find that box." He bent over so his eyes were level with hers and she tried not to cringe at his closeness. It was hard because his breath smelled of smoke and bad halitosis.

"I don't know what box you…" The back of his hand hit the other side of her mouth, and she whimpered.

"What the fuck did you do with the rest of his things that were left at the apartment?" He grabbed her face and squeezed it hard. "I'm going outside for a smoke, and when I come back you better have an answer or I swear I'll beat you until you remember." He pushed her face, and she fell back against the couch.

The door closed and she couldn't stop the tears. She had no idea what he was talking about but if she didn't tell him, he was going to kill her. She couldn't believe that she'd been so stupid as to not check with James or Bull before she'd left the office building. She'd just been so tired and wanted to go home, so when her secretary told her James had called and wanted her to meet him at the back exit, she didn't think twice. Of course, her phone was dead so she couldn't text him before she left or she would have known that it wasn't James that called.

When the receptionist told her something was wrong with Danny, she didn't even check outside before she stepped out. Then it was too late. Marc was there with a gun to her ribs. He never said a word, just shoved her towards the truck and made her get in. How could she be so stupid?

She could see his shadow going back and forth on the front porch and knew she didn't have long to come up with an answer. She had to tell him something, or he was going to kill her. She just had to stall for time until someone noticed she was missing and come find her. Who was she kidding? Nobody was going to think to look for her here, and she didn't even have her cell phone.

The door opened again and he stomped back into the cabin. She readied herself for him to ask her again, but he went straight to the fridge and grabbed a bottle of whiskey. She'd never known Marc to drink anything that hard before. He put the bottle to his lips and guzzled half of it before he lowered, he turned and glared at her. This was it, he wanted an answer, and like a gift from God an idea popped into her head.

"Well, where's the box?" He didn't come closer to her, but he stood holding the gun in one hand and the bottle in the other. She swallowed and met his gaze.

"I stored all of your things in the shed behind my dad's house." She hated the thought of Marc going close to her parent's place, but she knew they'd been staying with Stephanie and John since all of this started. It was a safety measure John and Keith had come up with, but John made it seem like it was all her dad's idea.

"So the box is there." He scratched his head with the barrel of the gun. It made her quiver.

"Everything belonging to you is there." She wasn't being dishonest because when he left, her sister helped her pack up the rest of his things, and what his friend didn't take, her father stored it.

"Is that prick home?" he snapped.

"No. Mom and Dad have been staying with Steph." She really didn't know if the box was there or not, but at least it seemed to appease him that it could be.

"We'll wait until midnight and then you're going to show me exactly where the stuff is." He walked towards her. "Maybe we could have some fun until then." Marina pulled her knees up to her chest and shook her head.

"Please, Marc, you don't want to do this," she begged. After everything he'd done, now he was going to rape her. When he stood in front of her, she closed her eyes and waited for the attack.

"You're right. I'd throw up if I had to stick it in you. I really don't know what he saw in you." He turned and walked to a door in the back that she'd assumed was a bedroom or a bathroom.

"What happened to you, Marc?" She had to ask because he was so different.

"You really haven't figured it out, have you? I guess it must be the blonde hair that makes you so stupid." He laughed. "I didn't change. I'm not Marc."

He really had lost his mind. "If you're not Marc, then who are you?"

He turned around. "He never told you about me, did he?" he spat at her. "So he was telling the truth. Oh well, I guess letting him die was probably a mistake."

"Who'd you let die?" Marina asked.

"Who do you think? Marc." He pulled a chair over in front of her and straddled it. "Let me tell you something about your loving Marc. He wasn't an only child. As a matter of fact, he was a twin and guess what? I'm the twin." Had he completely lost it or was he telling the truth?

"I don't understand." This had to be his imagination, some sort of delusion because of the drugs.

"You know the dumb blonde act is really getting old." He pushed himself up off the chair and stood directly in front of her. He was doing it again. Making her feel stupid.

"I'm trying to understand what you're telling me." She really was trying to keep the tremor out of her voice, but when he stood over her, it was intimidating.

"I'm not Marc, you stupid fucking whore." He grabbed her by the hair and pulled her up until she was stood on the tips of her toes. "Your precious Marc is dead and has been for a long time." He was hurting her, but what he was saying was starting to make sense. "I left him chained up in that trailer he wanted me to stay in, until he could tell you about me." He ran the barrel of the gun slowly down her cheek. "So I knocked him out, chained him up inside, and left him there to die." He laughed and his lips formed a sadistic smirk. "You didn't even know the difference when I showed up after he told you he had to take that trip for work."

"Oh. God." It finally made sense. The major change in his personality, not wanting to touch her, treating her like dirt—the violence. "My God you… you… killed him and took his place." Tears filled her eyes and sobs wracked her body so hard that she couldn't catch her breath. All this time she'd been hating Marc for putting her through hell. He let go of her hair and pushed her back on the chair. Marc hadn't become the monster she thought he was. The Marc she fell in love with was murdered by this crazy clone.

"Well look who finally caught on. I can't believe you couldn't tell the difference. I'm no where near the pussy that husband of yours was." He picked up the whiskey and gulped from the bottle again as he tossed the gun on the coffee table. He was being pretty careless with the thing. She didn't know much about them, but she was pretty sure you weren't supposed to throw them around. "And you've got that kid of yours just as soft. I never got the chance to give him a good smack because the idiot I hired to watch him went and overdosed and the kid got away. Smart little bastard, though. He managed to find his way out of here but when I get him again, he won't be so lucky. I need that kid to get what's due to me." It was then she realized once he found the box he was looking for, he was going to go after Danny again. Suddenly all her fear didn't matter anymore—all that mattered was keeping this crazy monster away from her son. While he went on with his rant she slowly moved forward until she was within reach of the gun. It was as if it happened in slow motion.

She grabbed the gun off the table, he turned around and as she raised the gun, the door burst open and then... *Pop, Pop, Pop.*

Chapter 25

James and John stood along the treeline in full view of the front entrance as the team of officers and Keith's security team swarmed the cabin. Then he heard the gunshots and time seemed to crawl waiting for someone to come out. John held him back from running into the house, and he was struggling to get free but it seemed every bit of strength he had, was gone.

"James, you can't go in there until it's cleared," Kurt shouted as he stood in front of him.

"I need to see if Marina's okay. For fuck sake, let me see if she's okay." It was then he realized he was on his knees with John holding his hands behind his back and Kurt kneeling in front of him.

"She's fine, James." He heard the crackle through the earpiece and he couldn't tell who said it, but all he knew was she was safe. He looked around Kurt and saw Rick walking with his arm wrapped around Marina. All the air whooshed out of him when he saw the splatter of blood across the front of her shirt.

"John, let me fucking go." James struggled, but this time John released him and he was running towards Marina. When she met his eyes, he felt like his heart was going to shatter in two because she held up her hand to stop him.

"Don't… please. Just… don't." Marina sobbed and leaned against Rick as he led her down the pathway to the awaiting cruiser. James watched her get in the car and then it drove off.

"She didn't realize he had two weapons and when she picked up one, he turned the other on her. Rick got him before he got a shot off. That was his blood splattered on her." Greg stood behind him. "Give her some space, buddy."

Martin Tapper was dead, and they were no closer to finding out what box he was talking about and what it had to do with Danny.

Marina was admitted to the hospital and refusing to see him. He just didn't know why. All he knew was, Stephanie came to take Danny to Doug and Janet's house, and nobody was telling him anything. Mason was spending the night with his parents because he was in no condition to look after him. So he sat in his living room staring at the wall wondering why Marina didn't want to see him.

"Why are ya sitting here feelin' sorry fer yarself?" Nanny Betty sat next to him on the couch. "Dis is not like ya, Jimmy."

"She doesn't want to see me and I don't know why." James pulled his hands down over his face.

"I see." Nanny Betty sighed. "Can I tell ya a story?" James turned to his grandmother and nodded.

"When I was sixteen years old, I was madly in love with dis handsome fella." She smiled at him.

"Grandda?" James smiled.

"No." She tilted her head. "Dis boy was my first love. I thought I was going to marry him someday. His family were very poor and me fadder wasn't too happy about me seeing de lad, but me mudder put him in his place." Nanny Betty chuckled.

"I guess you take after her, huh?" James forced a laugh.

"That I do. Anyway, we continued ta see each other fer over a year. Then his parents and two brothers died in a terrible fire. He had spent the night wit me so he wasn't home."

"I'm not understanding what this has to do with Marina." James was shocked his grandmother admitted to spending the night with a man she wasn't married to.

"Guilt my son. Tommy felt so much guilt about not being dere, he refused to see me anymore, and he left de province. I eventually got over him and fell in love wit my Jack but Tommy always held a piece a me heart."

"I'm sorry, Nan but I don't know how that compares to this."

"She's probably blaming herself fer not knowing de difference between her husband and his brother. She's probably blaming herself fer his death, and she's probably feeling all sorts of guilt fer hating him so much over the last few years. Remember, she thought her husband had beaten her, but really he was dying somewhere and she didn't know."

"How do you know that, Nan?" James asked.

"I overheard her tellin' her mudder." Nanny Betty smiled. "I went ta visit her, and I heard dem talkin'. Jimmy, ya've got ta think about it like this. She just found out the man she married died, and she's mourning dat man."

It finally made sense and he knew how it felt to lose someone you loved.

"I don't know what to do, Nan. I love her and how can I be there if she's refusing to see me?"

"Just give her time." Nanny Betty said. "In de mean time you can't be sitting here feeling sorry fer yarself. So clean yourself up. She loves ya and I know things will work out." She took his hand in hers and kissed his cheek.

"I will, Nan, and thanks." He said standing up. "Wait a minute. That guy you were talking about you said his name was Tommy. Are you talking about Tom Roberts?"

"My Tommy is long gone, and I don't know Tom Roberts." Nanny Betty patted his arm and left the room. His grandmother always said that people came into a life for a reason and sometimes they stayed forever, but other times they came to teach a lesson.

Maybe Tom Roberts was going to be for both, whether Nanny Betty wanted to admit it or not. At the moment his only concern was Marina and how he was going to get her back. It had been twenty-four hours and it felt like he hadn't seen her in months. His heart hurt, and he didn't know if he could take the pain of losing someone he loved again.

Two weeks passed by and he was trying hard to get on with his life, but it was a struggle every day without Marina and Danny. He even missed the damn dog, but the worst of it was Mason's constant questions about why Marina and Danny went away. He even asked if he'd done anything wrong. That almost killed him, to think Mason was blaming himself. The only one to blame for the whole mess was Martin Tapper.

John called him every day to let him know how Marina was doing, but no matter how many times he texted her, she never returned his texts or calls. It was killing him, but according to John, Marina was seeing a therapist to help with her trauma. He just wished she'd talk to him, but it didn't look like that was going to happen anytime soon.

James returned from work exhausted and irritated, and Mason wasn't in the best of moods either. James had told him several times to pick up his toys, but Mason didn't seem to want to do anything. He knew what was bothering the kid and there was nothing he could do about it. Marina hadn't been bringing Danny to daycare, so Mason was really missing his best friend. For the fourth time, James told Mason to pick up his toys as he went to answer a soft knock on the door. Mason whined as he slid off the couch to the floor.

"Mason, if I have to ask again I'll pick them up and they'll go in the garbage," James said firmly as he opened the door.

"I want you to be my daddy and I want to come home." James stood in the doorway his mouth hanging open as he looked down at Danny and Cloud. He looked around outside but there was no sign of Marina or anyone else.

"Danny, how did you get here?" James had to plug his ears when Mason came squealing into the foyer. The two boys were jumping up and down and Cloud seemed just as excited as he jumped up and down.

"I missed ya, buddy." Mason hugged the dog.

"Danny, does your mom know you're here?" James knelt crouched so he was eye level with Danny.

"No, I told Mommy I wanted to come here, and she said maybe soon but I didn't want to wait. So I left Unca John's and came home." It melted his heart to know that Danny considered his house home.

"You shouldn't have come here without telling someone, buddy," James said.

"I was tired of waiting to see you, Daddy." Danny looked down at the floor.

"I missed you too, but you can't just run off without telling anyone." James pulled out his phone to call his brother. Maybe this would force Marina to talk to him or maybe it could push her further away.

Chapter 26

Marina gazed out through the window of her sister's kitchen and realized it was the first time she'd been back in Hopedale since the whole mess happened. Her life had been turned upside down by all of it, but there was one thing she could finally do. She could finally stop hating Marc. He wasn't the one who put her through hell the last couple of months of her marriage. He did love her, and if it wasn't for his crazy twin brother they'd be raising Danny together but then where would that leave James. God, she missed him so much but in her confusion she couldn't pursue a relationship with anyone.

The therapist she was seeing was helping a lot. She'd suggested that Marina talk to James but she kept putting off facing him. She really didn't know why but being so close to where he lived was making it hard not to run straight to his house.

"Marina, where's Danny?"

She turned around to see her sister searching the back garden for Danny and Cloud. Marina slid open the patio door and called out to him, but he didn't answer. She tried calling out to the dog but there was no sign. She started to shake and ran out into the garden calling to Danny. Where the hell was he?

"Danny, answer me now." She didn't even realize she was shaking from the cold until her mother brought out her jacket.

"He has to be around here," Janet said. "Put this on and we'll take a walk up the road."

The level of panic she was feeling was making her heart pound in her chest, and she was struggling to pull on her jacket. Her father opened the door as John pulled his cell phone out of his pocket to answer it.

"Wait!" John held up his hand as he listened to the caller.

From John's side of the conversation Marina found out that whoever it was had Danny. She relaxed until John put the phone in his pocket and wouldn't meet her eyes.

"Where is he, John?" Marina asked, but in her heart she knew the answer.

"He's at James' house. Danny told him he wanted to go home." John met her eyes and her stomach flipped. It was time to face James, but was she ready?

"I'll go get him." Doug opened the door.

"No. Dad, I'll go get him." Marina snatched the car keys out of her father's hand but before she got through the door, John stopped her.

"Marina, before you go just listen." John grasped both her hands in his. "James loves you and he loves Danny, and it's obvious Danny wants to be there or he wouldn't have run off, but I can't let you go over there if you're just going to take Danny and not talk to my brother. He already went through hell when he lost Sarah and for what it's worth, losing you is harder on him because he knows you're still there. So if you're not ready to talk to him, let me go get Danny and Cloud." John held out his hand for the keys, and she stared at it.

"Rina, you know you belong with James. Don't throw this away because you're scared." Stephanie stepped up next to her.

"Marina, it's up to you." John still had his hand out for the keys and she scanned her family standing around the kitchen. They were all so worried about her, and she'd given them good reason because she'd shut them out. She'd shut out all the people she loved but over the past couple of days, she'd slowly let them all back in. Was she ready to let James back in too?

"I need to do this." Marina turned towards her family. "I love him, and I know the only way I'm going to feel whole again is with him. Danny made me realize James is my home." Marina ran out the front door and almost knocked over Ian on the way out. "I love you, Ian. He's my home." She laughed and kissed Ian's cheek as she ran around him and to the car. She glanced up at the step as she started her car and laughed when Ian was still standing there staring at her.

She pulled the car into James' driveway so fast that she ended up halfway on the front lawn. Without even turning off the car she threw open the door and ran up the driveway to the front door. James opened it, and she launched herself into his arms.

"I'm so, so sorry, James. I've been an idiot for shutting you out. I never meant to hurt you. I know I've got no right to ask you this, but I love you and I'm a complete fool that it took my four-year-old to tell me that this is home. You're my home. Everything that happened with Marc or Martin had nothing to do with how I feel about you. It was just the guilt of hating a man that didn't do anything and..." James covered her mouth with his hand.

"You needed time to process everything, Marina. I understand and all I need to know is you're coming home. To me and Mason." He moved his hand from her mouth and stared into her eyes. Oh how she missed those blue pools of his, and just like the first time she gazed into them, everything seemed to fall into place. James O'Connor was the love of her life and no matter what happened that wasn't going to change. She'd said her goodbyes to Marc and she'd made peace with the fact that she didn't cause his death. It was a relief to know that she hadn't been wrong about the man she'd married. That Marc really was a good man, that he loved her but there was still the mysterious box his crazy brother kept referring to.

"I'm home and I'm never leaving again." Before their lips met, they heard the happy squeals of two boys peeking out from the living room.

"You think we should check with them to make sure they're okay with you and Danny coming back?" James chuckled.

"I'm pretty sure they're good with it." Marina smiled and cupped his face with her hands. "I love you so much." The next thing she knew, James covered her mouth with his and the faint sounds of the boys in the background made her smile against his lips.

"You think they'll ever stop getting grossed out by me kissing you?" James pressed his forehead against hers.

"Do you still get grossed out by your mom and dad kissing?" Marina raised an eyebrow.

"Good point." James laughed and wrapped his arms around her. "I really love you, Marina, and I missed you so damn much," he whispered in her ear as he hugged her and she knew at that moment she was home.

In the days that followed, Marina, James, Stephanie, Keith and Sandy dug deep into the lives of Marc and Martin. Sandy managed to open the adoption records on both brothers, but it didn't lead to any answers. It did shed new light on why Martin was so screwed up. The family who adopted him was abusive and he ended up in foster care once he was removed from that family. His foster families were not the best role models either. Marc had been luckier even though his adoptive parents had died when he was eighteen. None of that information led to the box Martin had been so desperate to find.

So the next task was going through the things Marina had stored at her parents. She wasn't sure how she felt about everyone going through Marc's things, and they'd agreed to let her look through them first. The shed held at least twenty boxes of things she'd stored there but she didn't know which contained Marc's things.

She did finally remember where she'd seen the key before. Marc had put it on a chain for her and told her it was the key to his heart. It had been in her jewelry box. That was why it was in the middle of her closet the day of the break-in and she hadn't noticed anything missing from it.

So the task was to go through each box one at a time. While James and John pulled the boxes down from the shelves, Marina opened them and glanced through them. When she knew it wasn't Marc's she'd hand it to Stephanie to sort.

It seemed they'd been in the shed for hours and were almost through all the boxes, but there was still nothing that required a key to open it. John pulled down one of the last three and set it in front of her. She pulled open the cover and gasped. It was Marc's belongings and there on the top was a black, steel box with a pad lock.

"James, pass me the key." Marina pulled out the box and set it on the floor next to her. James dropped the key into her hand. She unlocked the box and looked up at James, John and Stephanie. James nodded and she swallowed hard. "Do you guys mind if I do this alone?" she asked.

"We'll be in the house if you need us." James touched her cheek and left the shed behind Stephanie and John. The door closed behind them, and she stared at the box. After a couple of deep breaths, she opened it slowly. It was full of papers, old pictures and a large yellow envelope that was sealed and folded in half.

The pictures were of a young couple, both of them holding a small child. On the back was written *Me, Hilda, and our adorable boys Marc and Martin*. Marina turned the picture back over and looked at it closer. It was Marc's parents holding him and his brother. Tears formed in her eyes and she blinked to clear her vision. They had such a sad family history. The other pictures were similar. Pictures of the couple and the boys but the last one made her gasp. Marc and Martin were sat on a step with their father behind them. It was like looking at Danny, but she always knew he favored Marc.

The papers in the box were documents of birth certificates, marriage certificates for both Marc's parents and his adopted parents as well as their birth and death certificates. Nothing in the box would be worth money. Then she spotted the yellow envelope she'd put aside. She unfolded it and written on it was a note. It was only to be open in the event of the death of the O'Reilly's, but it didn't look as if it had ever been opened. Carefully, she opened the flap and pulled out a thick folder of papers.

"A letter to my son and my last will and testament." Marina read the typewritten letter on the top of the papers and flipped the top page. She sat back and began to read.

Marc,

If you are reading this letter, then your mother and I have passed. I hope this letter finds you well and that you understand what these documents mean for the rest of your life.

As you know, we had a modest lifestyle. I only wish we had the wealth to leave to you and your future family. However, your birth mother came from a wealthy family. When we adopted you, we were given these documents to give to you when you reached the age of thirty. The documents state that there is a trust for you in the amount of five million dollars that will be released to you on your thirtieth birthday. It also states that you have a brother of which we were not told about until we received this document. I'm hoping by the time you read this we will have already told you about him, but if we haven't it's because your brother has taken the wrong road in life. He too has a trust fund. It also states that should you or your brother refuse the trusts or have yourself passed away, then the money would be put into trust for any children either of you have produced and kept there until they have reached thirty.

Son, since you're adopted, you are not aware of your real family's secrets, but you need to know your true heritage and who your family really is. Your father, Clifford Tapper himself was an orphan, but your mother Helen Mann Tapper, her family is much more tragic. Your mother's grandparents were devout Catholics by the name of Liam and Constance Doyle. They lived in Witless Bay and were well respected by the community. Your grandmother, Dorothy, was an only child and given an extremely strict upbringing.

However, the family took in a young man who had lost his family in a fire when your grandmother was just seventeen. The story of how your grandmother and this young man ended up together is not really clear, but your mother was a result of their short affair. The young man was sent away, and your grandmother was forced to marry Herbert Mann. He took on the responsibility of your pregnant grandmother and claimed your mother as his child.

How do I know this story, you may wonder? Well after your parents' untimely death, all of their possessions were sent to the orphanage and when we adopted you they were given to us. We didn't look through the old trunks until we found out about your brother. The boxes contained journals of your grandmother and mother and told the whole story. Also, in there was the name your mother's birth father. He never knew about your mother, because according to your grandmother's family, he was beneath them. His information is also included with these papers and I hope this letter finds him still living so he can get to know you. We tried to find him so you could get to know him, but we were not able to locate him. We were told he no longer lived in Newfoundland.

One last thing, be happy and we always loved you as if you were our own. Never forget that.

Wilfred and Sadie O'Reilly

Marina dropped the papers into her lap to wipe the tears from her cheeks. Marc's family was one tragedy after the other and it was sad none of them seemed to live a happy, content life. To make it worse this was Danny's family.

She picked up the papers again and moved to the next page. It was the will of Marc's birth parents. She wasn't good with legal documents so she put them aside to have Mike check them out. If the letter was true, Danny would be the beneficiary.

She flipped through the rest of the pages which looked to be pages from a book. As she glanced through them she realized they were the pages of the diary referred to in the letter. She flipped through them until she came to a birth certificate with Helen Doyle on it. She scanned through it and noticed the father's name. She couldn't believe her eyes. What were the chances he was Helen's real father?

"Holy shit! That makes him Danny's great-grandfather." Marina struggled to her feet and grabbed the papers while she shouted. "James, Stephanie, you're not going to believe this."

Chapter 27

James sipped his coffee that Janet had poured him and stared through the window at the shed where Marina was going through a can. One that had gotten her son kidnapped as well as her. She seemed to be taking forever and he was getting edgy.

"She'll be fine, James." Janet placed her hand on his back.

"I'm just worried there's something that may upset her." James was more concerned it was something that would take her away from him again.

"Nothing in that box is going to change how my daughter feels about you." Janet smiled at him. He was about to thank her but the yelling coming from the shed had him and Janet running out the back door.

"You're not going to believe this." Marina shoved a piece of paper into his hand, and he glanced at it. It was a birth certificate for a Helen Doyle.

"I don't know who this is." James was baffled. He didn't know why Marina was so excited.

"Of course you don't. You didn't read this, but Helen Doyle is Marc's birth mother. This is a copy of her original birth certificate." James still didn't get all the excitement.

"Okay, but what does this mean?" James shrugged and glanced at Janet who seemed to be just as confused.

"Look at the father's name." Marina pointed to the name.

"Thomas Roberts." It took a second for it to sink in. "Tom Roberts is Marc's grandfather?"

"Yes! It's a whole sordid story with crazy religious parents but what it boils down to is Tom didn't know he had a child. He was sent away but he was never told why."

"Holy shit!" James said. "This means Tom is related to Danny."

"Yes, and according to the letter he didn't know about the baby," Marina said.

"So what you're saying is Danny is Tom Roberts' great-grandson." Janet seemed to be still trying to catch up.

"Yes, and from everything I know about the man, Danny is his only relative." James said.

"I've got to go talk to him. If he didn't know about his daughter, he deserves to know. Your grandmother also deserves to know why he didn't come back for her. He broke her heart and she deserves to know why." Marina said but he didn't know if his grandmother wanted to know or if opening that can of worms was a good thing.

James searched through his wallet for the business card that Tom had given him after Marina and Danny's accident. In all her excitement Marina would probably tell him everything over the phone and scare the man to death.

"Why don't we invite him to the house for supper?" Marina suggested. "We can tell him everything then. Of course we can also invite your grandmother but not tell her who the other guest will be." Marina wrapped her arms around his waist and grinned up at him.

"She probably wouldn't show up if she knew Tom was going to be there." James laughed as he pulled his phone from his pocket and tapped in Tom's personal number.

Marina was on pins and needles as she scurried around the house cleaning and tidying things that didn't really need to be. She was so on edge about the other papers she'd handed over to Mike to look through. James didn't understand a lot of the legal jargon in the will but if he was understanding it correctly, Danny was going to inherit a lot when he was older. That was if he was the only living relative, but as far as they knew Martin had no children, Danny was Marc's only child and there were no other siblings.

The knock on the door had Marina wringing her hands and him wondering if she was going to relax at any point during the night. He opened the door and Tom stood on the front porch but he wasn't alone. Nanny Betty was on the steps giving him what his father would call the evil glare. It was a look his grandmother had perfected to keep her kids and grandkids under control, but it only seemed to be amusing Tom. That was only going to piss her off even more.

"Jimmy, what is the meaning of this?" she pushed by Tom and entered the house.

"We'll explain, Nan, but it's something you need to know so please give us a chance." James asked but he wasn't confident that she would stay.

"Why does he have ta be here?" She hitched her thumb over her shoulder at Tom who was still standing on the front porch.

"It'll all make sense soon. I promise." Marina interjected and helped Nanny Betty with her coat. "Tom please come in. We've got a lot to tell you, too." Tom entered and shook hands with James. It was obvious Tom was leery of what exactly he had been summoned for.

James was in awe of the way Marina had treated the delicate subject they were discussing. Tom's reaction was obvious but his grandmother was another story. She sat stone-faced as Marina read the letter that had been in with the papers. When she finished reading it Tom took the letter with a trembling hand.

"I'm sorry you never got to meet your daughter or grandsons," Marina said.

"Me too, but at least I know now why they were so quick to get rid of me." Tom's voice trembled.

"I did find the journals of her and your daughter. They were actually still in the attic at the family home." Marina had found out through researching Marc's family that their family home still stood in Witless Bay, abandoned. He'd gone with her to the town hall with the deed for the house and found out that there was no other family left. It was a couple of days but they were able to gain access to the house and were devastated that it had been badly vandalized. Most things had been stolen or destroyed, but when they found the attic they were surprised to find the trunks filled with journals and family treasures.

"I'd like to read them, if you'll allow me," Tom said.

"I've got them boxed up in the spare room. You can take them when you leave." Marina smiled and clasped Tom's hand. James glanced at his grandmother. Her stone-faced glare was starting to fade.

"I'll take good care of them and make sure you get them back for Danny." As if just realizing what all this meant, he sat up straight. "This means…"

"It means dat our Danny is yar great grandson." It was the first time Nanny Betty spoke since they'd broke the news.

"Elizabeth, I want to explain what happened with Dorothy." Tom seemed embarrassed.

"It's none a me business." Nanny Betty stood and straightened her dress.

"I still want to tell what happened." Tom glanced at him, and James nodded to Marina.

"We'll leave you two to talk," Marina said.

"No. I want all of you to hear this, but please, Elizabeth, I'd like you to stay and listen as well." Tom was definitely begging and it was probably what it would take to get his stubborn grandmother to listen. James held his breath waiting for her answer.

"I'll stay but if ya call me Elizabeth once more I'm going ta slap you up de side yar head." Nanny Betty pointed her finger in Tom's face and James coughed to cover the laugh. If he laughed Nanny Betty would slap him.

"Agreed." Tom chuckled as Nanny Betty sat again. "First of all just to make it clear I didn't know about any of this. When I went to live with the Doyles it was after the fire. The night I got there, I was angry. I had to leave without talking to you, Betty. Mr. Doyle came to the station and picked me up. When I told him he had to take me to see Betty. He told me he would do no such thing and I was to forget my life in Cape Broyle." Tom clasped his hands together and stared down at them.

"The first night, I'm ashamed to say, I stole a bottle of whiskey from Mr. Doyle's liquor cabinet, and I snuck out into the woodshed. I was about half way through the bottle, and half way through a letter I was writing Betty, when Dorothy came in. I won't bore you with how things happened, but it did and I was so ashamed I tore up the letter. I figured it was better if you'd hate me rather than find out that I betrayed you." Tom reached out to touch Nanny Betty's hand, but she pulled it away. "I guess it worked, because even after all these years, you still do. Anyway, for the next few weeks I worked with the Doyles at their home. Then Mr. Doyle told me he was shipping me off to his brother's farm in Alberta because he needed the extra workers. He did agree to take me to Cape Broyle to say goodbye to you but when I got there your father told me you were seeing Jack O'Connor and I was to leave you alone. I left and never came back."

Nanny Betty didn't say anything for a few minutes, and James looked at her, trying to gage her reaction. James hadn't seen Nanny Betty this quiet since the day his grandfather passed away and it worried him.

"Nan, are you okay?" James asked and for a second she didn't seem to hear him, but then she turned to James and nodded.

"Tommy, I'm sorry me fadder lied ta ya but it was over a year after you left dat I took up wit Jack. My dad had introduced us because Jack was on his fishing boat, but dere was nothin' going on. He'd just ended an engagement." James had never seen his grandmother so unsure of herself. "But Jack was an amazin' husband, father and grandfather. I wouldn't change a second of me life wit him. We had a good life."

"I'm glad Betty. I'm glad you were happy." Tom smiled.

"Why didn't you ever marry?" Marina blurted out and James had a feeling he knew the answer. One of the articles he read on Tom stated that he'd lost the love of his life and nobody ever came close to her. James had a feeling his grandmother was that woman.

"I just didn't find anyone who could hold a candle to Betty." Tom smiled and James saw his grandmother blush for the first time in his life, but it wasn't long before the Nanny Betty he knew appeared again.

"Okay enough a dis malarkey, I came here fer supper and I'm ready ta eat." Nanny Betty stood up and headed to the kitchen. That was the Nanny Betty he knew and loved.

In the months that passed, Tom and Nanny Betty spent a lot of time together. Tom was also ecstatic when Danny and Mason started to call him Granddad. The only thing James had left to figure out was how he was going to propose to Marina and make them a family.

He'd been sitting in the living room on his day off when Mason ran into the living room with Danny not far behind him. He climbed onto his lap as did Danny they both stared at him for a moment before James spoke.

"What's up, boys?" James asked.

"What do propose mean?" Mason asked, but the word came out more like propros.

"Where did you hear that word?" James really didn't need to ask because Mason probably heard it from someone in the family.

"Nanny Kathleen told Aunt Cora it was time for you to propose," Mason said and James tried not to roll his eyes.

"What they mean is, it's time for me to ask Mommy to marry me." James couldn't think of any other way to explain it, and he needed to talk to his mother and aunt about their conversation topics with the boys around.

"Can we help?" Danny asked and like a light flicked on, an idea came to him.

"You can help, if you can keep a secret," James said.

"I won't say not a word, Daddy," Mason said excitedly.

"Me either." Danny jumped off his lap and jumped up and down.

"Well since Mommy's at work, we need to go shopping." James said. Tonight would be the night and the boys were going to help.

Chapter 28

For the first time in a long time Marina felt a sense of calm and happiness. In less than a month it would be Christmas but there was nothing she wanted that she didn't already have. She had a wonderful man that she loved and loved her. Danny was happy and she had another boy in her life that now called her Mommy. Her life was just about perfect. The only thing that was causing it to be not quite perfect was she wasn't feeling well over the past couple of days. She was tired and she'd been nauseous all day. She'd hoped to avoid the stomach bug going around her office, but on the drive home from work she realized she didn't.

She turned onto the main road to Hopedale as a text came in on her phone. She pulled into the side of the road and opened her phone. It was a text from her sister asking her to drop by before she went home. Marina groaned because she'd hoped to get home and relax. A second text came in before she could decline telling her it was important.

"Damn it." Marina tossed her phone into her purse and turned down the road where Stephanie and John lived.

"Come in, come in. Hurry. I want you to be the second person to know." Stephanie almost knocked her over as she met her on the front step.

"Holy hell Steph, calm down." Marina laughed.

"Sorry, I'm just so excited." Stephanie pulled Marina into the house, just barely giving her enough time to remove her boots.

Stephanie dragged her into the kitchen where John was leaning against the counter grinning from ear to ear. When Stephanie dragged her to one of the kitchen chairs and sat in the chair next to her, Marina couldn't help but laugh at her sister's expression.

"The reason you're the second is because John was talking to James about..." Stephanie started to say but John cleared his throat and Stephanie covered her mouth. "Well what they were talking about is not important. Well, it's important but it has nothing to do with my news and its amazing news and John told James..." Marina covered her sister's mouth with her hand and turned to John.

"Is she going to get to the point soon, or should I just let you tell me?" Marina laughed because John knew as well as Marina that Stephanie rambled when she was excited and nervous.

"I'll let her tell you, but you may have to let her ramble on for a bit." John chuckled, and Marina laughed when she turned back to her sister.

"Can you get to the point because I'm tired." Marina giggled when Stephanie narrowed her eyes at her, but Marina removed her hand from Stephanie's mouth.

"I'm pregnant." Stephanie squealed and Marina gasped not because it wasn't good news but it was at that point she realized it may not be a stomach bug she had.

"Oh dear God." Marina stood up and started to pace.

"Marina, this is happy news." Stephanie seemed hurt by her reaction.

"I know, Steph, and I'm happy for you both really. It's just...." Marina stopped because if it was what she thought, James should be the first to know. "I'm sorry, Steph, I have to go but congrats to both of you." Marina yanked on her boots and ran out through the front door right to her car.

"Marina, wait." Stephanie yelled from the door.

"I'll talk to you later, Steph. I've got to go to the store before I go home." The drugstore to be more specific.

She rushed into the house so fast that she didn't even see James or the boys. She just called out a hello as she ran upstairs to the bathroom. For a moment she sat on the bathroom floor and stared at the door. Could she just be over-reacting? She was on the pill but things had been crazy a few weeks back and she couldn't be sure she's taken every pill. She pulled the box out of her purse and tapped it against her hand. Could it really be the reason why she'd been so tired?

"Marina, are you all right?" James called through the door. It hit her that maybe he wouldn't want this. He had suggested condoms the first time but she'd told him she was on the pill and it wasn't a lie. What if he didn't want another child? "Sweetheart?"

"I'm fine. I'll be down in a few minutes." Marina hoped her voice sounded normal because at the moment her hands were shaking.

"Okay. Me and the boys have a surprise," James said.

"Sounds good. Give me a few minutes." Five minutes to be exact and she might have a surprise herself.

The timer on her phone seemed to be ticking down in slow motion as she waited for it to buzz. She gazed at herself in the mirror. Did she look any different? Her cheeks were flushed, but it was really warm and she'd been pacing the bathroom. The buzzing sound from her phone startled her.

"Well, this is it." Marina picked up the stick and closed her eyes. A couple of deep breaths and she opened her eyes. She held the stick up and stared at it. "Wow," she said as she lowered herself to the floor. "At least I know I'm not sick."

Marina wasn't sure how to break the news to James but if she was being completely honest with herself, she was actually happy about this, but maybe James wouldn't be. They'd never really talked about having more children. Hell, they hadn't even discussed getting married.

"Mommy, hurry up. It's time for the surprise," Danny yelled from the hallway.

"Yeah, it's time for a big surprise," Marina whispered to herself as she walked out of the bathroom and was immediately greeted by two very excited smiling boys.

"You taked forever in there," Mason said when she came out.

The boys led her downstairs and told her she had to close her eyes before they brought her into the kitchen. Letting two little boys walk her blindly into another room probably wasn't a good idea, but she was sure James was close by.

"Surprise!" Mason and Danny yelled together. Marina opened her eyes and gasped. The kitchen table was set for four and candles stood in the center of the table. All four plates were covered with domes and four wine glasses stood next to the plates. All four were filled with milk. She assumed that had been the boys' idea.

"What's all this?" Marina turned, and James stood behind the boys.

"First you need to have a seat." James smiled at her and there was a twinkle in his eye that made her shiver. Marina sat down on the chair and placed her hands in her lap.

"Daddy, is it time?" Mason looked up at James and he nodded. The two boys walked over to her, and James walked behind her.

"Mommy, we all love you very much." Danny took one of her hands.

"And I love all of you." Marina squeezed his hand gently.

"Shhh, Mommy, you can't talk yet." Danny said. Marina closed her lips together and looked at Mason.

"I like having you as a mommy." Mason took her other hand. Mason looked over her head, and he must have gotten a cue from James because both he and Danny knelt down on the floor in front of her.

"Mommy, will you marry Daddy?" Mason and Danny said slowly together.

Marina stared at the boys for a minute before it sank in what they were actually saying. She turned her head to see James and he was on one knee holding a black velvet box in front of him. Marina covered her mouth with her hands and tears started to roll down her face.

"Mommy, don't be sad. This is a happy day." Mason seemed so concerned.

"I'm not sad, Mason. These are happy tears," Marina said.

"Girls don't make sense." Danny shook his head.

"Sweetheart, you haven't answered the boys' question." James reminded her and she turned back to the boys.

"I would love nothing more than to marry Daddy." Marina kissed them on the cheeks.

"Daddy, give her the ring," Mason ordered.

"Marina, I love you so much." James took her hand and slipped the ring onto her finger.

"I love you, too." Marina sobbed and cupped his face in her hands. "And I love that you included the boys in all this." She brushed her lips against his.

"Ewww, no kissing." The boys stepped in between them.

"I guess that will have to wait until later." James winked and held her hands in his.

"Can we eat now?" Danny said as he and Mason climbed up into their seats.

"Yes, we can." James turned Marina's chair into the table and with a flourish he removed the dome from her plate.

"The boys' gourmet cheeseburgers and salad." James chuckled and Marina smiled at the simple meal in front of her. She had no doubt the boys had chosen the meal.

"Well this looks so delicious." Marina smiled.

The four of them sat at the table. A real family and Marina couldn't be happier. The boys were chattering on about shopping for the ring and cooking supper, but Marina barely heard them because her eyes hadn't left James. They were going to be married, and she couldn't be happier.

"What took you so long in the bathroom, Mommy?" Mason asked and like someone poured a jug of cold water over her, she froze.

"Marina, are you okay?" James must have seen something on her face because he jumped up from the chair.

"I'm fine." Marina lied as she glanced at the boys.

"Boys, if you're finished you can go play in your room before bath time." James said but his eyes never moved from her and she could see the concern on his face. The boys jumped down off their chairs and ran out of the kitchen.

"I'll clean all this up." Marina was suddenly very nervous to be alone with James.

"No, you don't. Now what's wrong? Your face turned completely white." James pulled her towards him.

"I'm fine," Marina said but she couldn't meet his eyes.

"Marina, look at me." James put his finger under her chin and tipped her head up so she had to meet his gaze. "Talk to me."

"I've got something I need to tell you, but I don't want to ruin the night." Marina hated the way her voice trembled.

"Marina, you're scaring me. Are you sick?" Now she felt terrible, he didn't need to worry about her being sick. It was probably his biggest fear of someone he loved getting sick again.

"No. No, I'm not sick but I am…" She stopped and closed her eyes.

"You're what?" James asked.

"Pregnant," she whispered and at first she didn't think he heard her but she was afraid to open her eyes. Then she was spinning through the air and she opened her eyes and looked down at his grinning face.

"Shit. I'm sorry. Did I hurt you?" James put her back on her feet and held her by the shoulders.

"I'm fine, James." Marina smiled. "So you're okay with this?"

"Okay? I'm thrilled, sweetheart." James took her hands. "We're gonna have a baby."

"Steph and I are going to be pregnant together. Are you sure the O'Connor clan can handle two pregnant women?" Marina laughed.

"I know I can and I'll keep the rest in line." James pulled her into his arms and stared into her eyes. "I love you so much, baby."

"I love you, too." Marina whispered as his lips brushed against hers.

"Can we keep this between us for tonight?" James smiled. "I want you all to myself once the boys go to bed, and if we tell the family, it'll be like a swarm of bees." James laughed.

"I'm fine with just us for tonight." Marina smiled and wrapped her arms around his neck. Tonight would just be for them to celebrate their engagement and a new life growing inside her. She was in heaven.

Chapter 29

They wanted to be married before the baby came and before Marina and Stephanie started to show too much, they'd planned the wedding for New Year's Day. The families were ecstatic. Mike had also pushed the papers through for her to adopt Mason and James to adopt Danny.

Since Tom had become so close to them, he insisted on holding the ceremony at his home. He'd gone all out with decorating the place and had heated tents erected in his garden. The whole place was decorated with thousands of twinkle lights and flowers everywhere. The way the lights glowed off the snow was so beautiful.

The boys loved Tom and called him Granddad Tom. Nanny Betty had also become a constant in Tom's life. It made Marina chuckle every time the older woman got flustered if someone asked her about Tom. She'd tell people the they were just friends and immediately change the subject.

Marina stood in one of the largest bedrooms she'd ever seen waiting for the cue for her to descend the stairs and marry the man of her dreams. They'd still not told anyone in the family that she was expecting, because she didn't want to steal Stephanie and John's thunder with their news. They'd decided to announce it during the reception as well as let the boys know the adoption news.

"Come on, Marina. Time to get hung." Marina turned to see her sister and James' cousin Kristy standing in the doorway to the bedroom.

"You look so beautiful," Stephanie covered her mouth with her hand and Marina giggled. Pregnancy was making her sister an emotional wreck.

"Oh dry up the tears, Stephanie." Jess entered the room behind them followed by the rest of her bridesmaids Sandy and Isabelle.

"She's been a waterfall all day." Sandy laughed.

"Leave me alone." Stephanie pouted. "I'm allowed to be emotional."

"I don't know about these O'Connor boys. They keep taking my little girls." Marina's gaze moved back to the doorway. Her father stood there in his tuxedo and her mother linked into his arm.

"Oh stop it, Doug. Those boys are like sons to you." Janet scurried into the room and kissed Marina's cheek. "It's time, honey."

****

The ceremony was a blur to him except for the beautiful woman sat next to him at the head table. The only thing he would remember about it was how beautiful she looked walking towards him, and to top it off they were going to bring another child into their family.

"Before we start the party can I have everyone's attention." John held the microphone. "The bride and groom have a few things they want to say before we get to the dancing." John handed him the microphone and James squeezed Marina's hand.

"First of all, thank you Tom for everything you've done for us. You are a tremendous person and we're so happy to have you as part of our family. Secondly, thanks to our families for being there when we needed you because without you guys, we wouldn't be here. Finally, I want to thank my beautiful bride for coming into my life. I love you, Marina." James kissed Marina's hand.

"We do have a couple of other things we need to say but before we do we need Danny and Mason to join us up here." The sound of running feet could be heard all over the tent as the two little boys made their way up next to him and Marina.

"We'd like everyone to know that as of one week ago Marina has legally adopted Mason, and I've adopted Danny."

Marina crouched down in front of the boys. "That means I'm Mommy to both of you and James is Daddy to both of you, and both of you are brothers now." Marina took each of their hands. Danny looked around and seemed confused by everyone clapping. He started to speak but nobody could hear him because of the clapping. James motioned for everyone to be quiet and held the microphone in front of him.

"Is this why you had this big party?" Danny asked looking up at James.

"That's part of it, yes." James chuckled.

"Well gee, Mommy, all you had to do was ask me and Mason. We figured we were already brothers. I told Mason he was my brother and he told me I was his brother," Danny said, and the whole tent erupted in laughter and applause.

"Well I guess we don't have any more questions about that, but we do have one more thing to announce." James held Marina's hand as she stood back up.

"Are you gonna tell them about the baby now?" Mason yelled. Marina burst out laughing.

"How did you know about the baby?" James asked.

"Uncle John said Aunt Stephanie was havin' a baby," Mason said.

"Yes, she is but the other news is we're expecting a baby in July," James said. The next thing he knew they were surrounded by family and being hugged more often than he thought possible. Once he was able to slip out of the crowd he made his way outside and stared up at the sky.

"Thanks, Sarah, for bringing love into my life again." James blew a kiss towards the sky.

"Thank you, Sarah, for showing me the way to James." He turned around to see his bride watching him. It was embarrassing being caught talking to his late wife but Marina smiled and walked up to him and he pulled her into his arms. "I'll be forever grateful to her."

"I'm sorry to disappear like that." James touched her cheek.

"I understand." She smiled.

"I love you so much." He pulled her into his arms and stared into her eyes. "You came into my life when I thought it had ended and you helped me feel again. I need to thank you for that."

"You showed me how to love and trust again and you gave my son the father he never had." A tear ran down her cheek. "I love you more than I ever thought I could love anyone. You, Danny, Mason and this new little one are my life and my heart," she said as if she had read his mind because he felt the same way and he looked forward to the rest of their lives together.

****

He watched her from the entrance of the tent. He'd fucked up so badly with her and he didn't know if they'd ever get back to where they were. He'd hurt Sandy when he stood her up to meet with Colleen and ended up spending the night with her. How she managed to seduce him after the way she left him he'd never know but the next day she was gone again leaving him with a note saying she'd made a mistake and she was sorry. Sorry didn't cut it for him because everything with Sandy was screwed now.

"Standing here staring at her isn't going to get her to talk to you." James stood behind him his arm wrapped around his new bride.

"I'm not staring." Ian grumbled because he didn't mean to get caught.

"I know she still cares about you, Ian." Marina smiled at him. Care and trust were two different things, and he could tell by the way she acted when they danced during the bridal party dance, that it was uncomfortable for her to be in his arms and when he asked her if they could talk, she declined. Well she didn't exactly say no but the glare was enough to tell him no.

"You guys leaving soon." He said changing the subject and when James and Marina laughed he realized, they got the point.

"We're just going to say our goodbyes and then we're heading to the hotel. Thanks again for watching the boys while we take a short honeymoon." Marina reached out and touched his cheek. "They love spending time with you."

"I love spending time with them, too." Ian leaned in and kissed her cheek.

"Hey just because you can't get your own woman don't be trying to take the groom's." This was just what he wanted right now.

Aaron poking fun at him because of Sandy. He was ready to punch his youngest brother as it was with the way he was flirting with Sandy. Not that she seemed to mind, but it made him want to kill the youngest O'Connor.

"Fuck off, A.J. Don't you have a date to irritate?" Ian snapped.

"She's in the lady's room, so I came over here to keep you company." Aaron slapped him on the back.

"Well we're going to make our rounds," James said as he and Marina walked away.

"Sandy looks hot tonight." Aaron wiggled his eyebrows.

"I know what you're trying to do, A.J., and it's not going to work." Ian pushed by his brother and headed towards his two nephews. It was time to get the hell out of Dodge before he really did punch his brother.

****

She watched him out of the corner of her eye and sighed. He looked so sad, and something told her it was her fault. She just couldn't get over him standing her up to meet with his ex. Not because he went to see her, but because he'd never had the courtesy to call her and let her know they'd have to put off their date. Well she wasn't even sure if it was supposed to be a date, because all he had said was let's go out to dinner. Maybe she'd read too much into it but he still could have called.

- 384 -

Actually if she was being honest with herself, she wasn't angry until she knew he'd spent the night out. She knew what must have happened, and it broke her heart. She'd been in love with him for so long and things between them were just starting to move in the right direction.

"You should see if he needs help with the boys while James and Marina are gone away," Kristy whispered into her ear. Ian's cousin had become like a sister to her and she knew almost as much as Stephanie knew about her feelings for Ian.

"I'm sure he'll have all the help he needs. Maybe he'll call his ex." Sandy tried not to gag on that comment.

"I doubt he'll call her because he's crazy about you and she's been out of the picture for a long time. I don't know what happened between them and neither do you for sure but I do know Ian hasn't been able to take his eyes off of you all night," Kristy said.

"You know that guy Bull he's been eyeing you all night too." Sandy chuckled at the crimson colour her friend's cheeks turned.

"Whatever, besides he thinks he's too old for me. I mean he's only six years older than me." Kristy sighed. "I hate when you do that."

Sandy always had a knack for changing the subject when she didn't want to talk about herself. It came from lots of practice when she was supposed to keep her employment under wraps but with

Kristy it was easy. All she had to do was bring up the big, muscular Dean Nash otherwise known as Bull.

"Aunt Sandy, we're going home now." Sandy glanced down to see Marina's son Danny tugging on her hand.

"Oh and you came over to give me one of your special hugs." Sandy crouched so Danny could give her a hug. She loved kids, and had come to care deeply for James and Marina's two little boys.

"I have a special hug for you, too." Mason wrapped his arms around her neck and kissed her cheek.

"Well I'm the luckiest girl in the world to get a hug and kiss from such handsome young men." Sandy smiled.

"Uncle Ian, you give her a hug and she'll be real lucky then." Sandy froze and her eyes traveled up the tall figure standing behind the boys.

"I don't think mine are as lucky as you two," Ian said meeting her gaze.

"I'm sure Uncle Ian needs to keep his hugs for other people." Sandy stood slowly and ruffled the boys' heads.

"I'm sure Uncle Ian has one he can give to Aunt Sandy. Right boys?" Stephanie said from behind her. She'd never wanted to smack her best friend so hard as she did at that moment. Then before she knew what was happening, she was being dragged by two determined boys.

"Hug her," Mason demanded and Ian looked down at his nephew. Sandy's heart was pounding in her chest and she wanted to run, but the boys had both of her hands. "Go on," Mason insisted.

Ian wrapped his arms around her waist and she held her breath because if she got a whiff of him she'd melt. He pulled her against him and hugged her tightly. Sandy closed her eyes and she tried not to melt into him but as if they had a mind of their own, her arms wrapped around his neck

"I'm sorry." He whispered into her ear and then he kissed her temple before he stepped back. "Let's go, boys." He bent and lifted both boys into his arms and with a soft smile he walked away with the two little boys waving frantically.

"Go after him." Kristy nudged her.

Sandy stared after them for a few minutes and then turned and ran as fast as she could in the opposite direction. She wasn't going to let him break her heart again. She'd had enough heartbreak in her life and Ian O'Connor wasn't going to add to it.

About the Author

What does someone say to describe themselves? You could start with giving what others say about you. Scratch that. It doesn't really matter what others think about you. It matters what you think of yourself. So here we go.

First of all, I'm a wife and mother. I'm also a grandmother. That alone would fulfil any woman's life and to be honest it does. But...

I'm also a writer. Someone who loves to tell stories of love, suspense, heartache and of course happily ever after. For most of my life, I've written those stories for myself. A type of therapy, I suppose. I love the characters I create. They become part of who I am because there's part of me in them.

So... Now that you know this about me. I hope when you read my books, you fall in love with them.

You should also know that I'm a Newfoundlander. What is that you ask? Well we're a proud people who live on an island, off the east coast of Canada. Some people believe Canada ends with Nova Scotia. It doesn't. If you keep going east, there is a beautiful island full of amazing people and magnificent scenery. That is where my stories are set because let's face it. The best stories always come from the places you know and love.

If there is anything else, you would like to know about me. Follow me on:

Facebook - https://www.facebook.com/rhondabrewerauthor
Twitter - https://twitter.com/rhondabrewer67
Instagram - https://www.instagram.com/rhondabrewerauthor/
Website - http://rhondabrewerauthor.wix.com/home

Made in the USA
Lexington, KY
05 April 2017